I0631796

THE ADVENTURE OF THE VOODOO MOON
THE COMPLETE CASES OF THE
LADY FROM HELL, VOLUME 2

BOOKS IN THE ARGOSY LIBRARY:

THE

THE ADVENTURE OF THE VOODOO MOON

THE COMPLETE CASES OF THE LADY FROM HELL, VOLUME 2

EUGENE THOMAS

ILLUSTRATED BY

JOSEPH A. FARREN

POPULAR PUBLICATIONS · 2025

© 2025 Popular Publications, an imprint of Steeger Properties, LLC

First Edition—2025

PUBLISHING HISTORY

"The Adventure of the King of Diamonds" originally appeared in the September 21, 1935 issue of *Detective Fiction Weekly* magazine (Vol. 96, No. 4). Copyright © 1935 by The Frank A. Munsey Company. Copyright renewed © 1962 and assigned to Steeger Properties, LLC. All rights reserved.

"The Adventure of the Maharaja's Wife" originally appeared in the September 28, 1935 issue of *Detective Fiction Weekly* magazine (Vol. 96, No. 5). Copyright © 1935 by The Frank A. Munsey Company. Copyright renewed © 1962 and assigned to Steeger Properties, LLC. All rights reserved.

"The Episode of the London Queen of Crime" originally appeared in the October 12, 1935 issue of *Detective Fiction Weekly* magazine (Vol. 97, No. 1). Copyright © 1935 by The Frank A. Munsey Company. Copyright renewed © 1962 and assigned to Steeger Properties, LLC. All rights reserved.

"The Adventure of the Dragon Claws" originally appeared in the October 19, 1935 issue of *Detective Fiction Weekly* magazine (Vol. 97, No. 1). Copyright © 1935 by The Frank A. Munsey Company. Copyright renewed © 1962 and assigned to Steeger Properties, LLC. All rights reserved.

"The Adventure of the Headless Statue" originally appeared in the January 25, 1936 issue of *Detective Fiction Weekly* magazine (Vol. 99, No. 4). Copyright © 1936 by The Frank A. Munsey Company. Copyright renewed © 1963 and assigned to Steeger Properties, LLC. All rights reserved.

"The Adventure of the Voodoo Moon" originally appeared in the February 1, 1936 issue of *Detective Fiction Weekly* magazine (Vol. 99, No. 5). Copyright © 1936 by The Frank A. Munsey Company. Copyright renewed © 1963 and assigned to Steeger Properties, LLC. All rights reserved.

"The Adventure of the Cayenne Fugitives" originally appeared in the February 15, 1936 issue of *Detective Fiction Weekly* magazine (Vol. 100, No. 1). Copyright © 1936 by The Frank A. Munsey Company. Copyright renewed © 1963 and assigned to Steeger Properties, LLC. All rights reserved.

"The Adventure of the Dying Dictator" originally appeared in the February 22, 1936 issue of *Detective Fiction Weekly* magazine (Vol. 100, No. 2). Copyright © 1936 by The Frank A. Munsey Company. Copyright renewed © 1963 and assigned to Steeger Properties, LLC. All rights reserved.

ALL RIGHTS RESERVED

No part of this book may be reproduced or utilized in any form or by any means without permission in writing from the publisher.

Visit ARGOSYMAGAZINE.COM for more books like this.

TABLE OF CONTENTS

THE ADVENTURE OF THE KING OF DIAMONDS

When Vivian Legrand Turns Good Samaritan and Saves the Life of a Man—For a Quarter of a Million Dollars!

1

THE PERFECT SET-UP

AN AIR OF electrical tension hung over the occupants of the little table in the grill room of the Carlton. It was the same kind of tension that falls over a quivering wolf pack the instant before the kill, or that strange, quivering alertness that blankets a regiment a second or two before the zero hour.

The narrowed greenish eyes of Vivian Legrand were following every movement of the two waiters who were arranging an adjoining table with silverware and napery, and to anyone who knew the Lady from Hell this was significant. The Lady from Hell never wasted interest on matters of no importance.

The eyes of Adrian Wylie, the companion of the Lady from Hell, were apparently roaming aimlessly about the room, but in reality he also was not missing a single move at the next table. But then, Adrian Wylie, extraordinary criminal that he was, rarely missed the import of anything that was happening in his neighborhood.

His eyes stopped for a moment on a party of three at a table across the brilliantly lighted room, studied them without seeming to do so. One of them he did not know. The other two were criminals whose activities had been a source of fruitless interest to Scotland Yard for some time.

Death glittered in the
Barron's eyes as he crouched

The Lady from Hell followed the direction of his gaze and her greenish eyes narrowed as she saw the three men. Their presence might indicate that more than one wolf pack was on the trail of this particular prey… and again it might be a coincidence.

Then Wylie's eyes came back to the adjoining table and what he saw there caused him to snap his lighter into flame, lean across the table and light the cigarette the woman held between her scarlet lips, saying swiftly as he did so:

"Two places at the table tonight. Usually he dines alone."

Vivian Legrand nodded. There was nothing about her, as she sat there, elbows on the table, smoke from the cigarette curling in front of her inscrutable green eyes, to indicate that she was as deadly—and as merciless—as a striking snake. The lights caught her red hair and caused it to take on the appearance of a quivering flame above the exquisitely modeled exotic face.

"He's harder to get to than the king himself," she said. Her eyes rested thoughtfully for a moment on the man who was her chief of staff and partner in every criminal enterprise that she had engineered—those crimes that had already made them two of the wealthiest criminals in the underworld of three continents. "He's the first man I've ever seen I couldn't find a way of contacting."

"He has a right to be exclusive, with a fortune of twenty million pounds sterling in his pocket and more piling up all the time," Wylie responded.

"A fortune that we are going to have a good share of," Vivian returned. Her voice, despite its momentary grimness, was low and rich and marked by a huskiness that was rare because it was musical. She resumed her scrutiny of the room.

THE MAN THEY were discussing, and whose arrival they were so eagerly awaiting, was Wolf Bernhardt, South African diamond king, who was on a visit to London. For two weeks Vivian Legrand and her companion in crime, Adrian Wylie, had been striving desperately for some point of contact with the King of Diamonds, and up to now had failed utterly.

Bernhardt had rented a whole wing of an upper floor of the Carlton, and to reach him one went through as many secretaries as though he had been royalty. Vivian was shrewd enough to realize that none of the usual feminine tricks would suffice to make his acquaintance, gain his confidence.

Not that the man was a saint. But he was as prudent in his affairs with women as he was savagely ruthless in his business dealings. It was the latter that had gained for him the nickname of "Wolf" Bernhardt. His career from diamond prospector in South Africa to the commanding position he held in the diamond world was marked by the wreckage of men he had used and cast aside when their usefulness was ended.

The two criminals had, themselves, procured rooms on the same floor with Bernhardt, and by judicious use of the funds at their command had managed to secure several lines of information—the head waiter in the grill room who always looked after Bernhardt when he dined in public, a chambermaid in the wing the millionaire occupied, and the elevator man who ran the private elevator car the King of Diamonds and his suite used.

For more than ten days scarcely a move of the diamond millionaire had been missed by Vivian or her men. They had been close on his heels when he visited various offices on appointments; they had a complete list of the men with whom he talked, and, if they did not know, in all cases, what he discussed with these men they had a fair idea of what the conversation was about.

The Lady from Hell could have enumerated what Bernhardt had eaten for breakfast, or lunch or dinner during any one of those ten days. And the King of Diamonds would have been amazed had he known that the contents of his waste baskets, instead of being burned each night, were delivered to the Lady from Hell.

From the fragments of letters fitted together she had gained an amazing knowledge of the millionaire's personal affairs.

But all that was sorry recompense for the time and money spent, for beyond this they had not been able to go.

Not a single point of contact had they been able to establish with the man himself. True, they did know something of the nature of his business in London, and there was also the fact that he expected to have a knighthood conferred upon him, an honor which the Diamond King desired even more than any other thing in his life.

A remarkable judge of men, Vivian had realized early in her investigations that with Bernhardt it would have to be a bold stroke with him or nothing. And she realized also that any attempt to beguile him with her beauty would, in all probability, lead to failure. The man who owned more diamonds than any other man on earth had never given a single thought or stone to a woman.

SUDDENLY THE LADY from Hell stiffened. The indifference had gone out of her movements. She seemed to tighten, draw herself together like the slow curl of a steel spring. There were men in Manila, in Malaysia, in France, in Turkey, who knew that there was trouble brewing when the Lady from Hell looked like that. And Wylie, better than most, knew the danger signal.

"Trouble?" he asked, the single word barely reaching the other side of the table.

"Look at Bernhardt's companion," the Lady from Hell responded, without moving her lips.

His back to the door, Wylie had not seen the tall, broad-shouldered form of Bernhardt enter. Now, as the millionaire came into his line of vision, he too stiffened with surprise as he saw that the man's dinner companion was Franz von Weltheim, a lone desperado, who had spoiled many a blackmail and swindling set-up for others by loss of temper and blundering resort to violence when guile was called for.

He was a tall, powerfully built man, with broad shoulders and long arms. His face, a strange dead white, was disfigured by a long scar running from eye to ear.

With a gesture of her hand Vivian summoned the hovering head waiter.

"Your guest of honor has a companion tonight," she said pleasantly. "That is unusual, is it not?"

"Ah, yes," the man responded. "The Baron von Weltheim. He is now in the service of Mr. Bernhardt." The man leaned a little closer and said confidentially, "He is a kind of bodyguard, I believe, to protect Mr. Bernhardt against people who would fleece him."

Then, catching sight of an important guest entering the door, he hurried away.

"And that," Wylie said bitterly, "is that. He beat us to it."

"Perhaps not," Vivian said. Her brain was clicking with machine-like precision, working coolly, judicially, and the set of her lips, the look in her narrow eyes as she sat there did not augur well for the Baron von Weltheim. "As a matter of fact, he has provided us with the entering wedge we needed. The presence of the Baron von Weltheim provides us with the perfect set-up."

For a moment she studied Wolf Bernhardt speculatively. He was a big, loosely angular man, perhaps forty-five years old, tanned, with watchful eyes that were faintly sardonic, and lips that were thin and inclined to be both cruel and a trifle self-indulgent.

"We've got to work fast," she said slowly, "and if we've

any luck tonight we take the first step toward acquiring a part of Wolf Bernhardt's fortune."

And Wylie asked no questions as he got to his feet and followed her from the room. He had early in their career discovered that the Lady from Hell never took a step in one of their schemes without the next step being clear before her.

2

CROOKS IN MASQUERADE

IT WAS AFTER eleven when Wylie and Vivian stopped in front of the room occupied by Franz von Weltheim. Not for an instant would any of their London friends have recognized in the couple the lovely woman and the debonair, suave, well-dressed gentleman they knew. Gone from Vivian was any suggestion of the stately woman of the world, any suggestion of the clever, lying adventuress that she was. She was a chambermaid now, a rather pretty one, but still a chambermaid in the distinctive garb of the Carlton service. And the man with her was the typical conservatively dressed gentleman's valet that may be found in any of the better British hotels.

In thus disguising themselves Vivian and Wylie were following one of the cardinal principles that motivated their criminal activities… never to leave a trail that could be followed. This was one of the things that baffled the police of three continents. There was rarely a trail that led to one of the Legrand gang.

To a passerby, Wylie might have seemed merely working with a refractory lock. In actuality, in less than five minutes he had picked the lock of Von Weltheim's room and the two of them were inside with the door closed behind them.

"Do you suppose Von Weltheim will fall for it?" Wylie inquired dubiously in a low tone.

"He'll fall for it," she said confidently. "Von Weltheim's a fool, a blundering, utter fool who thinks himself clever. He'll see in it a chance to doublecross us and take the whole thing for himself, and that's where he'll wind up behind the eight ball—or in a grave."

The cold menace in her tones left no doubt of her willingness to carry out the threat her last words contained, should the occasion arise.

All her life Vivian Legrand was guided by what Wylie maintained was a rare sense of intuition. But whether it was that intuition, or whether it was the superb intelligence that the police of three continents credited her with, that something made her perfectly confident of Von Weltheim. The man's greed would blind him to whatever flaws the plan might have and his propensity for blundering through a situation instead of calmly reasoning it out, would cause him to play into their hands.

But Wylie was not as confident as his companion in crime and said so. "There's still a chance of the thing backfiring," he argued.

"Exactly what I want it to do," Vivian responded, and then she stiffened. "He's at the door," she breathed through half closed lips. Turning, she slipped noiselessly into a closet, left the door slightly ajar.

And then Wylie did a strange thing. Even as the rattle of the key in the lock told him that the occupant was entering the room he turned his back on the door, opened one of the drawers of the desk and began running through the papers it contained. He was still engrossed in this so that he apparently did not hear the door open or Von Weltheim enter.

It was only when the man was in the room and the door closed behind him that Wylie sprang to his feet with a start, a look of fear on his face.

"I—I was arranging your papers for you, sir," he said hesitantly, and his eyes darted about the room as the eyes of a man who was caught, trapped, would flit from one point to another, seeking a chance to flee.

"So," the German said suavely, "you were arranging my papers, eh?" In his voice there was scarcely a trace of foreign accent. "And you think I believe that?"

HE STRODE FORWARD threateningly. Wylie, cringing, shrank back, moved so that Von Weltheim stood with his back to the closet door.

"Tell me the truth about what you're doing here, or I'll break every bone in your damned body," he roared, and raised his hand threateningly.

The closet door behind him opened. The slight sound of it in the quiet room almost spelled disaster. It warned Von Weltheim. He whirled like a cat, and his eyes met those of Vivian's in startled astonishment. From him came a gasp as he realized that it was a trap, and for one instant his steely eyes flashed from the man to the woman, the hard, reckless features in the dead white face working with fury.

Then, with a growl that came from deep in his throat, the man snatched out a knife. Its long blade gleamed in the pale London sunlight pouring through the windows. Death glittered in the Baron's eyes, narrowed to slits, as he crouched.

In that instant it would have taken but the merest straw

in the wind to wreck the entire scene that Vivian had so carefully built up. Although she was armed, Vivian dared not use her revolver. The sound of a shot would bring the whole hotel staff swarming in upon them.

Like a huge cat Von Weltheim suddenly leaped at Wylie. Like a tongue of darting flame the knife tipped in, straight for Wylie's heart.

And in that instant Vivian Legrand leaped also—leaped and struck him with the edge of her palm across the back of his neck. A deadly, paralyzing blow, the product of the jujitsu art that knows no mercy; the blow, learned in the Orient where Vivian's criminal career began, that can be used by the weakest of woman to fell the strongest of men.

The man dropped the knife as the exquisite, paralyzing pain of the blow ran through every nerve of his body, rocked for an instant, then crumpled.

"Tie him up," Vivian snapped.

In a moment the man's hands and feet were tightly lashed and Wylie shoved him contemptuously into a chair, before searching his pockets. It was another minute or two before Von Weltheim came to and gazed up at his captors.

"Don't try to call for aid," Vivian warned him, and the businesslike little automatic she produced gave weight to her words. The man got the implication. The incredible and merciless savagery of this woman was, for the moment, deadly evident in her voice.

"What do you want?" gasped Von Weltheim.

Vivian knew the dramatic value of sudden attack, and she counted on it in this instance to play in her favor. "We want a fifty-fifty split of everything you get out of him—or you'll go out of here in a box."

HER VOICE WAS biting. Her tone carried menace in its every note. Von Weltheim shrank back in his chair. For a second he stared at the tall, red-haired woman with sharp apprehension in his eyes.

"There's no way of getting anything out of Bernhardt," he said slowly, and there was truth in his tone. "Not a chance. He's led the most circumspect life possible since he's been in London. No affairs with women—nothing."

"Nothing that you know of," Vivian said significantly, and tossed a sheaf of letters on the table. "He'll pay through the nose to get those back."

It had taken Wylie hours to forge those letters, and to a casual observer they appeared to be in the handwriting of the diamond king. Vivian held one of the envelopes up for the man to see, and he gasped when he read the name of the woman inscribed there—a woman famous on three continents for her wit and beauty, a woman who stood, and still stands for that matter, so near the top of England's peerage that she was almost royalty.

The man gazed at the letters enviously, his resentment at these two already vanished. It was obvious to Wylie that he was already figuring how much of a gouge Bernhardt would stand.

"You've got the *entree* with him," Vivian went on, "but you haven't a card to play. We haven't the *entree,* can't even get near enough to talk to him, but we've got all the trumps." Her cold eyes slashed at the other's face. "So, the idea is this: we turn the letters over to you, you collect ten thousand pounds from him in exchange for the letters, and split fifty-fifty with us. But don't forget," she warned him, "that we'll be watching you, and one single false move on your part will be your last."

"I'll throw in with you," he said eagerly.

"Good," Vivian said. "We need a clever man to handle this." And, picking up the knife that the Baron had dropped, she slashed his bonds.

Half an hour later she rose from her seat from beside the table and handed Von Weltheim the package of letters. Irony lurked in the depth of her green eyes as she gave him a final word or two of instructions.

Once in the corridor Wylie looked at her inquiringly. She held up a cake of soap which she took from the front of her dress. Its surface bore the impression of several keys.

"Every key on his ring," she said with triumph. "One of them is for Bernhardt's room." Then she laughed again and nodded at the blank panels of the door. "That poor fool in there. Won't he be surprised when Bernhardt tells him that the letters are forgeries and orders him out before he is thrown out. Yes, it's a good thing for us that the Baron von Weltheim has a very hasty temper."

3

MURDER BY PROXY

THE HOTEL CORRIDOR was deserted the following morning as Vivian and Wylie made their way up the stairs from their room to the wing on the floor above occupied by Wolf Bernhardt—deserted for very good reasons, each one of which had cost Wylie a hundred pounds or more.

From a safe vantage point they watched as Weltheim opened the door of Bernhardt's sitting room and went in. Then they made their way quietly down the corridor and Wylie tried first one of the keys made from the impression in the soap, and then another, until he found one that with a little skillful maneuvering shot the tumblers in the lock.

Bernhardt was talking as Wylie opened the door the merest crack, and his voice, as dry and keen as a new ground sword, came to them through the opening.

"Letters," he said curtly, "there isn't a letter in the world that I'd be willing to pay a pound to recover, much less ten thousand."

"You will these," they heard Von Weltheim say confidently, and then the man quoted a phrase or two from them.

There was a moment's silence. Vivian, placing her eye at the crack of the door, could see Bernhardt, his back half turned toward the door, staring at the would-be black-mailer stonily.

"Get out," he finally said curtly. "Get out before I break your damned neck, and don't let me ever see your face again."

Von Weltheim's answer was to toss one of the letters on the table.

"Read that," he said with triumph. "And you needn't bother to tear it up. I've a dozen or more, addressed to the same person, and they're hidden where you'll never get your hands on them until I get the ten thousand pounds."

Bernhardt picked the letter up, glanced through it, and then tossed it back on the table with a short laugh.

"A forgery, and a damned poor one," he said. For a moment it was as if a chilling wind had sifted through the room. Bernhardt smiled a thin-lipped smile, like a trap opening and closing. "I didn't write it, and I don't even know the woman to whom it is addressed." He sprang to his feet. "Now get out, before I wring your neck."

VON WELTHEIM WET his lips. Anger, that anger that had more than once defeated his schemes, was rising in him like a tide, and Vivian, peering through the crack of the door, could see his hands slowly clenching; knew that she had not been mistaken in her man.

Suddenly the slender fingers of Von Weltheim's hand caught Bernhardt's shoulder, sending him backward, and his ever-ready knife slashed viciously at the millionaire's body.

Neither of them had noticed the slow opening of the door. With a swift movement Wylie was inside the room, and, before Bernhardt had caught sight of him, the blackjack Wylie carried crashed down on the head of the Diamond King. He never knew what struck him.

Von Weltheim gave a startled gasp. His eyes flashed in amazement from the form that had crumpled in his grip and slid to the floor, to Wylie. Then he strode toward Wylie and Vivian menacingly.

"The letters were forgeries," he said angrily. "What kind…"

But the sentence was never finished.

Wylie's blackjack descended on his head. He crumpled to the floor beside the man he had attempted to blackmail.

Wylie's blow had been expertly given. Wolf Bernhardt was out like a light for some time. When he came to it was to find himself on a couch in his living room. A man and a woman were bending over him with anxious faces. He tried to struggle to his feet, and Adrian Wylie pushed him down again with professional firmness.

"You mustn't move," he said gently. "You might start the wound to bleeding again."

"Yes, you must lie quiet until the ambulance comes," Vivian told him, crossing to the couch. In the leisurely, flowing quality of her movement there was something of the cat, and her husky, musical voice was that of a woman who knows the full value of an engaging personality. "And then, too, I imagine the police will want to ask some questions."

"Police? Ambulance?" Bernhardt looked at them with a puzzled expression, then he sat up with sudden agitation. "Good Lord, what happened?"

"Mrs. Legrand and myself were passing the end of the corridor that leads into this wing," Wylie told him, "when we heard what sounded like a struggle. We investigated. This door was partly open and I looked in just in time. Just as you hit this gentleman. I am Dr. Adrian Wylie, by the way," he added, "and this is Mrs. Legrand."

Vivian's smile was gracious, with just the right amount of solicitude mingled with it, but in her heart was not the slightest particle of pity for the terrific shock that was in store for the man.

"You must be quiet for a time to give the wound on your shoulder a chance to heal," Wylie went on in his best bedside manner. "But the doctors at the hospital will look after that, of course."

"I haven't time to go to any hospital," Bernhardt told him with visible annoyance.

"Oh, but as a doctor, I must urge that you do," Wylie told him. "You couldn't possibly stay here. Besides, as soon as the news of this gets out you will be overrun with reporters."

"REPORTERS!" BERNHARDT EXCLAIMED, as the full import of the situation burst upon him. Wylie and Vivian, watching, could almost read the thoughts that flitted through his mind. The fish was taking the hook—reporters meant publicity. He might say that the letters were forged, but the fact would still remain that he had been injured in a quarrel over them. A scandal, such as would inevitably result, would kill any chance of his securing a knighthood.

"The fact that I have been wounded must not be advertised," he said decisively. "Have you already notified the police—the hotel management?"

"Not yet," Wylie said with a puzzled air. "There has been no time. I thought that perhaps you might wish to call your attorney… that you might wish to have him here when the police arrive."

"There are reasons why I prefer not to notify the police," Bernhardt said slowly. "No one must ever know that this thing has happened. After all, it is a small matter. I am the only one harmed, and so long as I do not wish to advertise it there is no reason to call in the police."

"A small matter!" Wylie said in utter astonishment. "Do you call killing a man a small matter?"

Bernhardt sat bolt upright in astonishment.

"What do you mean?" he ejaculated.

With a gesture Wylie stepped aside and indicated the white-sheeted form on the floor.

"I mean," he said in a low voice, "that in your quarrel you killed the other man."

Bending over he drew back the sheet from the face of the man on the floor.

Bernhardt stared in stupefaction at the drawn face of Von Weltheim, at the trickle of scarlet that had matted his hair and dyed the whole side of his face.

"My God!" he whispered through white lips. "I killed him?"

Wylie nodded.

"You struck him with that," and he indicated a scarlet-stained brass candlestick which lay on the floor near the still form, "just as we opened the door. He never moved after he fell."

"I must have been mad," Bernhardt said. He looked suddenly much older than his years. "I remember nothing—absolutely nothing."

"The world has not lost anything by his death, if that is a

consolation," Vivian said suddenly, and Bernhardt looked at her in gratitude.

"It is a shame," Wylie said with a sigh, "but that, I am afraid, is not the attitude that Scotland Yard will take." He turned toward the telephone. "I had better ask the office to send a constable up here at once. As it is, we've waited longer than we should."

"Wait," Bernhardt said horsely. "Isn't there something we can do—some way of handling this without calling in the police "

Wylie stopped, his hands on the telephone receiver.

"You mean," he said politely incredulous, "cover this up?"

"Exactly," Bernhardt went on. "After all, as this lady has said, the world loses nothing by his death. My killing him was an accident. I have a position in the world—much to lose."

4

HIJACKING A HALF MILLION

IN THE SILENCE that followed the Lady from Hell watched him closely.

"You seem to forget," Wylie told the man coldly, after a moment, "my position in the matter. I am a reputable doctor. I have everything to lose. The slightest breath of suspicion, of publicity that I am assisting in covering up a murder and my practice is gone."

Bernhardt shivered at the word "murder." Vivian smiled thinly. Bernhardt started to speak, but Wylie cut him short.

"In addition," he said evenly, "even were I to consider such a preposterous suggestion, you seem to forget the body. That cannot be left lying around, indefinitely, you know."

Bernhardt's face lit up. "I could throw the body out of the window," he said. "The fall would remove any traces of his being killed before he was thrown." He was thoughtful for a moment while the two watched him in silence. "He has a room on the floor above, just above this room. It would appear as though he had fallen through his open window."

Wylie went on: "You would inevitably be questioned. The man worked for you. Someone might have seen him come in here." He shook his head.

"It is too big a risk for me to take. I must think of myself."

Bernhardt looked at him quietly a moment.

"You will pardon me if I seem impertinent," he said slowly, "but I take it that you are not a wealthy man."

Wylie laughed shortly.

"What doctor, unless he be a fashionable West End specialist, is wealthy these days? No. I make a comfortable living out of my practice, but I can't afford to risk losing that."

"But, look here—I am a wealthy man," Bernhardt said. "I know this sounds preposterous, but suppose I deposited a substantial sum in your bank to your credit… wait," he said hastily as he saw a gathering frown on Wylie's face. "You must not look at it as a bribe. You are a physician, and as such the confidences of a patient are sacred. You are my doctor: I have confided in you that I killed this man during a quarrel. As such my confidence is sacred. And your fee for attending me is—shall we say a thousand pounds." Deep anxiety rang in the man's voice.

WYLIE SHOOK HIS head. "It is not that I have scruples against concealing this matter from the police. I feel much the same as Mrs. Legrand and yourself. The world lost nothing by his death. But I must think of myself." He gave a dry laugh. "Sell my career for a thousand pounds—and then what?"

Vivian stepped forward.

"I think I see Dr. Wylie's viewpoint," she said. A subtle, warm beauty radiated from her. Bernhardt took his eyes away slowly, in spite of the tension of the situation. "I think possibly I can make it clearer to you than he has. A thousand pounds is not an exorbitant fee for a doctor to receive from a grateful patient—in fact, a doctor often receives much more than that for merely performing his duty.

"You are requesting Dr. Wylie—I do not count—to do something that is not only altogether against his professional inclinations, but also something that menaces his entire future. And I believe that what he is trying to tell you is that his fee for saving you from prison and possibly the gallows should be in proportion."

"No, no," Wylie said hurriedly, angrily. "I could not do it."

"You are quite right," Bernhardt said quickly. "What fee do you think would be commensurate with the service?"

"Fifty thousand pounds," Vivian said quietly.

There was not the slightest suggestion in her veiled green eyes, in the frankness with which she spoke, that this was the turning point of their scheme. She had worked carefully to make every suggestion—save this one as to price—come from the man himself. If he became suspicious now…

"Fifty thousand pounds!" Bernhardt exclaimed in astonishment. His face darkened. "But that is nearly a quarter of a million of your American dollars."

Vivian nodded. The carelessness with which she spoke was a triumph of artistry. "Is that too high a price to place upon your freedom, and possibly your life?" She shrugged. "I'm afraid I was looking at it from my own standpoint— from the viewpoint that a person has only one life to live. Possibly it would be better if we just slipped away quietly, forget what we have seen, and leave you to dispose of the body of the man you killed as you see fit."

"Yes," Wylie said nervously. "Yes, that would be best. I think it would be best if we went away without saying anything."

"No," Bernhardt said slowly. "It is high—but not too

high." He turned toward Wylie. "I will pay your fee, Dr. Wylie."

THEN HE TURNED a startled face toward the door of his bedroom as it was flung open. Standing in the open was a tall, soldier-like figure. He carried a short, awkward looking rifle, with a little box on the end. Instead of a mask he wore a criss-cross of black sticking plaster which effectively distorted the essential outlines of his face.

And Vivian recognized him in spite of the disguise of sticking plaster. He was one of the three men in the restaurant whose presence had attracted her own and Wylie's attention.

"What the hell does this mean?" Bernhardt demanded savagely.

"It's a snatch," came back the answer in a voice that was distinctly American, "and in case you don't know what that means, the answer is that we're taking you as security for the half a million dollars that you're going to be damn glad to pay us in a damned short time." His glance flickered across the little group. "Just keep still, all of you. This box affair at the end of my rifle is a silencer. I don't want to have to use it—but if I have to, I will."

He turned toward Vivian and Wylie.

"You two get over there in the corner," he said curtly, and followed their movements with his rifle. Then he turned to Wolf Bernhardt. "In there with you," he said and jerked his head toward the door behind him, where another man, similarly armed could be seen.

"You can't get away with this," Vivian said.

The man with the rifle studied her for a moment.

"That'll be enough out of you, sister," he said warningly.

"You'd be surprised at what a man can get away with, if he really tries. Now you just stay quiet for five minutes, and you won't be hurt. After that, do what you want. Turn in the alarm, if you want to—if you can think of a good explanation for your being in here with a dead body on the floor."

He laughed a little, and nodded toward the door again.

"Inside," he said to Bernhardt.

For a moment Bernhardt stood motionless, staring at the rifle that covered him. Then he stepped through the open door into the other room.

The gunman laughed, stepped through the door behind him and kicked it shut with one foot. There was the sound of a key turning in the lock.

Wylie swore deeply in a low voice.

"Bilked," he said. "A quarter of a million dollars snatched right out of our hands."

"Temporarily," the Lady from Hell said succinctly, a flame of scorching anger, sudden as the outburst of a smouldering volcano, searing her face. Swiftly she snatched off the sheet that covered Von Weltheim; the sheet that had prevented Bernhardt from seeing that the Baron's hands and feet were tightly tied. Roughly she shook the drugged form of the man whom Bernhardt had believed to be dead. "There are ways—some of them unpleasant—for making our friend the Baron talk as soon as he recovers consciousness," she said, "and then, we'll have that quarter of a million dollars in our hands again."

The expression on her face, as she worked over the unconscious form, did not speak well for the safety of the man who had snatched her victim from beneath her very nose.

5

KIDNAPER'S LAIR

AN HOUR LATER Vivian Legrand faced the Baron von Weltheim, a grim smile of triumph flickering across her face.

In a tumble of words, their flight winged by the lash of fear, Von Weltheim poured out his story. He was a member of the gang that had planned the kidnaping of Bernhardt. He had been their contact man on the inside. But for some reason which he did not understand, the date had been advanced.

"Where is this house to which Bernhardt has been taken?" Vivian asked.

He gave them the address, an isolated place on the outskirts of London.

"How many people are likely to be there?" Vivian asked.

Van Weltheim enumerated them, and Vivian's eyes were thoughtful.

Eight men! It would be no easy matter to snatch Bernhardt back from his captors. Any attempt at force would be out. They dared risk nothing that might attract the attention of the police, and there was always the possibility that if Madison and his men were cornered, Bernhardt might be killed to prevent his identifying his captors. It was a situation in which guile and strategy must be used.

Swiftly she plied the baron with questions, and as he talked, gradually a plan began to take shape in her mind.

A MAN MADE his way up to the front entrance of the big house on the outskirts of London the following morning. Wylie had become a ruddy-faced Briton. He wore a small mustache, his eyebrows were bushy and the cut of his clothes was typical of the British working man.

The door opened. A man appeared, tall and wiry, with a hard set jaw, broad shoulders and a pair of smouldering ink-black eyes. He stood squarely in the doorway, blocking entrance, and there was nothing in his manner to indicate the trained servant.

"Yes?" he asked.

"Police matter," Wylie said briefly. "I want to see Mr. Joyce."

"Mr. Joyce sees no one," the man said firmly.

"Give him this," Wylie said firmly, thrusting a card on which the ink was barely dry into the man's hand. "I'm from the Acme Detective Agency. The owner of this house is a client of ours. Recently there's been a number of burglaries in the neighborhood, and the owner wired us from Paris to check the burglar alarms in this house."

"I'll see," the man said doubtfully and closed the door, leaving Wylie standing on the doorstep. In a moment or two the man appeared, motioned Wylie in.

"Mr. Joyce will see you," he said.

They passed into the hall. A man stood at the foot of the stairs. This, Wylie knew, must be Madison, alias Joyce, the man who had held them up in Bernhardt's room and snatched the diamond millionaire from under their noses.

"What can I do for you?" Madison inqured curtly. Cold steel of suspicion was plain beneath the mask of courtesy.

Wylie repeated his story.

"Very well," Madison said. "What is it you wish to do?"

"Primarily to check the locks and burglar alarms on the doors and windows," Wylie returned.

"Go ahead," the man said curtly. "There is one room, however, that I cannot permit you to enter—Mrs. Joyce's room. She is resting, and in addition, the news that there have been burglaries in the neighborhood might prove very upsetting to her."

"That will be quite all right, sir," Wylie returned, "if you'll look after the window fastenings in that room yourself."

THEY FOLLOWED THE servant up the stairs. At the top the man indicated a closed door at the left.

"That is Mrs. Joyce's room," he said, and Wylie nodded. In that room, if Von Weltheim's story was true, Wolf Bernhardt was being kept a prisoner.

"Where is the rear staircase?" Wylie asked.

"There's only the one at the front," the man responded.

"How many entrances on the ground floor?" Wylie went on.

"Two," the man responded. "The one you came in, and the one at the back."

"I'd like to look them over," Wylie said.

The guard followed him down the stairs. It was while Wylie was examining the lock on one of the library windows that he managed to slip a small triangle of steel into the window catch. The window was now unfastened and would afford an entrance for Vivian Legrand—and an exit in case of an emergency.

Meanwhile the diamond king lay tightly bound on a long narrow table in the room on the top floor that was the object of Vivian and Wylie's attention. Above him was a brilliant light. It was as strong as the glaring rays of the sun and Bernhardt even with his eyes closed could feel the glare of it against his eyeballs.

Of a sudden his eyes were startled open by the sharp, sudden rattle of a key in the door, followed by the turning of a knob.

Then he was conscious of a shadowy form beside him.

Vivian Legrand stepped out of the cloaking dark, her face as grim as the gun she carried. Behind her was Wylie. They had been lucky in that they had been able to make their way from the library without being observed after Wylie had knocked out the guard who had escorted him about the house.

Swiftly she kicked the door that shut and turned to Wylie.

"Cut Bernhardt loose," she said curtly, and, snapping on the electric lights, turned the key in the lock. Then she ran to the window. Below was a tangle of shrubbery; then a vista of lawn, empty in the moonlight. There was escape that way. But how to get down.

On the far side of the room was another door. She flung it open, and her eyes lit up in triumph. It was a bedroom. Swiftly she snatched the sheets from the bed, the heavy draperies from the window, and ran back into the room where Bernhardt, now freed from his bonds, was sitting up rubbing his legs to restore circulation.

He started to speak, to whisper his gratitude, but even as he did, there was the clatter of running feet in the corridor from outside; a pounding upon the door.

Vivian fired point blank at the panels, and from outside came the sound of a yell of pain.

"There are plenty more where those came from," she called clearly. For a moment there was silence, then retreating footsteps. But Vivian knew they would return—and soon.

Two minutes and the sheets and draperies were knotted into a strong rope. Flinging it outside the window, Vivian tied it securely to the legs of the table on which Bernhardt had been strapped.

With a swift gesture Vivian snapped out the lights and plunged the room into darkness, save for the faint light of the moon that came through the window.

"Down the rope," she said to Bernhardt. "Make it as fast as you can. Five minutes more and they'll have that door down. Can you make it?"

"I can make it," the millionaire said grimly. "How about you?"

"Don't bother about me," Vivian shot back at him. "Go on down."

Without another word the millionaire climbed through the opened window, slid over and down. Then the rope went slack.

"Next," Vivian said curtly to Wylie and without a word he crossed to the window, slid out and down.

Even as Wylie slid down out of sight, one of the door panels splintered. As Vivian climbed hurriedly onto the window sill and prepared to slide down the rope, an ugly gun muzzle was through the hole in the panel. A dagger of orange flame stabbed the darkness. Sudden fire stung Vivian's shoulder and she knew that the enemy had scored a hit.

She swung herself out over the sill and seized the rope. Something warm was trickling down her shoulder. She started to slide down, even as she heard a tremendous crash and a babble of excited voices in the room she had just left. The door had given away.

The ground seemed leaping up to meet her feet as she slid down, the cloth burning her palms. She crashed through the bushes and landed on the ground with an impact that jarred her.

And as she landed a gun blazed from the window above. Another, the aim made uncertain by the tricky, mystifying moonlight. Wylie's gun answered. Then Vivian was on her feet and the three of them were fleeing through the night toward the clump of trees where Vivian and Wylie had hidden their car.

A FIRE GLOWED softly in the living room of the house in London that Vivian had rented. The Lady from Hell, her wounded shoulder bandaged, was lying back in a big easy chair. A pendent light turned her hair to flame. Wolf Bernhardt, a half emptied brandy and soda in his hand, was standing with his back to the fire.

"I have tried several times in the last hour," he said slowly, "to express my gratitude to Doctor Wylie and yourself for what you have done for me. I don't suppose I'll ever be able to express it adequately."

"I imagine," she said thoughtfully, "that Doctor Wylie felt that, since he had already become deeply involved in the matter, that the only thing to do was to see it through. You need not worry," she added, "about the episode of the body in your hotel suite. The man, er, fell through an open window. An unfortunate occurrence."

He breathed a sigh of relief. "I had been worrying," he confessed. "I wondered what had happened after my kidnapers took me out of there."

"There was no need to worry," she assured him. "You had engaged Doctor Wylie, as your personal physician, to perform a certain service. So, being a man of his word, he performed it regardless of the kidnaping."

"And I," Bernhardt said, "am also a man of my word. Tomorrow I will instruct my bank to transfer fifty thousands pounds to Doctor Wylie's account." Then he smiled. "But I am still deeply in your debt. I want you to go with me to the best jeweler in London, and whatever you select I will buy you, regardless of the cost."

She laughed. It was a husky, musical laugh, and he did not see the slowly eddying light of amusement in her eyes.

"You are clever and you are a brave man. But neither your cleverness nor your bravery will be of any aid to you, unless you use your head. You must not go to a jeweler's or anywhere else for a time. As a matter of fact, you must not leave this house. Here you are safe. The men who kidnaped you will never be able to locate you here. You must stay here until all danger of your being kidnaped is over. Then I will remind you of your promise to buy me a little something to remember you by."

And Bernhardt agreed. But he would not have agreed so readily could he have read the mind of the Lady from Hell… had he realized that to her one millionaire safely under her thumb was much more likely to be profitable than several millionaires loose in London.

THE ADVENTURE OF THE MAHARAJA'S WIFE

Sinister Vivian Legrand Uses Her
Charm on a Man and Her Nerve on a
Woman to Get the "Kohinoor Double"

1

VIVIAN LEGRAND FLUNG the letter she had been reading onto the pile on the table of her London house with
an angry gesture.

"Not a line, not a word in any of his letters that we've
opened to give us a hint of the real reason Wolf Bernhardt
is so anxious to leave us and return to his hotel," she said
thoughtfully.

Adrian Wylie, Chief of Staff in all of the criminal activities of the Lady from Hell, picked up the letter she had
flung down, inserted it in its envelope and resealed it so
cleverly that not even the most suspicious of men could
have detected that it had been opened.

"Can he be suspicious?" he queried. A scholar by inclina-
tion, Wylie could never have reached the pinnacle in crime
that he did had it not been for his association with Vivian
Legrand. He lacked the rare initiative and cold, deadly
ruthlessness which she amply provided. "After all, we did
take Bernhardt for nearly a quarter of a million dollars on
a frame up. Perhaps he's beginning to have doubts that he
did kill Von Weltheim."

The Lady from Hell shook her head decisively, her green
eyes narrowed in thought. She abhorred the unknown. All
through her criminal career the unsolved riddle, the unexplained situation inflamed her imagination, drove her until

she had solved it… usually to the advantage of her own bank account. And for days her mind had been hovering over this problem with relentless tenacity.

"No, it isn't that," she said. "He's grateful to us for getting him out of the mess he believed he got himself into. He didn't miss the quarter of a million dollars he paid us to cover up a crime he didn't commit."

She laughed softly to herself at the memory of the bound and gagged form of the German adventurer, Von Weltheim, lying beneath a white sheet on Bernhardt's bedroom floor, while she and Wylie convinced the diamond millionaire that he had killed the man.

"No, it's something else," she went on. "Something that he's expecting news of by mail. He's as eager for his letters as any lovesick boy for a note from his sweetheart. That is one of the things that made me arrange to have his mail delivered to us first, so that we could go through it."

"How about Clarke… his secretary?" Wylie asked. "Would he be likely to know?"

Vivian shook her head, a slightly scornful smile on her face at mention of the name.

"He's just a fool who wants to be bad and doesn't know how, but thinks he is because he buys the women he wants through Priell down in Limehouse. I've had him tailed night after night when he leaves here and almost invariably he ends up there. No, he knows nothing."

SHE REACHED THOUGHTFULLY for the envelope that Wylie had cunningly opened and extracted the sheet of paper it contained. "We won't be able to keep him here as our guest much longer. A day or so more and he'll insist on returning to his suite at the hotel."

The two, Wylie and Vivian, had rescued Bernhardt from the hands of kidnapers who had snatched him from beneath their very noses during the course of their own blackmail scheme. After this, Vivian, sensing that there might be more money to be had from him, insisted on the man remaining as their guest instead of returning to his hotel suite. Fear that he might again be kidnaped was the lever she used to insure his presence.

The Lady from Hell unfolded the sheet of paper and read it thoughtfully.

"The Maharaja of Indrapoor writes that he is in London and will be glad to see Bernhardt at his

Carefully she swung the little basket out over the window

convenience on the matter that he has already discussed with Bernhardt's agent," she said. She tapped the paper thoughtfully on the table. "The Maharaja of Indrapoor? That's the man who married the French girl and almost got himself bounced off the throne, isn't it? Now what could he be wanting to see Bernhardt about?"

She sat in silence for a moment or two while Wylie watched her intently. Her green eyes glittered in her beautiful white face. Suddenly she gave vent to a soft exclamation.

"It clicks," she said. "It clicks! The Maharaja of Indrapoor is the owner of the Kohinoor Double, the diamond that's fully as large as the Kohinoor itself. It's been common knowledge that he's been hard up for money for sometime. His French wife is proving an expensive luxury." She turned and faced Wylie. "It fits, every bit of it. Wolf Bernhardt is the diamond king of the world. If the Maharaja is putting the Kohinoor Double on the market, then the logical man to purchase it is Bernhardt. I'll stake everything you want to name that this is the letter he's been expecting, and that he's buying the stone."

"So what?" Wylie asked.

She flung out of her chair impatiently and took a long turn up and down the room. Presently she came back and stood in front of Wylie.

"I mean to have that diamond," she said, and her face had lost some of its beauty; it had tightened into a grim, expressionless mask.

Her companion shook his head forcefully. "Don't force your luck, Vivian," he said. "The Maharaja is royalty— Indian royalty to be sure, but royalty none the less—and when you meddle with visiting royalty in England you're stepping squarely on the toes of Scotland Yard."

"That's precisely why an attempt to lift the diamond is likely to be successful," the Lady from Hell explained. "The more Scotland Yard men there are around, the less they'll suspect that anything will be attempted."

"It's out of the question," Wylie told her decisively. "It's too big. The stone is too well known to attempt to sell it. And to take it to Amsterdam and have it cut up into smaller stones is running too great a risk."

"I mean to have that stone," the Lady from Hell said quietly.

And then all expression was wiped from her face with such complete and startling abruptness that it left only a mask in which the green eyes alone seemed alive. For she had caught a glimpse of a face between the portieres of the door—the face of Rodney Clarke, Bernhardt's secretary. It was there for just a moment and then it vanished. When the Lady from Hell reached the spot where it had been there was no one in sight. She knew she had not been mistaken, but she did not know how much of their conversation Bernhardt's confidential secretary had overheard.

She swung around, and there was a murderous flame in her green eyes.

"Clarke was listening," she said curtly. "I don't know how much he heard, but whatever it was, it was too much for his own good. Come on, Adrian, we've got to work and work fast."

2

THE EVENING WAS just getting under way in Priell's place in Limehouse. There were dark things whispered about that place when men gathered to talk. And even uglier rumors flowed about the owner Georgie Priell, whose business was women and liquor, and who deliberately made a bid for society slumming trade in order that their presence might cloak his real objectives.

Although it was scarcely dark outside, the place was fairly well filled. Here and there furs, jewels, and the black and white formality of masculine evening attire could be seen at tables, cheek by jowl, with sailors ashore for a binge and longshoremen out to make a night of it. And those furs and jewels were as safe—safer perhaps than they would have been in the grill room of London's swankiest hotel. Every habitue of Priell's place knew that retribution, swift and painful, would follow any attempt at annoyance or pilfering of guests. As long as the police believed that the place was a set-up for slumming West Enders, Priell could carry on his real trade unmolested.

A man with bloodshot, cynical eyes peering out of his slightly tanned mask of a face, drank deeply from a streaked glass and then turned to watch the couples bobbing slowly about the floor, clinging to each other with maudlin affection. After a while he dropped his head to his folded arms and snored hoarsely.

Even the closest of friends would not have recognized in the white-bleary-eyed man the dapper, trim Adrian Wylie, the companion in crime of the Lady from Hell.

And the Lady from Hell herself sat at a table in a corner, a black wig hiding the red-gold of her hair. Deft strokes with a make-up pencil had altered the lines of her face, made of her a different woman. The Lady from Hell was playing a dangerous game tonight—a game that might lead her to the gallows, and she was taking no chances on leaving a trail that might be followed.

Her face was cold as though it had been chiseled from lifeless marble; the yellow light gleamed on the white of her face above the sheer redness of her gown. She was alone, and not by the slightest sign did she betray the fact that the apparently drunken man two tables away was her chief aid.

In the fashionable bag on the table before her was a deadly little automatic. For she was on the hunt tonight—on the hunt for Rodney Clarke, Bernhardt's secretary. She knew that, unless he varied his usual routine, he would turn up at Priell's place sooner or later.

Chords rippled and crashed from the fingers of a man at the piano. A girl with a low cut dress and a mouth like a crimson scar danced with a drunken man. He stumbled, fell, tried to drag her down with him, but she jerked his hands free and kicked him where he lay. Then she walked unsteadily toward the table where the Lady from Hell sat.

"You're new here, ain't you?" she said, resting her hands on the table and peering at Vivian Legrand.

"Yes," the Lady from Hell answered in a low voice. "This is my first time here." Then that husky, musical voice of hers dropped to the faintest whisper, barely perceptible to the girl on the opposite side of the table. "Has he come yet?"

"You'll like it here—if you ain't too particular," the girl said, with a harsh laugh as she snatched a bottle and glass from the tray of a passing waiter. He started to strike her, but desisted as the Lady from Hell tossed a bill upon the table. "He's here," she responded in the same tense whisper in which the question of the Lady from Hell had been put. An almost imperceptible gesture of her head indicated a door at the further end of the room. "Came in the other entrance a minute or two ago."

THE YELLOW LIGHT accentuated the shadows under her eyes, the sagging lines of her face. She smiled sardonically as she refilled her glass. A man staggered against the table, pulled at her shoulder.

She pulled away and clawed at him viciously with curved fingers. Crimson drops oozed suddenly against the brown of his neck where her nails had raked. He stared stupidly at her for a moment, then lurched away.

"Get out of here," the Lady from Hell said softly. "Get out of it while you've still got time. There'll be trouble any minute."

She was watching, out of the corner of her eye, Georgie Priell, the owner of the place, as he came rapidly across the hall, shouldering aside the dancers as he came. He had seen the incident and noted also, the fact that one of his girls was talking to a patron. He did not encourage that unless he knew something about that patron.

"You don't need me?" the girl queried tensely. She, also, had marked the oncoming figure. Sharp apprehension flashed in her eyes. "That's Priell coming this way. I don't want to get mixed up with him. It's not healthy for a girl to talk too much around here."

"I don't need you," Vivian said. Unperceived by anyone her hands slipped a folded five pound note into the girl's hand. Then she raised her voice. "Get away from my table," she snarled. "I'm not buying free drinks for all the lousy sluts in the place. If you want a drink, get a man to buy it for you."

With a muttered curse the girl slouched away and Vivian Legrand looked up from beneath screening lashes at the man who stood beside her table.

"Was she annoying you?" he queried. His eyes, slight with suspicion, swept over her.

She shrugged. "Not at all. She merely asked if there was anything that she could do to make things pleasanter for me."

She turned away with a definite gesture of dismissal and after a second's hesitation the man left. In the big room the hard eyed pianist touched the keys again and a melody rippled from beneath his fingers. A woman laughed—a laugh harsh from too much liquor. For a moment or two Vivian searched the room with quick, hard eyes.

Then, screened by the crowd on the floor she got to her feet and drifted slowly the length of the room toward the corridor at the rear. No one saw her, or if they did, paid no attention to her movement. She reached the corridor opening, gave a quick glance around, saw that Wylie was also slowly weaving his way down the floor behind her, and stepped out. Even as she did Priell turned from his place at the far end of the long bar and she could not be sure whether his glance marked her figure or not. If he had seen her, it could not be helped. She could not stop now. And Wylie would be on guard in the corridor to warn her. But she knew that she must hurry. On her left a door opened off from the corridor. She lifted her hand and knocked three times with a peculiar rhythm. For a long moment there was no sound, then the door opened and Rodney Clarke looked out.

There was smiling expectancy upon his face as he saw the woman standing upon the threshold. His eyes swept her figure boldly. Then the smile faded somewhat as with a quick gesture she flung the door open and stepped into the room, closing the door after her. For a moment there was ominous expectancy in the room. Then the Lady from Hell laughed.

THERE WAS SOMETHING about her, something about that laugh, that seemed to drive recognition home with all its ominous meaning. It showed in his eyes. He whipped about and stared full into the ugly muzzle of the little gun that she had produced from her bag. His face went ashen, his jaws dropped.

"So you do recognize me, in spite of this wig." She pulled off the black wig that covered her flaming hair and tossed it on the table. "Well, no matter. I came here to find out how much of my conversation you repeated to Bernhardt."

The man backed away from her, his eyes fixed on that gun. He thrust out a hand in frantic protest.

"I don't—don't know what you mean," he stammered.

"Don't lie." Cold steel of menace was plain through the

cloak of her words. "It's your play. How much did you tell him?"

"Nothing," the man faltered. "I haven't seen him. He has been away on business all afternoon."

From the corridor outside came a shot. Wylie's gun. Whether a shot at a living target or a shot to warn her of danger she did not know. Followed a bedlam of cries from outside, the shrieks of women. The next instant the door was flung open and Wylie was in the room. Swiftly he locked the door.

"Hurry," he said.

Wylie's presence seemed to break the almost hypnotic spell in which Clarke had been held. He screamed, partly from fear, partly from the snapping of the tension, and his hands clawed for a knife that lay upon the table, Vivian's hand flicked the merest trifle. There was the hammer of an explosion and Clarke toppled, fell to his knees and slowly pitched to the floor, blood welling from a hole under his heart. From outside came a hammering upon the door.

Without a backward glance, the Lady from Hell ran toward the window and flung it up. She did not need to ask where the alley on which it opened led. She knew. In an instant she had vaulted the sill and was standing outside. Wylie joined her. And, even as they ran toward the end of the alley, where their car waited, the Lady from Hell was changing her appearance. Hastily she combed her ruffled hair and swift strokes with a handkerchief eradicated the lines of black that had changed the contour of her eyebrows. Thus leaving behind them another mystery to which the police were never to find a clue.

3

WOLF BERNHARDT WAS in an exceedingly pleasant humor as he lay back in his chair in Vivian Legrand's pleasant living room. In a few hours he would see his efforts crowned with success and then—a knighthood—perhaps even a peerage. He would purchase the great diamond, almost as famous as the Kohinoor itself, present it to the king, to be treasured as one of the crown jewels. It would be expensive, but he could afford it.

The Lady from Hell, sitting opposite him, stood up with effortless grace, every line of her seeming to be inspired by an intense fire, bright as that which glowed in her hair, and slowly poured two cocktails.

Seeing her thus, it seemed impossible that an hour earlier her hand had dealt death to a man—a death inspired by nothing more than the fact that the man stood in her path. That was like Vivian Legrand, and one of the reasons for her nickname of the Lady from Hell. Throughout the whole course of her career as the world's most successful blackmailer, she permitted nothing in the way of scruples to stand in her way. She swept a man's life away as ruthlessly, as surely, as she would his career or his reputation.

She picked up a glass and passed it to Bernhardt.

"Shall we drink to the success of your mission with the Maharaja?" she queried, raising her own glass.

Not by a word or intonation did she betray the fact that her whole scheme hung upon Bernhardt's reaction to that apparently innocent, but in actuality cunningly phrased question. And she saw, with a sense of satisfaction, that she had struck home as he stopped the glass he was raising, a look of suspicion upon his face.

"My mission with the Maharaja?" he queried. An undercurrent of anxiety troubled the cautious tones.

"Yes," Vivian said innocently. "About the diamond, you know."

She looked at him with an unreadable, faintly slant-eyed gaze. He put down his glass with a hand that was not quite steady. No one in the world save the Maharaja and himself knew that the great glittering gem was in London; that he contemplated purchasing it—and now this woman spoke of it as though the news were public property.

"May I ask," he queried, "how you know about my mission with the Maharaja?"

A glow flared and died in her green eyes. Vivian knew now that her hunch had been right. Up until then she had been working in the dark.

Bernhardt had spoken slowly and very thoughtfully. He seemed to be appraising the woman who had sunk down into the corner opposite him, her untouched glass still in her hand. Now her free hand flew to her lips in cleverly simulated dismay.

"But how thoughtless of me," she cried. "I should not have mentioned it to you. It is a secret, of course. I understand that. And believe me, this is the first time that I have spoken of it."

"How did you come to know of it?" Bernhardt's voice was coldly suspicious.

"I am afraid I am betraying a confidence, but—" She seemed pretty confused for a moment. "I have a friend in Scotland Yard." She played with her glass, twisting it so the stem shone in her fingers, a pale, metallic splinter of light. "They have been asked to take extra precaution while the Maharaja of Indrapoor is here, to guard some great gem that he has, and to watch everyone who enters the house except yourself. So naturally…" She made a gesture and did not finish.

Bernhardt breathed a sigh of relief. Coming in the way it did, the story sounded plausible enough.

"It's tomorrow night, isn't it?" she queried casually.

"No. Tonight. In fact, I must leave you in about an hour," he declared, with a glance at his wrist watch.

The Lady from Hell hid the start of alarm that his words caused her. Tonight! Then they would have to work fast indeed. Unperceived by the diamond millionaire her hand opened the little vanity case in her lap and extracted something from it.

"Then by all means, let us drink to your mission," she said, and picking up his glass, handed it to him. And he did not notice the swift gesture of her hand across the glass; failed to notice the tiny white pellet that dissolved almost as soon as it struck the amber fluid.

"To your success," she said, and picking up her own glass drained it.

THE NEXT FEW minutes were anxious ones for the Lady from Hell. Bernhardt had to be kept there and unsuspicious until the pellet worked, and to this end she exerted all of her charm. And so successful was she that ten minutes later his head dropped forward and he slumped against the arm of the easy chair in which he sat.

Laughing softly she got to her feet.

"Au revoir," she said to the unconscious figure. "I hope you enjoy your sleep. Because, when you awake, you will probably be very much displeased to know that I have the Kohinoor Double."

THE FLAT THAT the Maharaja of Indrapoor had taken was on the top floor of a house in a quiet street. That fact was the keynote of Vivian Legrand's plans, otherwise she would not have been lying on the parapet of the roof directly above the window that opened into the Rajah's sitting room. The moon was rising, but the spot where she lay was still in shadow. The next house, ten feet away, and a story higher, cast its shadow across her. Her only danger was that someone in that house might glance out of a window and see her shadowy form hugging the roof.

Beneath her, she knew, Adrian Wylie was carrying out his part of the plan. It was one of the few times in her criminal career that Wylie and herself had been separated. Usually they worked as a pair, but with her usual far sightedness, she knew that they would never be able to leave the Maharaja's flat alive with the great diamond in their possession, should they attempt a commonplace robbery. Hence the elaborate plan that had been worked out, with Wylie, bearing a forged letter of introduction from Bernhardt posing as the representative of the diamond millionaire.

Suddenly she tensed. A shadow had passed across the lighted window beneath her. Swiftly she uncoiled a light line at the end of which swung a little basket and lowered it down until it was level with the window sill, but to one side out of the line of vision inside the room.

As clearly as if she had been in the room herself she saw the grave, courtly Wylie, holding the glittering gem in his hands, take a step nearer the open window as he examined the gem through his jeweler's glass. There was silence in the room below.

Then came the signal. The lights in the room flashed out. The servant they had bribed had done his work to the split second. Carefully she swung the little basket out over the window and saw a hand come out of the window and grope for it. She steadied the basket, saw a flash as a stray ray of light caught the great faceted gem as it dropped in the basket; then she hauled it swiftly up again. Wylie, she knew, had instantly replaced the real gem with a false one the instant the real one had been dropped into the basket.

The little jeweler in Soho who had made that false gem for her was equally as famous as any jeweler in Covent Garden, London's great diamond center—but for a different reason. To him came ladies of the peerage for imitations of their family jewels, so that they might wear the replicas and keep the real stones securely hidden in bank vaults. Ladies of the night who had achieved a substantial footing on the ladder of success in their profession came to him for imitations of gems, so that the gentlemen responsible for the rent of their flats might never know that the real gems had been sold and the proceeds salted away for the inevitable rainy day. And the imitation of the famous Kohinoor Double he had made for the Lady from Hell would have passed as the original anywhere, except with an expert.

Swiftly she hauled up the line, dropped the gem in the specially prepared pocket of the trousers she wore and rose to her knees—and then catastrophe struck.

SUDDENLY FROM THE room below had come the sound of a slamming door—and a loud voice raised in angry tones—Bernhardt's voice.

For a moment Vivian stood there on the roof top. This was the one thing that her agile mind had not prepared for. Either Bernhardt had fooled her—had not tossed off the drugged cocktail—or its effect had been less potent than she had believed. His presence there meant that Wylie was trapped. And she knew that Bernhardt, a jewel expert, would distinguish at a glance what the Maharaja would not have discovered unaided—the fact that his gem had vanished and in its place was a substitute, cleverly made, but a substitute none the less.

Her eyes went swiftly about the roof. There was, of course, the rope ladder by which she had gained the roof. She might, if necessary, draw it up and drop it down to the level of the window through which Wylie had passed the diamond; gain entrance to the room below that way. She shook her head. That plan had many disadvantages and should be used only as a last resort.

At the rear of the roof was a tin capped affair some three feet square. Undoubtedly this covered the opening which gave access to the roof. Below it, she knew, there would be either a ladder opening into a storeroom or a steep stairway. She moved along the parapet to the ventilator.

It took all of her strength to get the cover up. It had

evidently not been used for a long time but finally she raised it and dropped it back on the roof, making as little noise as possible.

She peered down into the well of blackness below. A steep ladder-like flight of steps disappeared into the darkness.

Leaving the trap door open, an avenue of quick escape should it be necessary, Vivian picked her way cautiously down the stairs to the floor, feeling her way along a wall of shelves until she came to a door. Evidently the ladder led into a storeroom.

Carefully and silently she opened this door and stepped out into a hallway that ran the length of the building. The house was in utter darkness—such utter darkness that the senses were almost swallowed by it. She groped her way, step by step, down the hallway, listening now and then for any sound. The blackness about her was unbroken by a single ray of light.

Her search was rewarded by the discovery of a door. Her trailing fingers found the knob and she knew that luck was with her, for the door opened silently inward and she stepped through.

Moonlight falling through a window showed her that she had entered the kitchen of the Maharaja's establishment, and on the further side she saw an oblong of darkness that could only be the door to the dining room. Standing in the center of the kitchen she stood waiting and listening for a minute or two; then she tiptoed toward the dining room door.

Suddenly she stumbled against a chair. The sharp noise it made as it skidded across the polished floor was like a volley of shots cannonading through the dark silence of the room.

From the room beyond came a sudden exclamation—a movement.

Beside one of the windows stood a tall sideboard, the angle between the heavy piece of furniture and the angle of the wall forming a pool of black shadow. Almost simultaneously with the movement in the next room Vivian glided into that pool of shadow, crouched there.

SHE WAS NOT a moment too soon. The door was flung open and a woman stood in the oblong of light, her figure silhouetted sharply against the brilliant glow that streamed into the dark dining room.

Stealthily Vivian felt for her automatic, and caught her breath with a little gasp as she realized that it was gone. Sometime during that tussle with the roof opening it must have dropped out of her pocket and the loss had gone unnoticed.

"Who is zat?" the woman in the doorway said, as she peered into the darkness.

Vivian held her breath. If the woman remained where she was—did not come further into the room or search it, she was quite safe there in her pool of shadow. But if she were discovered Vivian was quite prepared to throttle her—choke the other woman into unconsciousness to prevent the alarm being given.

This woman was evidently the French wife of the Maharaja, the woman with whom he was so madly in love that he could deny her nothing—the woman whose extravagances were responsible for the sale of the Kohinoor Double to

Bernhardt. And suddenly Vivian Legrand's agile brain perceived a way out of the dilemma.

Tense there in the shadows Vivian watched. If only the woman would go back into her room and permit her to start putting into operation the daring, harebrained scheme. And, as if the thought had leaped from Vivian's mind to hers, the woman turned away, stepped back into her room and closed the door.

Waiting a moment in silence to make sure that she was not returning, Vivian made her way cautiously through the kitchen to the hall and began feeling her way down toward the door behind which Wylie was held prisoner.

4

MEANWHILE, IN THE Maharaja's sitting room, Adrian
Wylie faced a group of hard-eyed men. Revolvers had
suddenly appeared in the hands of the two attendants
who were a part of the Rajah's retinue. Bernhardt's strong
fingers closed and unclosed as if with a desire to seize the
throat of the man before him.

Wylie felt a thin trickle of fear that was like an icy
finger, a sensation that came to him with the sight of those
moving fingers. It was not cowardice; he could not have
existed as the companion of the Lady from Hell as long as
he had and been a coward. It was simply the sensation of
the wild thing that finds the jaws of a trap closing about it.

Bernhardt moved toward him slowly, while the Maharaja's glance flitted from the one man to the other with cold
suspicion. He had eyes like sloes, had the Indian potentate.
They seemed to be pinched between cheeks and brows.
There was something Mongolian in his features, something
masklike, with the Oriental fold to the eyelids. And, like
an Oriental, he was quick to suspect treachery.

"What are you doing here?" Bernhardt demanded
of Wylie.

"I came as your representative," Wylie answered
smoothly. He was quite cool, but his mind was working
fast. He was in a bad spot and he knew it. And he knew that

he was going to need all the sidelights, however feeble, that might illuminate the tense situation that confronted him.

His glance flickered to the piece of black velvet upon the table, wrapped about the imitation gem. It was only a matter of time before Bernhardt would glimpse the stone, realize that it was an imitation. His eyes flitted rapidly about the room, seeking an avenue of escape. By now, Vivian would be gone from the roof, he knew, half way to their quarters with the diamond.

"Don't lie," the diamond millionaire warned him viciously. "You know that you're not my representative. You came here to try and steal the Maharaja's diamond."

"I came here as your representative," Wylie insisted. He tried to keep cool and collected. He had known, from the moment that Bernhardt had burst into the room, that he was trapped. He was talking, not from any hope of convincing Bernhardt of his innocence, but of gaining time to find a way out of the trap. "You were ill—unconscious. I knew that you had an appointment and rather than see you lose what you so evidently desired, I kept the appointment for you."

"And how did you know that I had an appointment with His Highness?" Bernhardt's voice was silky, suave, and its tone told Wylie that whatever his answer might be, it would serve but to close the jaws of the trap tighter about himself.

"From your secretary," Wylie said.

Instantly Bernhardt pounced upon the statement. "He did not know of the appointment," he said triumphantly. "You came to steal the stone. There is no doubt of it."

Wylie gestured toward the Rajah. "You may ask him if

there was any question of my taking the stone away with me. I simply made arrangements to have it delivered to you in person tomorrow."

"That is right," the Maharaja said. His English had, the accent of an Oxford man, for he had been educated there. His black eyes flitted suspiciously from one to the other.

"He meant to steal the stone," Bernhardt said positively. "I do not know how, but he would not have come here otherwise." Then he spoke sharply. "Has he the stone on him?"

"It is there," the Maharaja said, gesturing toward the little heap of black velvet upon the table.

Wylie gathered himself together tensely. It had come. He must act now, or not at all. And a blunder now—the smallest of missteps—would wreck him.

WITH A QUICK flip of his fingers Bernhardt flung back the velvet and peered down at the stone. Then a bellow of rage tore from his lips.

"He's substituted, a fake," he cried. "This isn't the real stone!"

He made a lunge toward Wylie.

And as he moved, Wylie moved also. The chair on the back of which his hand had rested skidded across the rug like a live thing and crashed into Bernhardt's knees sending him to the floor with a howl of mingled rage and pain. And in the same instant his arm, continuing the movement which had sent the chair skidding into Bernhardt, struck the shaded lamp upon the table; sent it crashing to the floor. In the resulting darkness he dived for the door upon the opposite side of the room.

But he had underestimated the quickness with which

the Rajah's guards could move. Before he had covered half
the distance to the door, hands were upon him, hands with
a grip like tempered steel.

In the same instant he heard a warning cry from the
Rajah and, although his knowledge of the Indian's tongue
was not perfect, he grasped the fact that it was an order to
use the knife, not a gun.

One hand went up under Wylie's left elbow, reached up
to grasp his fist. The hand reached its mark and Wylie was
caught, held in a human vise.

Another hand seized him, hands went about his throat
as lights in the wall brackets flashed on.

"Got him," Bernhardt said with a grunt of satisfaction
as he rose from the wreckage of the chair on the floor.
"Search him."

He swore in anger when the search disclosed nothing.

"Call the police," he said. "Give him his chance of returning the stone or going to prison."

"I wouldn't if I were you," said a voice from the doorway
that cut through the air like a metal tipped whip.

Stunned, the little group turned.

Leaning nonchalantly against the door frame was the
Lady from Hell. In the excitement following Bernhardt's
dramatic entrance no one had thought of locking the door,
and it had been an easy matter for her to slip into the
room. Her eyes, fixed on the little group, were the color of
sun-washed ice. Killer's eyes.

"To call the police would be equivalent to throwing your
diamond down the drain pipe," she said with a charming smile for the Maharaja. But Wylie knew, even if the
Maharaja and Bernhardt did not, what cold ferocity, what

deadly cunning, that tone could mask. "You see," Vivian went on, "I have the diamond—or had it, until I disposed of it securely before I entered your apartment."

Bernhardt ripped out an oath and the gun he carried flashed into view.

"So," he said, "it is you who are behind this?"

His tone was grim, and there was a tight anger about him that at once warned Vivian that he was extremely dangerous.

"Quite right," she said metallically, and there was a curious iron note in her voice that caused the Maharaja to lift his eyes and give her a sharp narrow glance. With the intuition of the Oriental he knew that there was something in the wind that was not apparent upon the surface. The air was suddenly electric, filled with the portent of danger, and the sense of it was strong in the minds of the men who faced her. "I am behind it. I engineered it—and it seems to me that the answer is obvious. I have the diamond. You want it. An elementary business transaction of seller and purchaser."

"Search her," Bernhardt said thickly to the guards.

HIS FURY-FILLED EYES held no recognition of the fact that she was a very beautiful woman; only the fact that she was a woman who threatened to thwart his plans.

And then Vivian did a surprising thing. Before the two men Bernhardt had ordered to search her could reach the spot where she stood, she had crossed the room in swift strides and flung open the door at its end—a door that disclosed a bedroom and a woman in negligee who rose in surprise from before a mirror. The same woman and the same room that Vivian had seen a few moments before.

"You may search me if you wish," she said clearly, "but before coming in here I gave the little parcel containing the diamond to a confederate. If I am not out of this house in…" she glanced at her wrist watch…" ten minutes, he is to drop the parcel down the nearest drain pipe."

Out of the corner of her eye she saw the Maharaja's wife draw nearer, curiosity in her face. The brilliantly lighted room turned her blue-black hair to lacquer and outlined her figure clearly through the thin violet silk of her negligee.

"I don't believe you," Bernhardt said flatly. "You're not fool enough to throw away the only thing that would buy your safety. And if you think you're playing poker, you'll find your bluff called."

He reached out and picked up the telephone receiver. Vivian did not stir from her position at the door.

"But me through to the nearest police station," he ordered the operator, and when he got his connection, gave his name and asked that a couple of policemen be sent at once to the Maharaja's address.

Then he turned back to the others in the room.

"I think you had better let me handle this," he said to the Maharaja. "I've probably had more experience in handling thieves and crooks than you have." He looked steadily at Vivian. "It will take probably ten minutes for the police to arrive. You have just that length of time to produce the diamond and go free. After that, you will have to make your bargain with a British judge. And don't imagine that you can escape through that door that you have so conveniently opened. I would have no scruples about shooting you if you attempt it."

"I have no intention of attempting to escape," Vivian's voice rose bitingly. Her eyes, like twin green rapiers, flickered to the woman who was standing near her now. "And what you do is a matter of complete indifference to me. If His Highness is willing to risk losing the diamond that he was selling, that is his affair. Perhaps his wife will not mind going without the things that she could have bought with that money."

"What ees zat?" the woman said alertly. There was a stillness in her poise, a stillness in her black eyes that told Vivian plainer than words could have done that her shot had gone true. She came past Vivian into the room. "Ze diamond— Eet has not been lost, *non?*"

"Not entirely," Vivian assured her. She knew that she must work fast. This woman—her insatiable desire for the good things of life—was the crux of Vivian's whole scheme. "Within a few minutes, however, the diamond will be lost forever, along with the money that Mr. Bernhardt would have paid His Highness, unless, of course, His Highness can be made to see reason. But he seems to be stubborn."

FOR A MOMENT the woman's hard black eyes stared into Vivian's green ones; appraised her after the manner of a jungle beast that has discovered an intruder in its lair.

"And why should ze diamond be lost?" she queried dangerously.

"Because I have stolen it," Vivian told her with superb calmness. She ran no risk of misjudging this woman. She knew the type from top to toe and saw in her the sort of predatory creature that will go to any extreme to avoid losing a precious possession—or to gain something ardently desired. "It would be quite easy for your husband to get it back. He has simply to add ten thousand pounds to the price he asked Mr. Bernhardt, pay that ten thousand to me, and I return the diamond. Refuse, and it is lost forever."

"She's got the diamond on her," Bernhardt said furiously.

The woman turned on Vivian like a vulture swooping onto its prey and ran her hands over her, turning the pockets of Vivian's trousers inside out. A moment or two later she turned away and shrugged.

"It is not zere," she said.

"And while you wait," Vivian said softly, "the police are on the way and once they arrive the diamond or what it represents to you in money, is lost to you forever."

The Maharanee turned ominously to her husband. That thrifty French peasant soul of hers which hated to see anything, no matter how trivial, go to waste was fussing with the knowledge that the loss of the diamond meant the loss of the things she craved. And the resulting flame was the thing upon which Vivian had counted.

"Zo," the Maharanee said. "And what about me? What about ze new car? And ze necklace of emeralds?" Her voice rose shrilly. "What will you do about them?"

"He prefers," Vivian put in smoothly, fanning the flame still higher, "to gamble that I am lying and to take the chance of losing it forever."

Fury flamed in the woman's face.

"Zo? Zat is no gamble. Eet costs you nozzing. You raise your price, you pay ze difference to zis ladyee—and I get ze things I weesh."

"But I have made the price, given my word that I would sell at that figure," the Maharaja protested. "I cannot change it."

"And I won't pay the difference," Bernhardt cut in. "She's lying, I tell you. A woman as clever as she, wouldn't take the risk of losing a stone like the Kohinoor Double. Toss her in jail and you'll get it back soon enough."

Vivian shrugged and turned to the Maharanee. No woman living, save the Lady from Hell, could have had the supreme effrontery to rob a man of a great diamond such as the Kohinoor Double and then return to the scene of her crime to blackmail the man she had robbed. But it was such breath-taking daring that had carried her from her father's gambling house in Shanghai to the pinnacle of crime upon which she stood. And, with the uncanny intuition that had never deserted her, she knew that the fact of her spectacular and daring presence there in the room, unarmed, when she could have made good her escape, had left the two men bewildered, shaken, uncertain.

"I am willing to gamble if you are," she said to the Maharanee.

FOR A MOMENT the two women stood there facing one another, black eyes boring deeply into green ones. Then the wife of the Maharaja turned suddenly to Bernhardt:

"Zo, you weel not pay more, eh?"

"No," Bernhardt said grimly.

"I zink zat you weel pay zat ten thousand pounds more, and be glad to do eet."

"Not for the devil himself," vowed Bernhardt.

"No," mocked the woman, "but eet is perhaps possible zat you weel do eet for an outraged woman, eh? Zat, Mon Cher Monsieur Bernhardt, is mooch, mooch worse zan ze devil. See…" a slender white hand flashed to her shoulder, ripped the filmy fabric of her negligee across her shoulders to shreds… "You come here to see my hoosband about ze diamond. He ees not here yet so you make what zey call in America ze passes at me. I struggle. Zese people, my zo dear friends zey hear me scream. Zey rush in—how ees zat, eh? Yes, I zink you weel pay."

"That, Your Highness," Vivian said softly, "is what is technically known in the trade as the badger game—with variations."

"But…" began the Maharaja.

His wife silenced him with a gesture and a swift sliding flow of words, swinging into the French with which she was more familiar.

"Keep quiet," she flung at him. "You may wish to run the risk of losing the diamond, but I do not."

Vivian turned to Bernhardt with a triumphant smile. "The little lady is very clever," she said sweetly. "Oh, I know that it is an old device. But it works, my friend, it works—especially when the woman in the case is the wife of an Indian ruler—and unrest seethes in India. Do you think that the British government will go easy with you? There is nothing they will not do to keep the news of such an insult to the wife of a ruling Indian prince from reaching India. You pay, or when the police that you have called arrive, I shall tell my story. They will call Scotland Yard. Scotland Yard will get in touch with the Prime Minister…" She shrugged with a little gesture of triumph.

Vivian's eyes were very bright; little red flames danced in their green depths. The Frenchwoman was playing into her hands even better than she had planned. She knew that she would win unless Bernhardt's stubbornness got the better of him.

"He will pay," the woman said confidently. For a fleeting second a bond seemed to have been established between Vivian and herself—two women leagued against their common enemy, man. "The price that you were to pay was one hundred thousand pounds. It is now one hundred and ten thousand pounds."

"I won't pay it," Bernhardt vowed again, but there was no conviction in his voice. He knew all too well the fact that England tolerates no insults to its native princes of India. And such an accusation against him would mean not only the loss of the knighthood he so strongly desired—it would mean disgrace, the withdrawing of favors; possibly his retiring from business—if not punishment.

"It seems to me," Vivian said calmly, "that the best way to handle the matter is for Mr. Bernhardt to pay Her Highness here the money for the diamond. She will, in turn, deliver to me the money I demand and I will deliver the stone to her. You see," she added with a charming smile, "I do not trust Mr. Bernhardt. He would be quite capable of setting a trap for me. But Her Highness, I think, is too desirous that the transaction go through to attempt to trap me."

She did not mention that the diamond, all the time, had been securely hidden in the crevice of the parapet on the roof above, and that there it would remain until the money had been paid her. Once she got her hands on the money she would inform the Maharanee, or whoever delivered the money, of the location of the stone. Otherwise it was stalemate.

THE DOORBELL SHRILLED loudly in the silence. For a long minute the four stared at one another.

"Quick," she said. "That is the police. Will you pay? Or shall Her Highness stage her—shall we call it 'act'—for the benefit of the bobbies?"

"Shall I begin to scream?" asked the Maharanee ominously.

"I'll pay," Bernhardt said, anger boiling in his voice.

"Very good," Vivian said. She turned to one of the guards. "Inform the police that they are no longer needed. And now, my companion and myself will go."

She turned to the Maharanee.

"It has been a pleasure to meet you, Your Highness, and I look forward to having lunch with you tomorrow at the Carlton. You will bring Mr. Bernhardt's little remembrance with you?"

"I shall bring it," the Maharanee said decisively.

And Vivian knew that she would; knew there would be no trouble when the Maharanee appeared with Bernhardt's ten thousand pounds.

THE EPISODE OF THE
LONDON QUEEN OF CRIME

*It Is a Duel Between Two Diabolic Women
When the Green-eyed Vivian Legrand Faces
the Ugly Queen of London's Underworld*

1

AN UNSEEN MENACE

IN THE SOFTLY lighted showroom of Henriette and Cie., one of London's most famous dressmaking establishments, Vivian Legrand surveyed the gown the mannequin was displaying for her, and then shook her head decisively.

"That is not my style," she said. "Too simple—too girlish. I do not look well in simple things. I must have something with more chic—more daring."

"Madame, of course, can wear the daring things," the saleswoman agreed. "But, unlike most women, she looks equally well in clothes with more youthful lines. However, we have something that I am sure will please madame. I will have the model display it for you."

Herding the model before her she disappeared through a door in the rear. Vivian's eyes wandered idly to her own reflection in the full length mirror that the body of the saleswoman had hidden from her view. And that casual movement saved her life. Had the saleswoman been an instant slower in stepping from Vivian's line of vision; had the eyes of the Lady from Hell not wandered to that mirror, her criminal career would have been ended an instant later.

She saw through the mirror a movement in the curtains of the fitting room behind her—saw them stir slightly—

*She saw the curtains part and a hand
clutching a dagger slip through*

part—and a hand clutching a gleaming dagger slip through
them.

With a lithe, cat-like motion Vivian sprang from the
chair she had been occupying and the slashing vicious
blow that would have plunged the knife to the hilt in her
back was futile.

Before the wielder of the knife could recover from the
blow that had gone wild, Vivian's hand darted out like the
head of a striking snake—a fraction of a second too late.
Her clutching fingers grazed a feminine wrist and hooked
in a link bracelet of odd design. The hand gave a convulsive
jerk, the slender bracelet snapped beneath the strain and
the hand vanished through the curtains again.

Long in the telling but brief in the action. Scarcely fifteen seconds had passed between the time that the Lady from Hell glimpsed the gleaming knife, until the moment that she sprang to the dressing room curtains where the hand had been, and flung them aside. The room was empty, but a tapestry that masked a doorway on the farther side still shook, betraying by its movement the fact that someone had just passed. Vivian Legrand quickly crossed the room and tried the door. It was locked.

With a grim look on her face the Lady from Hell turned back into the salesroom, picked up the slender trinket that she had plucked from the arm of her would-be murderer. Light from the shaded lamps caught her bright hair and turned it into a halo of flames about her exquisite, exotic face as she examined the bracelet. The thing was not expensive. They were turned out by the hundreds in Naples—Vivian knew the little shop on a side street where they were made and sold—but they were not usual in London.

This thing had been planned, carefully planned. The girl had been planted there, undoubtedly, by someone who knew the Lady from Hell, knew her movements, knew that she bought most of her gowns from Henriette and Cie. **HER FACE WAS** exceedingly thoughtful as the saleswoman opened the door in the rear and ushered in a mannequin wearing another gown.

"I am afraid that I shall not have time to look at the gown now," Vivian said with a charming smile. "I had forgotten the time, and I am late for an appointment now. Perhaps tomorrow."

Then she extended the slender chain that her fingers had snatched from the wrist of her attacker.

"I found this on the floor,"she said. "Very pretty thing, and apparently valuable. Doubtless one of your customers dropped it."

Her narrowed eyes watched the saleswoman keenly for any sign of recognition of the trinket. There was nothing in the eyes of the woman as she took the bracelet from Vivian's outstretched hands and turned it over.

"I don't know who could have dropped it," she said doubtfully. "I do not remember a customer wearing it."

The mannequin took a step forward in curiosity and then gave a little exclamation of surprise.

"Why," she said, "that belongs to Bianca Forli, one of the mannequins. She was sick today, and after trying to work was excused to go home, just a few minutes after you arrived. She will be glad to know that she has not lost it."

There was a gracious smile on the face of the Lady from Hell but in her green eyes flamed the spurt of fire that turned their greenness red as flame. Then the lids dropped softly as she turned and made her way out of the shop.

A few doors away she stopped at a public telephone and called Adrian Wylie, her companion in crime and chief of staff in all of her criminal enterprises.

"Adrian," she said sharply, when he answered. "I want a report on a girl named Bianca Forli. She's a mannequin, works for Henriette and Cie. I want to know where she lives, how long she has been living there—anything about her that you can find."

She did not tell him why she wanted the report, and he did not ask. The two, Adrian Wylie and the Lady from Hell had worked together in too many criminal ventures for either of them to demand explanations when an emergency arose. She knew that as soon as Wylie left the telephone a man would be at work tracing the girl who had attempted to kill her.

And on his part, Wylie knew that the Lady from Hell knew what she was doing. He had implicit faith in her judgment, and, while there were times when he argued with her against some course of action, he always ended by doing exactly what she said.

VIVIAN LEGRAND, LIKE many good sailors, could sense a storm before it made its appearance above the horizon. And now, as she and Wylie waited in the sitting room of the house they had rented in London, for a report on Bianca Forli, the sense of impending trouble that had been growing ever since the attack upon her, was heavy in the room.

She turned to Wylie with a little gesture of exasperation.

"I know that you've been laughing at me for three days," she said. "But I tell you there is something in the wind—something that means trouble."

Wylie smiled tolerantly. The two had just pulled off their second big criminal job in London. Their already well-filled bank accounts had been augmented and, to him, everything seemed rosy. He was tall and lean and gray-haired and impressive, a whimsical yet prudent and incalculably gifted criminal now turning fifty and still unknown to the principal authorities of the world charged with the suppression of crime. As a matter of fact, many of the exploits of the Lady from Hell would still be cloaked in secrecy if, years later, Wylie had not told some of them. Half dreamer, half distorted genius, he had only lacked the rare initiative and cold ruthlessness which Vivian Legrand amply provided. Directly they had met in Manila, where Wylie had been chief assistant to Mandarin Fi Tu, oriental underworld lord, their partnership had come into being.

"We've nothing to worry about," he said. "You're attaching too much importance to what happened in that dressmaking establishment. That knife might not have been intended for you at all. The girl might have mistaken you for someone else. Aside from that, everything is calm."

"The calm before the storm," she said ominously. "I feel it. I know it." She leaned forward earnestly. "You've heard the old saying about rats deserting the sinking ship. Well, that hits home to us, Adrian."

"We're not sinking," her companion retorted with a smile.

"No," she answered with emphasis. "But some of the rats think we are. Look at the trouble we've had getting a report on this Forli girl. Three days and we know no more about her than we did. Take Benton, for example. He made a good sum out of us by impersonating old man Ashebrooke in the Ashebrooke will case. He was scheduled for a good cut in this next job we're working on. Three days ago you assigned him to check on the Forli girl. And within an hour he was run down and seriously injured by an automobile."

"An accident," Wylie retorted.

"Perhaps," the Lady from Hell responded. "What about L'Estrange?"

"He was honest enough about it," Wylie said. "He wants to spend what he has made—enjoy life for a time."

"So he said. Went to the Riviera almost immediately. Expects to be there six months. But he didn't decide that he wanted to drop out until after he'd been assigned to work on the Forli girl."

"Just coincidences," Wylie said. "Coincidences do happen you know."

"Perhaps," Vivian answered evenly, "except for the fact that I saw L'Estrange today in London—and you saw him off for Monte Carlo yesterday."

FOR A MOMENT the last phrase hung suspended in the air. It was as though each article in the room repeated it, echoing it again and again against some distant mountain of understanding. Then Wylie sat up alertly.

"L'Estrange—you saw him in London?"

She nodded. "In Soho. He didn't see me. I took good care that he shouldn't. But that was all I needed. I've felt for days that something was wrong. That attempt to knife me confirmed the feeling. Benton's accident made me more sure, and now the fact of seeing L'Estrange in London when he is supposed to be on the continent leaves no doubt in my mind." She leaned forward earnestly. "Adrian, we're facing trouble. Just what kind of trouble, I don't know, except that I'm sure it isn't the police. It may be the outgrowth of one of our jobs in Paris, in Turkey—I don't know, but whatever it is, it means trouble, and serious trouble at that, I'm sure."

She turned as a servant appeared in a doorway.

"Mr. Burt, Mrs. Legrand," he said.

"Show him in," Vivian ordered, and the two waited in silence until a tall, slim man appeared in the entrance. Burt was a recent addition to the Legrand gang. He was a private detective, and through underworld channels and connections, Vivian had found that he was in league with a gang of jewel thieves. Burt would map out a robbery and then, when a reward was offered return the jewels in his capacity of private detective and collect the reward. With her usual acumen, Vivian had contacted the man, given him his choice of becoming a member of the Legrand forces or having his entire record placed before the police. This was his first job with them.

"Listen," he said, seating himself across the table from the Lady from Hell. "There's something funny about that Forli woman. I don't like it. Here's her address." He tossed a folded slip of paper across the table to Vivian. "She's a mannequin at Henriette et Cie., all right—earns five pounds a week—and lives in a flat in St. John's Wood that costs a cool thousand pounds a year. It's not the usual answer either. There's no man. She lives alone. Has a few friends who come in now and then, but not a hint that any of the men might be paying her bills. I checked with—"

A muffled coughing sound, simultaneously with the clear tinkle of breaking glass behind Burt cut short his sentence. Amazement appeared in his eyes—amazement that faded to blankness as he slowly slumped forward onto the table, a slowly spreading stain on the back of his coat.

Ignoring the stricken man Vivian sprang for the switch and plunged the room into darkness, then ran for the window and peered out. A bright moon turned everything to silver. There was no one in sight. Nothing living save a bat that noiselessly cut the night, swift and soundless as the shadow of a phantom. But she saw immediately where the shot had come from. There was only one possible spot, and mentally she cursed herself for not having taken precautions against that one vulnerable spot. Doors sheathed in steel. Windows guarded by iron grilles. Yet, bounding the paved areaway outside was a brick wall, almost on a level with the windows of the room in which she stood. On the top of that wall marksmen had stood or knelt and fired across the intervening space at their target in the brightly lighted room.

She turned back, drew the curtains and snapped on the lights as Wylie straightened up from the figure slumped across the table. She nodded slowly.

"Dead," he said curtly. "Killed almost immediately."

Vivian's face had tightened into a grim expressionless mask. Behind her clung her shadow, black, motionless, vengeful against the wall. "It's war," she said. "War to the bitter end, with the disadvantage of not knowing whom we're fighting—not knowing where the next shot is coming from. But we've got an ace in the hole that they don't know about." She held up the folded slip of paper that Burt had tossed to her. "The address of the Forli woman."

2

DEATH DARES VIVIAN LEGRAND

NOT ONE OF the dozens of people who witnessed the little scene on the crowded street realized that a kidnaping was taking place under their very eyes. Not one of them realized that the slender girl, walking between the tall, red-haired woman and the gray-haired well-dressed man was as much a prisoner as if she had been behind iron bars, held in the bonds of fear inspired by the gun in the pocket of the man and the smaller, but none the less deadly gun in the muff that the Lady from Hell carried.

It had been easy for them to drift quietly up on either side of Bianca Forli as she left Henriette et Cie. A swift, whispered word or two, a significant glimpse of the guns, and the girl, pale beneath her rouge, had walked quietly on with them. A hundred or so feet away a car waited at the curb, its engine purring softly. Within ten minutes they had vanished into London's afternoon traffic.

Once inside her own house, the steel sheathed door bolted, the curtains drawn across the iron grilled windows, the Lady from Hell turned toward the girl who stood defiantly in the center of the room, her glance touching her briefly; a look unlightened by the loveliness of her. Bianca Forli was young and amazingly beautiful, Her black hair was parted at the little widow's peak on her forehead and combed sleekly back over her ears. Her eyes, too, were black beneath the dark curved lines of her brows. But it was the lips that gave an index to the character. Beautifully shaped, they were cruel, sensuous, and marred what might have been an almost perfect ensemble.

Just now, shock of finding herself the captive of the woman she had tried to kill had tightened her eyes. In the diluted light of the room her face was dead white, but she was, nevertheless, holding a tight rein upon her emotions.

"Take off your hat," Vivian told her smilingly. "I'm sure you will be more comfortable."

"My stay will not be long enough," the girl told her curtly, her trapped eyes shifting from one to the other, "to make it worth while."

Vivian's answer was swift and thoroughly in keeping with the reputation that had caused her to be nicknamed the Lady from Hell. Before the Forli girl realized what was happening Vivian had lashed out with her open palm and struck the girl on the face. Bianca gasped under the impact and staggered against the wall.

"Take off your hat," Vivian blazed. Her green eyes flared and the girl had a glimpse of another woman. That glare chilled her, hardened though she was.

Slowly the girl's hands went to her head. She lifted off the hat and dropped it on the table.

"You are wrong about how long you will stay," Vivian told her. The threat was as plain as words could have made it. "Your stay will not be brief, in any event, and the length of it depends entirely upon yourself."

"You won't dare harm me," the girl said. Her eyes were

darting nervously from one to the other and her hands trembled. There was no courage in her voice and her manner when she went on. "If you weren't a fool you'd get out of London, without adding to the trouble, already brought upon yourself."

"Oh, we wouldn't dream of harming you," the Lady from Hell said, a little red flame leaping from behind her green eyes and she permitted herself a slow, deep smile. "You won't die—although you might perhaps wish that you had. There is nothing so pathetic as a beautiful girl who finds herself suddenly hideous."

CLEARLY, EVER SO clearly, her words dropped into stillness, flogging the girl's rising fear with their sinister suggestion. Bianca's hand went unsteadily to her throat.

"What do you mean?" she demanded.

Her answer was a scream from the next room, shrill, inarticulate, rising with a soulless quaver—a scream that resembled a call of despairing madness that summons death to strike and have done. It was a fearful thing, that cry, and the agony of death was in it.

The girl's startled eyes flew to the door from behind which the scream came, and her face blanched, her lips tightened. Vivian watched her with a cold, grim smile.

That silence of hers was calculated, artful. It was a wall as blank as her eyes. She waited for the effect of the scream to strike home before she spoke. "Perhaps," she said, "it would be better to leave your face until the last. Yes, I think it would be better. The arms and shoulders first. Then, if you should desire to talk, the only harm would be that you could never wear an evening dress again. But the face would be preserved."

There was an unsteady note in the girl's voice as she spoke.

"Don't you realize what you're up against?" she said frantically. "Don't you know that within half an hour this place will be ringed about with armed men, and, if they cannot gain entrance, you will never leave it alive."

"No," Vivian said regretfully. "I don't know it. In fact, I don't believe it! Now, my child, we wish to know why you attempted to kill me—and we want to know who is behind you. If you are willing to talk, that pretty white skin of yours will not be harmed. If not—well, Doctor Wylie here is a very skillful surgeon as well as an eminent scientist."

She crossed the room and flung open the door behind which the scream had come. It was a room done all in white, white walls, a bright light suspended low above a white metal table over which two men bent.

"In here," she said curtly to the girl, and motioned her to enter.

Reluctantly Bianca came forward; stepped through the door. As she did so the two men straightened up, picked up a limp form from the gleaming table and placed it upon a stretcher—a form of a man stripped to the waist. He was unconscious but even in his unconsciousness he was moaning slightly from the pain of the hideous scars on his face and chest. His lips seemed to have been almost burned away by some corrosive acid—his face seemed to be one great raw wound and the hair had been burned away in a great slash across his head and where the hair had been was a raw wound.

The men passed slowly by the girl, giving her time to take in the full hideousness of what she saw, but not lingering long enough for her to realize that it was entirely a matter of makeup—skillful, painstaking make-up that had taken the clever Wylie several hours to apply.

DRY SOBS CAME from the girl's throat. Her manicured fingers clutched at her face, as if already feeling the horrible scars at which she was gazing on the face of the man. Her eyes, horror stricken, clung to the motionless form on the stretcher.

"That," Vivian said, and her voice was as soft and purring as that of a cat, as the door behind the stretcher closed, "was a man we thought could tell us something that we wanted to know. But we were wrong. He was evidently telling us the truth when he said that he did not know."

The shadow of the callous thing she had just witnessed had not left the girl's face. Over it had come a strange gray tint as if the sight she had beheld had reminded her of something more terrible than death. Little beads of perspiration sprang out upon her forehead. A door behind her opened, and a man entered silently, bearing a bag which he placed upon the floor.

"I hope for your sake," Vivian went on, "that you know what we desire to learn."

She made a signal and the man behind the Forli girl seized her in an iron grip before she had realized he was there. Wylie sprang to his aid, and in a moment the girl was strapped to the long table in the center of the room. With swift movements Vivian ripped off her dress at the throat so that the girl's arms and shoulders were bare.

With leisurely movements Wylie took off his coat, opened the bag that the servant had brought and arranged the instruments it contained on a little side table. Then he picked up a scalpel and tested the keenness of its edge critically, as the girl watched with horror in her eyes.

"Blindfold her," Vivian ordered.

Once the bandage had been securely adjusted the Lady from Hell asked:

"Are you ready to talk?"

Fear clung to the girl like a tangible aura, but still she was not willing to talk. Something—some greater fear—it was evident to the two, held her, kept her silent.

"I tried to kill you because I hated you," she cried desperately but her voice cracked as she said it. "No one told me to do it."

"Don't try to run a bluff on me," Vivian said harshly. "You'll be glad enough to talk when we get through with you. You see, Dr. Wylie will start by making half a dozen or so slashes across your chest. Into these he will rub an ointment that will cause them to turn blue when they heal. That will be charming, will it not? Ready, Doctor?"

"Ready," Wylie responded.

Taking up a steel needle, he made a long scratch across the girl's chest, while the Lady from Hell squeezed warm water from a sponge onto the scratch. The trickling warmth gave the girl the impression of flowing blood.

She screamed once, twice, the sound cutting through the still room in a thin knife blade of terror, Vivian said softly:

"Why waste your breath, my child? That is only the beginning—unless you are willing to talk."

"No," sobbed the girl. "I don't know anything."

"Again," rasped the Lady from Hell, and again the needle scratched the girl's chest; again the warm water from the sponge gave the sensation of flowing blood.

IT WAS NOT because of scruples that the Lady from Hell was refraining from actually torturing the girl, because she had no scruples. She was as ruthless, as cruel, as savage as a tigress in the jungle. It was because she had seen in this girl a possible addition to her own forces, and, past mistress in psychology that she was, she knew that the terror-ridden mind of the girl would convince her that she was being tortured.

"Wipe away that blood," she said sharply to Wylie as the girl strained forward against her bonds, gasping, greenish.

"No sense of permitting it to drip onto the table."

With a soft cloth she wiped away the warm water, and then said:

"Perhaps it would be better to start work on the face now. She seems stubborn. You might start here, perhaps," and she touched the girl's cheek.

The girl shuddered and then her nerve broke.

"I'll talk," she said wildly, "I'll talk. They'll kill me for it, but I'll tell you what you want to know."

"Talk," Vivian told her grimly.

"It's Madame Trescott—Madame Paula Trescott—who ordered me to kill you. You've interfered with her plans. She was afraid you might interfere with her again—"

She halted a moment gasping for breath. Vivian's eyes glowed. That single sentence had made things clear to her.

Paula Trescott. The woman who for years had been called the Empress, of the London Underworld. The woman Who had a finger in nearly every form of vice, crime and undercover activities. Vivian had never seen the old woman—few people had—and it was generally whispered in the underworld that she had retired from criminal activities.

"So," she said, "it is Madame Trescott who wishes me out of the way."

"Yes," the girl gasped. In a tumble of words, their passage winged by the terror that gripped her, she went on.

"It was Madame who planned the Ashebrooke case and it was Madame who planned the kidnaping of Bernhardt, and both of them you spoiled. She did not want to take a chance on her next scheme being upset."

"And what is her next scheme?" Vivian queried.

"I—I can't tell you," the girl whispered.

"No? What a pity," Vivian cooed. "You have such an attractive face."

"Please—" came tremblingly from the girl's pallid lips.

The Lady from Hell took a firm grip on the girl's head.

"Go ahead, Doctor. Start at the mouth and work up toward the left eye," she said.

"No! No! No!" the girl screamed. "I'll tell! I'll tell you anything you want to know."

"That's sensible," Vivian said. "All this stubbornness is such a foolish waste of time. And now, what is Madame Trescott's scheme?"

"Tonight," the girl said, "the jewels of the Duchess of Renwick. She is wearing them to a ball. Sometime during the ball—I do not know the details—she is to be robbed of them and the jewels delivered to Madame."

"So," Vivian said slowly. "The jewels of the Duchess of Renwick."

Her eyes were bright. Those particular jewels were fabulous. They had been in the family of the Duke of Renwick for generations, and in Vivian's card index of future jobs, those jewels were marked with a double star, indicating that they were particularly desirable.

For ten minutes she plied the girl with swift questions, and then turned to the servant who had been standing beside the door.

"Lock her in the corner room on the top floor," she said curtly. "See that she does not get out."

With a swift gesture she beckoned Wylie from the room.

"It was Napoleon, wasn't it," she asked, "who said that the only way to win a war is to strike the enemy first—and strike the hardest? Well, tonight we strike at Madame Paula Trescott."

3

THE SPIDER'S WEB

THE BUILDING BEFORE which the Lady from Hell and her companion alighted from their car that evening had the appearance of a magnificent country home. Every window was brightly lighted, and from it came faintly the strains of music played by an expensive orchestra.

For nearly an hour their car had stood hidden in the deep shadows beneath a group of ancient oaks beside the road, while the two watched. It was nearly eleven o'clock before a car that they recognized from the description Bianca Forli had given them roared past them and into the driveway. In that car, if the mission of Paula Trescott's agents had been successful, were the jewels of the Duchess of Renwick.

Neither of them had made any effort to disguise themselves. It was part of the plan of the Lady from Hell that they should be recognized and recognized as soon as possible.

They stood for a moment at the entrance to the club. The Lady from Hell knew quite well that tonight she was more conspicuous than ever before. She had intended to be. The flame of her dress brought out the sheen of her hair, edged it with little tones of flame, accentuated the lacquer-red of her lips into curved lines of beauty. She would not have been a woman had she not realized the arresting picture she made, and the shaded lights of the place brought out rather than dimmed the picture.

The partitions of the entire first floor had been torn out, turning it into one huge room. In the center was a dance floor, and about it were grouped little tables, most of them well filled. To the world in general the place was a fashionable and exceedingly expensive supper club. To the initiate, there were rooms upstairs where roulette and *chemin de fer* might be played and—to still others who cared nothing for gambling, there were other rooms where other vices, much less harmless, might be indulged in. In other words, it was the center of the spider's web of Madame Paula Trescott.

The head waiter hurried forward to greet Vivian and Wylie, his eyes flitting over the two appraisingly. A folded bill in Wylie's hand was slipped into that of the head waiter, and as if by magic, one of the reserved signs on a table beside the dance floor vanished and chairs were pulled forth for them.

Vivian's eyes flickered about the place. Beside the orchestra platform a man in evening clothes lounged beside a door. That door, Vivian knew from the Forli girl, led to the wing where Madame Trescott spun her webs, and to pass through it one needed to be sent for by the Queen of Vice, or to be vouched for with as much ceremony as a diplomat seeking an audience with a sovereign.

Both knew that it would only be a matter of minutes before they would be recognized. It stood to reason that more than one person in the entourage of the Queen of Vice knew them by sight. Vivian's evening bag lay open on the table in front of her. Her plan might work—and again she might have desperate need of the little automatic that snuggled among the feminine fripperies in the bag.

They had been in the place scarcely ten minutes when a man slipped into the other chair at their table.

"Madame Legrand," he said suavely.

"Yes," Vivian said.

She would have known the man to be a killer without being told. He had bad eyes, pale, uneasy and half hidden under heavy lids. They had a flat stare to them as deadly as nightshades. Very tall, perhaps six feet one, he had crossed to their table with a curious, gliding movement like a dancer advancing onto a polished floor. His head was hairless; not even on his brows nor fringing his drooping lids was there a hair. As his quick stare rested on them across the table, his right hand lifted instinctively toward the lapel of his tuxedo. But something in their attitude reassured him. His hand dropped back to his side, empty.

"Your visit is most welcome," he assured them, "even though it is unexpected. Madame Trescott will be most pleased to see you."

"Madame Trescott?" Wylie said with a note of well simulated agitation in his voice. "You mean that she is the owner of this club?"

ALREADY WYLIE KNEW more about this man than the man himself suspected. By the hairless head, by the accent of the voice, by the panther-like tread, he had already recognized him as King Curley, a former American boxing champion who had turned criminal.

"Quite right," Curley told him. "Madame Trescott is the owner of the club. And now if you will come with me—no, just leave that where it is," he snapped as Vivian's hand went out toward her evening bag. "I know quite well, Mrs. Legrand, that there is a gun in your bag, and that your companion has a gun in a shoulder holster. It would perhaps be better if he laid it quietly upon the table and covered it with a napkin."

"And suppose we refuse?"

Neither she nor Wylie had any intention of refusing. They had known that it would be an impossibility to gain the presence of Paula Trescott with a weapon. But to have acquiesced without a murmur might have been cause for suspicion.

The man's lashless lids lifted, exposing the flat stare of his uncurtained eyes. Vivian could smell death in the air as his gaze fixed upon her. Then he nodded at a heavy set man who stood near their table, a hand in his pocket suggestively.

"I am not without assistance, you see, and there are half a dozen others within call."

"I take it," Vivian said, rising to her feet, "that we have inadvertently stepped into the lion's jaws."

"Something of the sort," he agreed. "In fact, I might go so far as to say that you have come to the one place in London that it would have been wisest for you to stay away from. And now, if you will be so kind as to follow that gentleman." His nod indicated a man standing nearby. "I will follow you."

Once inside the little door beside the orchestra platform, the man stopped before them.

"I shall have to search you," he said briefly.

Wylie started to protest but Vivian silenced him with a

gesture. And then, Curley and the woman he summoned to his aid, proved that they knew a great deal about the Lady from Hell and her companion. The search was thorough, even to the examining of Wylie's cigar case and cigars and the heels of Vivian's brocaded evening slippers.

Something that might have been a gleam of triumph appeared in Vivian's eyes when he had finished, but her eyes, as they met Curley's, were wide and innocent. Her ace in the hole was still safe and she had no intention of betraying its presence by an unguarded look or movement.

Then, with a little bow Curley stepped aside and ushered them into a short passage. At its further end a door opened noiselessly, revealing a passage somewhat wider than the one they had left.

They walked on down the passage until, pushing aside a curtain of black velvet, they found themselves in a long room. And then, silhouetted blackly against a tapestry of rippling silk at the far end was a woman seated upon a throne—an incredible woman, ancient, haggard, wrinkled—and literally dripping in jewels. They were in the presence of the almost mythical Paula Trescott, born in Italy as Paula Trescotti, queen of London crime. Two dark eyes gleamed as brightly as any of the jewels she wore were all that remained of what must once have been great beauty. **VIVIAN'S EYES FLITTED** about the room, noting, verifying. There was, seemingly, no other entrance save the one through which they had come, but the walls were hung with black draperies and she knew from the Forli girl that the draperies masked at least one other door—a passageway close beside the throne-like chair on which Madame Trescott sat. The telephone on the long polished table against one of the walls she knew, also from the same source, was a private wire that did not connect with any of the other telephones in the house.

A sound—the soft whisper of bare feet on stone—caused Vivian to turn. On either side of them stood a man clad in black. They had materialized out of the darkness like somber ghosts. A slim, keen knife gleamed in the hands of each man.

A voice, a soft voice, with the oddest inflection imaginable—a soft slurring that was like no other accent that either of them had ever heard—a tonelessness that was like that of a person speaking in a dream.

"Greetings, Mrs. Legrand. And to you, also, Adrian Wylie."

For a moment there was silence. Then the old woman on the throne spoke again and there was a note of menace in her voice.

"Death waits hungrily in those knives."

Vivian answered her, flinging her words straight down the room at the shrunken figure upon the throne.

"If death is hungry, let it eat." For a moment there was a silence and the old woman leaned forward as if she had not heard.

Curley said quietly:

"Madame does not hear well, although she dislikes having the fact mentioned. You might raise your voice a trifle."

Vivian repeated her words in a louder voice and this time the old woman caught them. A hideous parody of a chuckle issued from the withered throat.

"A fool as always, eh? Well, no matter, a fool and his life

are soon parted. Here are my orders. Within forty-eight hours you are to be out of England—and you, too, Adrian Wylie. I care not where you go. The continent, America, back to Shanghai. It matters not. But death waits at your heels, and on the minute, forty-eight hours from the time you leave my door, death will strike if you are not beyond the boundaries of England."

Vivian laughed and said clearly, so that there might be no chance of the old woman's slightly deaf ears missing her words:

"And why should I take your threats seriously?"

"Because you love life, Vivian Legrand. I know you. I know how you fled from Shanghai after poisoning your father. I know how you blackmailed the British secret service in Rangoon, and snatched a political prisoner from under the noses of his jailers in the Andaman Islands, then sold him back again to the British. I know how you robbed the banker on the Riviera who was looting his own bank; how you outwitted Vediva Bey in Constantinople and escaped from a Turkish jail; know how you betrayed Wardell in Paris; know how you blackmailed Wolf Bernhardt here in London—and snatched what should have been mine."

VIVIAN'S OWN EYES narrowed as she saw the wild hatred which, for a brief instant, exploded in those beady eyes and she regretted, momentarily the hardihood which had made her invade the old woman's stronghold. True, she felt that her own cunning was more than a match for Paula Trescott's, but there was always the possibility that the scheme she had so carefully rehearsed with Wylie might slip. And she knew that the tiniest slip would mean death—quick and sudden—for the two of them.

"London is not big enough for both of us," the toneless voice of the old woman went on. "So you must go."

"And if I do not go?" Vivian questioned.

"You die!" Paula chuckled again. "I might have had you betrayed to the police, but I admire your courage. So I give you a chance,"

"Betray me to Scotland Yard," Vivian said. "That would be squealing"

"I call it expediency," the old woman said drily, and struck a small gong at her elbow. As the mellow tones of the gong died away the dim lights of the room slowly turned brighter, rising higher and higher as if the light were a tide on the flood. There was an odd touch of legerdemain about it, like the swift work of a maser magician. Vivian nodded her head approvingly. Herself a past mistress of effect, she could appreciate the stage setting with which the ancient queen of crime had surrounded herself.

"You are very beautiful," the old woman went on, surveying the Lady from Hell with beady eyes in which malice burned deeply. "I was like that a generation ago. More fascinating than Cora Pearl, lovelier than Castiglione herself who snared Napoleon the Little."

"We might do well together, you and I," Vivian said suddenly, taking a step or two nearer the old woman.

Paula shook her head, and her beady eyes had the merciless gleam of a bird of prey ready to sweep to the kill.

"No. I take no partners. I only work with women who are pawns in the game. It is not for nothing that I am called the most dangerous woman in Europe. I intend to keep my title." She peered at the two through bright eyes. "Remember—forty-eight hours before death strikes."

Wylie and Vivian exchanged glances.

"Forty-eight hours will find me still in London, and alive," Vivian said boldly. Behind her Wylie imperceptibly shifted his position nearer to the motionless figure on the throne-like chair. His nerves were tense. This was the closest that the two of them had ever seen death, and their game was nearer its climax. "I am not to be frightened from London by an old woman who merely calls herself the most dangerous woman in Europe," Vivian went on, and there was a deadly sweetness in her voice. "For you see, I *am* the most dangerous woman in Europe."

Again the old woman chuckled.

"Not yet, Vivian Legrand. Only when I am dead can you claim that title. Perhaps if your plan tonight had succeeded, you might have laid claim to it."

4

A WOMAN'S DARING

VIVIAN STARTED EVER so slightly, and her cold green eyes slashed at the other's face. Had this ancient hag penetrated her scheme? Paula seemed to read her thoughts with almost uncanny penetration.

"Aye, your plan has failed," she said. "I know what you have planned—I know that followers of yours were to slip quietly into the supper club under the guise of guests—force their way into my apartment and kidnap me." She chuckled again, a gleeful, wicked chuckle. "But one of them talked, and within five minutes after you entered my supper club every one of your men had been given a message from you—that your plans had been changed and they were to return to your house in London and await you." She struck the arm of her chair lightly to emphasize her words. "You thought you came here to open the jaws of a trap that would close on Paula Trescott—but you walked instead into a trap that Paula has set for you."

For a moment Vivian said nothing, but her brain was working swiftly. If the old woman's words were true, they were trapped. And there was no reason to doubt that Paula Trescott had done exactly what she said she had done. In her place Vivian knew that she would have done just that. Out of the corner of her eye she caught a glimpse of Wylie's face. It was a set, quiet mask, but she knew that consternation seethed in him as it did in her. But there was her ace in the hole—the weapon that Curley had overlooked in his search. A dubious weapon, but, situated as they were, the best at their command.

Vivian took a casual step forward, and flung out her hand in a gesture of resignation. Her tone was almost humble as she spoke.

"You are cleverer than I am," she admitted. "There is nothing that I can do—save accept your offer and leave London within forty-eight hours."

"No," Paula flung at her. "My offer is withdrawn. You bickered too long. And, besides, it will be safer for me if you die now."

Vivian paled. For a moment silence hung in the air between the two women. Then Madame Trescott gave a swift, curt command, and before Vivian could resist the guards had seized her wrists; held her firmly.

"Your ring interests me," Paula said almost in a whisper, leaning forward. At her command, one of the guards removed the massive gold ring from Vivian's finger and extended it to the old woman. She took it gingerly, and then, after a momentary examination, chuckled softly.

"So. You had this in store for me, did you? But I am Italian, and I, too, am familiar with the pattern of the ring that Lucrezia Borgia wore. A little pressure on the setting of the ring and a poison needle darts out, eh? You thought to poison old Paula, eh?"

Trapped, helpless, her last weapon taken from her, the clever mind of the Lady from Hell was still at work, seeking frantically a solution to the impasse in which she found herself. An idea lashed into her brain—a possible escape. She acted on it instantly. With a slight shrug she walked leisurely over to the table against the wall; leaned against it, her hands resting upon the table behind her.

"I had not thought that you would discover that weapon," she said.

There was silence in the room for a moment. But Vivian's brain was working coolly, methodically, and in her eyes was something more deadly and remorseless than any sudden flare of anger might bring. Wylie watched for a message. But her head was slightly bent. He could see nothing but her profile and that gave him no clue.

She was staring at a jeweled bracelet on her wrist. Slowly she undasped it and balanced it on the palm of her hand.

She said in a quiet voice, "This has brought me luck all my life, but now it has failed me. My luck has vanished. Take it."

WITH A SUDDEN movement she flung the glittering trifle into the far corner of the room. Every eye save Wylie's followed its passage. He alone witnessed the sudden gesture with which she placed her hand behind her; saw, even if he did understand the significance, the careful way in which she moved her body so that the actions of that hand were shielded from both Paula and her guards.

Paula's eyes flashed back to her captive.

"Luck cannot last forever," she said drily.

"I suppose," Vivian said, "that we have only a very brief time to live?"

Something in her tone caused Wylie to look at her

quickly. He knew that subtle intonation. Something was working in that brain of hers.

Paula Trescott laughed drily. "You are quite right," she said.

"Unless, of course," Vivian said slowly, "the police should come to our rescue."

"I do not think," the old woman said, "that you need hope for that."

"Scotland Yard," Vivian said, choosing her words with more than ordinary precision, her voice loud and clear so that the slightly deaf woman on the throne-like chair could not miss hearing, "at this moment is being warned that Madame Paula Trescott is holding a man and a woman prisoners in a room in a wing adjacent to her supper club and plans to put both of them to death."

Wylie wondered at the stilted, almost melodramatic way in which she couched her phrases. He swept the room searchingly from beneath lowered lids. But there seemed nothing to justify hope. Both of them were covered by armed men. He raised his eyes to Vivian's and it was with a tingling shock that he read unmistakable warning there. But of what? Furtively he swept the room again, not daring to let his eyes linger on the Trescott woman, lest she read in them some part of the emotion that flooded him.

"I am afraid that Scotland Yard will not be notified until later," Madame Trescott said comfortably. "And even then, the finding of the bodies of a man and woman in the river will not cause too great a commotion."

"How much time have we to live?" Vivian asked. "Sufficient for a last cigarette?"

"For a last cigarette, perhaps," the woman granted with a royal gesture.

Vivian alone knew how much had depended upon the woman's reaction to the request for a last cigarette. And now she was playing for time— Talking for time.

"May I have one from Mr. Wylie's case?" Vivian requested. "Mine are Turkish, and Turkish tobacco bums much faster than Virginian."

"Go ahead," Paula said pleasantly. She was enjoying the situation, playing with them as a cat plays with a mouse. Then she added grimly. "I realize that both of you have been searched and your weapons taken from you, but I might remind you that my men are both good shots."

WYLIE CROSSED THE room to Vivian, snapping his cigarette lighter into flame. And the movement brought him momentarily to Vivian's side. His eyes widened with amazement, and for a fleeting second comprehension flooded his face. Then he caught the warning look in Vivian's eyes and held the flame to the cigarette with expressionless face.

"Thank you, Adrian," Vivian said graciously. For a moment his eyes met hers. The almost imperceptible nod of his head told her that he also knew the desperate game that was being played. Then Vivian turned her head toward Paula. "Of course," she said, "you realize that I am making the cigarette last as long as possible. There is still time for the police to save us—if they are notified in time."

A hushed expectancy had shut down over the room like a tangible thing. Wylie was watching Vivian keenly, fully aware of the battle of wits that was going on and inwardly raging helplessly at his own inability to share it. He could not wrest his eyes from the slowly growing length of ash on the tip of the cigarette.

If only that cigarette lasted a sufficient length of time, the slender thread of hope upon which Vivian had hung their lives might be justified. And it might work. So tremendously simple, so ingenuous, so childish, that the very simplicity, the obviousness of it prevented detection. It seemed a preposterous thing to base a hope upon a plan so absurd, yet he knew that the absurdity of it made for its success.

On her throne, her chin cupped in her wrinkled hands, Paula Trescott watched the cigarette between Vivian's lips as if fascinated. She derived a certain sadistic pleasure from watching death creeping nearer as the glowing coal crept nearer to Vivian's carmine lips. And it irked her that there was no sign of nervousness, of terror, on the part of the Lady from Hell.

"May I ask how you intend to kill us?" Vivian queried. Her head was cocked to one side, as though she were listening for something. And Wylie, also, seemed to have that same, carefully guarded air of listening.

"Does it matter?" Paula queried with a chuckle.

"Not particularly," Vivian admitted. "But naturally we are interested."

A full inch of ash dropped from the cigarette. Every eye in the room followed it to the floor. Paula chuckled drily.

And then, suddenly, the black velvet drapes at the farther end of the room were flung open. Curley stood in the opening.

"Madame," he said hoarsely. "The police—they are in the supper club. They know that you have a man and a woman here—I do not know how they know—I have denied it—but they will search. It is only a matter of minutes before they will find the passage leading to your apartment—break down the doors—"

It was Vivian's turn to chuckle now. She dropped the cigarette on the floor, stepped on it, and then turned and replaced the telephone receiver which she had been holding back on its cradle.

"Great invention, the telephone," she said genially. "I opened a connection and the exchange girl heard every word that we have been saying. That was the reason that I spoke so loudly and distinctly. And so you see, Madame Trescott, Scotland Yard was notified."

KING CURLEY SWORE and a flood of curses poured from the lips of the old woman. The idea of the telephone had occurred to neither of them, and if it had, neither of them would have credited the Lady from Hell with sufficient audacity to call upon the police to rescue her. But it was precisely such audacity that had made her the clever criminal that she was.

"Just a few minutes," Vivian taunted the old woman, "and the police will be here, and then the great Paula Trescott will be trapped—with the jewels of the Duchess of Renwick still in the house."

"The jewels!" There was consternation in Paula's voice. "They will find them. I have not yet put them in the hiding place." She raised herself from the chair with an effort. "Quick! Bring them to me before the police break in. I must be gone when they arrive."

"Oh, no, Madame," Vivian said sweetly. "You must stay here. When the police break in, we shall very gladly tell them that the jewels of the Duchess of Renwick are here. There will very likely be a reward given us for recovering them. The presence of the jewels will be all the proof that will be needed to send you to prison. And don't attempt to kill us now, Madame. It is too late. It would be much pleasanter to go to prison for stealing the jewels of the Duchess of Renwick than to the gallows for murdering us. Because you couldn't possibly dispose of our bodies before the police discovered them."

As if to punctuate her remarks an agitated man popped into the room.

"Madame," he panted, "they have found the door to the passage, and are preparing to break it in."

"Good," Vivian said harshly, and her words hammered at the old woman. "Now, Madame, you have your choice. Give us the jewels and we will leave by the hidden door-way beside you there—ah, yes, we know of it. If not, we inform the police when they break in here, that you have the jewels."

Paula Trescott had not risen to her commanding posi-tion in the world of crime by indecision. She knew when she was trapped. And she did not make the mistake of underestimating the audacity of the Lady from Hell as many a man had done. A swift order and Curley ran out of the room, returning almost immediately with a little silver chest which he placed before her. With a quick move-ment Wylie opened it. It was filled with a glittering mass of jewels.

"Take them," she said hoarsely. "But you will pay for this night's work. It will be the last trick that you will play, Vivian Legrand."

"Perhaps," Vivian said unmoved. "And now, your own jewels. Adrian, get busy."

Under the baleful eyes of the old woman, the Empress of the Underworld was stripped of the jewels with which she was loaded—a fortune in themselves.

"Now," Vivian said with satisfaction in her voice. She reached out and picked up the ring which had been taken from her finger; replaced it. "We will take our departure, but I think it best that you come with us as—a hostage—shall we call it? That way, you will not be tempted to inform the police that we have escaped down your private passage with the jewels of the Duchess of Renwick. And from what the Forli girl told us of the passage, I think that it would be some time before the police found it, without guidance from one of your followers. And they will not dare, with you in our company."

She reached out and caught the old woman's arm. "I shall hold you like this," she told her. "You know something of this ring. The slightest pressure—the slightest intimation that you are betraying us—and the little poisoned needle plunges into your flesh. Now open the doorway to the passage."

With a choking sound of anger Paula Trescott raised one of the arms of her throne-like chair. There was a sliding sound behind the black velvet with which the wall was hung. Lifting the cloth, Wylie disclosed an oblong opening in the wall.

The little silver casket of jewels under one arm, the other clasped firmly about the wrist of Paula Trescott, Vivian stepped through the opening. From the distance came a tremendous crash as a door fell before the onslaught of the police.

"Au revoir," Vivian said sweetly to Curley. "I hope that you do not have too much difficulty with the police—and my thanks for the jewels of the duchess."

Wylie stepped through the opening behind her and dropped the velvet. There was a sliding rush as the panel closed behind them, and they turned their faces down the long passageway toward safety.

THE ADVENTURE OF THE DRAGON CLAWS

Fascinating Vivian Legrand Uses the Unsuspecting British Police Chief as Her Ally in a Conspiracy to End the Reign of London's Queen of Crime

1

SURPRISE ATTACK

THE LADY FROM Hell was in danger. Not that that was an unusual situation for her; she thrived upon such tension and peril as would have racked the nerves of any other woman of the international underworld. But this was a different situation. With incredible stealth, with nearly annihilating suddenness it had crept upon her, and she was utterly unaware of its presence.

The glow from a shaded table lamp made a halo about her flaming red hair and brought out to perfection the exquisite contours of her face as she bent over the papers on the table before her. A pleasant fire warmed the room, and rich draperies covering the casement windows shut out the blanketing grey-green oppressiveness of an autumn "pea soup" fog. All London had been groping its way through it all day. It was a perfect day for furtive actions and for crime, as Vivian Legrand herself might have decided, had not recent operations proved so profitable.

The Lady from Hell, with her adroit partner and Chief of Staff, Adrian Wylie, had dared to defy old Paula Trescott, uncrowned Empress of the English underworld. With surpassing boldness they had invaded old Paula's stronghold, snatched the proceeds of her most recent jewel

*The bullet bored into
the English telephone*

robbery from the ancient old hag and, in addition, had robbed her of her personal jewels, worth a fortune in themselves.

The haul had been worth nearly a hundred thousand dollars to them, even when the cut of the fence through whom they had disposed of the jewels had been taken out. But it had also gained them the bitter enmity of the old woman. And, as both Vivian and her companion in crime knew, the enmity of old Paula, entrenched in London's underworld for years, was not a thing to be reckoned with lightly.

Even at that moment, Wylie was in Soho, conferring with a certain Antonio Gonzales about a lucrative deal which might call the two master crooks to Madrid.

Meanwhile, Vivian sat before the table sorting and disposing of a variety of letters and documents. A maid would attend to her packing, but each of these missives had been saved for a purpose. Letters were sometimes as good as money in the bank.

Smiling sardonically, she read a lone one through, then put it carefully aside. When she got to America....

Two others she glanced at, and then let the glowing fire consume them. Yet another was grimly preserved. Nearly all men were fools, but not many of those she had duped remained alive and solvent over a term of years.

With a sudden low exclamation she picked up a small, tightly folded note, written upon grey-blue paper in a fine, distinguished hand. It was merely signed "C," but she would never forget the existence of the man who had written it. The writer was Colonel Sir Mark Caywood, who had been the British chief of secret service in the Far East. Crook though she was, The Lady from Hell had been of aid to Sir Mark. He had paid her price, and even written this note, thanking her and promising to help her if ever she should find herself in trouble within his jurisdiction.

And now, what was his jurisdiction? Vivian laughed aloud as she picked up a copy of the London *Times* lying upon the carved walnut table beside her armchair.

Circled in blue pencil was an announcement that General Sir Mark Caywood, G.C.S.I., K.G.I.E., D.S.O., had been promoted to the command of the entire police establishment of Greater London.

SHE FOLDED THE little message with more tenderness than she had ever shown one of her admirers. The most powerful police official in the country was obligated to her. And Vivian was not the sort of woman to permit ground like that to remain fallow.

She coughed, suddenly and raised one hand to brush

back the flaming hair from her forehead. She noted for the first time that her cheeks were burning, that her lips were dry and beads of unaccountable perspiration were standing upon her forehead.

What strange weakness, she wondered, was this that had so suddenly overtaken her. Even as she wondered, she caught her breath sharply and put her hand to her throat. It was becoming difficult to breathe.

Sharp apprehension flashed into her narrowed, greenish eyes. With an inward jolt of horror she thought of poison. Old Paula, frustrated and embittered—had she bribed a servant or somehow contrived to have her poisoned? The room was growing vague and cloudy, just as though the thick fog of the London streets outside was seeping through windows and heavy draperies. A queer, incredible, blinding vapor seemed to swim before her eyes.

The thought flashed over her that she was dying, alone, unattended. She staggered unsteadily to her feet in an attempt to reach the telephone—call a doctor.

A black gloved hand shot out from between the drawn curtains of one of the windows directly in front of her. A long black gauntlet covered the wrist halfway to the elbow. A small revolver of blue steel with a curious bulge at the end of the barrel was aimed by the black glove… not at her, but at the telephone. There came a sharp sound… a sound like the clapping of two hands together… the sound as of a stick being broken across a knee. The gun carried a silencer, and its report could not have been heard a dozen feet away. The bullet made a slightly louder noise as it bored into the cradle of the English telephone instrument, putting it out of commission.

Almost immediately following the report, a strange face showed through the curtain. The stifling vapor was an ever thickening cloud, but Vivian could see the weird face which was not a face, but a head protected by a gas mask of some foreign make.

Her eyes were dimming, her limbs heavy, her mind in a whirl. She wanted to cry out. But she knew that opening her tightly closed lips—one full gulp of the saturated atmosphere—would mean the end of consciousness. And so she mastered the very human instinct to call for help.

Her second thought—her very last thought—was for her partner, Adrian Wylie. That was the one Legrand loyalty. And in this case it was the one Legrand hope of counter-attack. She knew that she was beaten in this round. If Wylie could be warned in the remaining seconds of consciousness, he might take the next round with some hammer stroke of savage reprisal.

She was fiercely gripping the walnut table, pounding away at her remnant of strength and mental balance, compelling herself to remember what it was she still had to do. She felt her knees giving away. And even as she fell one arm shot out, a limp and seemingly uncontrolled gesture. A small silver cigarette box on the table was swept away. Five glittering pairs of eyes watched her fall. In a pitiable heap, this woman who feared no man lay helpless upon the Kerman rug. The window curtains were opening as the five masked and secret assailants stepped into the quiet room.

The Lady from Hell looked utterly beaten. But she was still alive; and the five agents of old Paula Trescott would have been surprised to know how good a chance Vivian still had to win.

2

THE KNEELING DEAD MAN

WHEN VIVIAN'S LAST desperate gesture swept the silver cigarette box out of its normal position, a tiny red eye of light had winked on in the vestibule of the house. That was the warning signal Wylie would see and understand.

The very day that they had moved into the house, Wylie had installed an electrical system of his own, and the clever trick of the cigarette box was only one of the devices. Every room in the house, apart from the servants' quarters, had a wire which led down to the control of the vestibule light. Every room contained some small and natural object that, on being disarranged, would break a contact and so flash the signal warning of sudden grave danger within.

In the drawing room the five black garbed invaders were communicating only by gestures. They made hardly a sound, hurriedly acting upon a well rehearsed plan.

Two lifted Vivian Legrand and placed her upon a divan. Two others removed from behind the curtains small pressure tanks from which an odorless gas, a bromated oxydrogine compound of recent discovery, had been projected into the room like fog from the nearly impenetrable streets of London.

The room was still impregnated with the gas. Vivian lay

on her back, pallid and fascinating even though the very hand of death seemed to have touched her. But evidently she was in no danger of death, for, when one of the five had taken her pulse, he gestured to a companion who at once set about binding her securely with stout black cords.

The five were not killers. Before accomplishing their purpose in the drawing room they had sought out, one by one, the four servants in the house, taking each of them by surprise, intimidating them, binding and gagging them.

They now, having overthrown every vestige of opposition, systematically searched the rooms which Vivian or Adrian Wylie occupied.

It was the safe they were looking for; but when one of them discovered it behind an antique cabinet, they found it unlocked and empty. Mocking them! The letters and papers Vivian Legrand had been sorting they carefully collected and put away in a black leather bag. The five moved swiftly on, hunting for the jewels and other treasures which Vivian and Wylie were known to have gained by their depredations since arriving in England.

THE FOG WAS not abating, and, though it delayed Adrian Wylie on his ride home from Soho, it likewise served him. He was close to his own house before a kind of sixth sense of instinctive vigilance warned him that something was wrong. At once he crossed the street, thankful now for conditions of climate which a moment before he had been roundly cursing.

When he saw the motor ambulance waiting, his first suspicion was that there had been some kind of violent encounter. Somebody had been hurt. Vivian knew well enough how to take care of herself. But if the police were in charge—

From across the street, in a momentary lifting of the blanket of fog, he discerned the bright, carmine gleam of his improvised signal light.

So it was the police!

Wylie hesitated, disturbed by the necessity of dealing with a situation whose barest outline was hidden from him. And as he waited, thinking hard, he saw something else which drove all thought of the police out of his mind. A slight, dark figure, moving with catlike grace and stealth, had suddenly come from the house—from his house and Vivian's—and hurried to the waiting motor ambulance.

Wylie heard an indistinct murmur of voices as this furtive messenger spoke with the ambulance driver. There was only one thing to be done, and Wylie immediately did it, crossing the street diagonally at a casual pace, hoping to put himself between the messenger, the ambulance and his evidently raided domicile.

The rage and vindictiveness of old Paula Trescott had already occurred to him as the motive force in back of this odd occurrence. And if Paula's adherents had taken the warpath on this gloomy, fog-bound day, it might mean that a considerable segment of the London underworld was lurking in the neighborhood. Whereas he was alone, and armed only with a sword-cane.

The slight, swift moving messenger was turning back to the house. He wore a black felt hat with the brim turned down, and his coat collar and muffler covered him to the eyes. Owing to the bad light, Wylie got not even a glimpse of the narrow slice of countenance exposed between hat brim and muffler. He was certain, however, from the other's manner and gait that he was some sort of Oriental, a Chinese, Malay, or Lascar.

Wylie was never disposed to worry about The Lady from Hell. He had seen her defend herself against amazing odds, and seize the offensive to the despair of her male antagonists. What worried him was his remembrance of the rich cargo of jewels and treasures which he and Vivian had gained and had only this morning been preparing to ship out of England.

Were other crooks giving Paula her revenge by despoiling thus crudely the two most artistic despoilers ever at large in London?

On impulse he abandoned his notion of speaking to the ambulance driver. Instead he wheeled suddenly, covered by a thick grey eddy of the fog, and darted down into the servants' entrance of the house.

He had a key to that lower door and he quietly let himself in. He made straight for the metal box he had put up close behind the electric meter, found his key for that, and opened it. Here were the switches for his cunningly contrived protective and signal systems. He threw the main switch with angry satisfaction. It was always on at night, but neither he nor Vivian had thought it necessary by day. **A LOUD, STRANGLING** yelp of terror informed him how near marauding hands had been to the accumulated treasure. Hesitating an instant, planning his next move, he heard the step of someone stealthily approaching.

Swiftly he withdrew into the cloaking shadows of an angle of the wall. Drawing the slender sword from his cane, he flexed it lightly, holding the cane-sheath in his left hand as a secondary weapon. The tip was loaded and would make an admirable blackjack.

Careless, because of the belief that every person in the house had been accounted for, the dark, cloaked figure came down the passageway. He had nearly reached Wylie when a stray ray of light gleamed for a moment on the bright polished surface of the sword. Wylie, watching alertly, saw a black gloved hand reach into the opposite sleeve for a weapon. He lunged forward, even as the hand swung back to hurl the small, steel hatchet.

The slender ribbon of Toledo steel leaped toward its mark, a deadly serpent's fangs with ten times the speed, weight and length. It pierced the young Chinese through the throat, spitting the very outcry he was about to utter.

The hatchet, too hurriedly aimed, bumped Wylie's head instead of carving a deadly furrow in his skull. His narrow dim world which was a basement passage rocked and heaved, and left him blinded and groping. He had suffered a terrific blow, cushioned opportunely by the fine Austrian hat which he wore. Thanks to his hat he was still clutching his sword, still on his feet, reeling weakly along a passageway in his own dwelling, sustained by a flickering gleam of conscious purpose.

Electricity safeguarded their treasures. He now must locate Vivian and interrupt whatever upstairs siege she was sustaining. After a few minutes of vague wandering, Adrian Wylie's shrewd wits were restored to him. He found the servants, trussed and gagged. He found the open safe behind the antique cabinet. But there was no trace of Vivian Legrand.

There was, of course, no lingering trace of the stupefying gas, which had been odorless even at the period of its greatest potency. In view of what the gasping, terrified servants had reported, he imagined that Vivian had been surprised before she could reach for a weapon. Doubtless she—unlike their help—had put up a fierce resistance. Perhaps she had been badly hurt; certainly she, with her untamed spirit, must have fought off the attackers until they beat her insensible.

Searching for some clue which he must have before he could organize a counter-attack upon their triumphant enemies, Wylie came now to the room toward which he would have immediately hurried but for the dazing collision with the hatchet and his mounting anxiety concerning his partner. Here at the library door he halted, sniffing. When he opened the door he recoiled, then forced himself to enter.

That sickening, smoky odor, at once both foul and sweetish, could mean only one thing. And there was the *thing*. Blackened and horribly contorted, in a gruesome praying posture before the fireplace!

Such treasures as Vivian and he had gained by superior craft had been similarly saved from this thief. The switch Wylie had thrown in the nick of time had electrified every metal part of the rich Old World fireplace. There was no fire to retard the intruder. He had come within eighteen inches of the hiding place of jewels and wealth. And then he had perished as if struck by a thunderbolt.

THE LUCKLESS FELLOW'S shoes had been ripped off by the terrific power of the current annihilating him. Wylie, turning from the charred body, studied the shoes with care. If these were to be all he would have to go by....

In the passage below he subsequently hunted for the other adversary, whose throat he had split. But there was no second corpse in the lately ransacked domicile, only an ugly stain of blood. They had found and carried away their wounded or dying. The victim of the fireplace they had not dared touch. His shocking doom had routed them.

Wylie switched off the current, examined the body, learned nothing. But Vivian, if her life was to be saved, must be traced, fog or no fog, traced in the underworld byways of London immediately.

Adrian Wylie paused to warn the still panicky and complaining servants; they must neither leave the house, talk to the police, nor admit any stranger during his absence. Then, having armed himself with a heavy automatic, he set forth into the grey, ghostly city. All of London's lights had been vainly blazing for hours. Wylie found a venturesome taxi, showed its driver two golden guineas, and invited him to risk a traffic accident or severe police reprimand for that attractive bonus.

"I'll do my best, guv'nor," said the taxi man. "Where to?"

Smiling grimly, his urgent, extravagant fare gave him the address of an Oxford Street bootmaker.

Wylie had discovered that address in the shoes of the electrocuted enemy. He was frantic to locate Vivian; and slender though it seemed, it was all the clue that he had.

3

DEN OF TORTURE

A SUDDEN STRONG breath of outdoor air, damp and cool, had begun to restore Vivian Legrand to consciousness. How long had she been helpless like this? Where was she, and what had happened?

She was in pain, and discovered herself tightly bound to a stretcher. It was being rapidly conveyed from her home to a waiting ambulance.

Pinned down as she was, she could only move her aching head a little, from side to side. She was not gagged; yet when she opened her mouth to attempt a frantic cry for help, she discovered the very muscles of her face were slack and leaden.

A feeble whisper of objection was all that she could manage. And now she was sliding into the immaculate interior of the private motor ambulance. She summoned those deep hidden batteries of her will and resolution, making a second attempt to limber the muscles of her aching throat.

A black gloved hand clamped down upon her lips.

Her head, to hide that flaming, unforgettable crop of hair, had been wrapped in a white towel. The mate to the stifling black gloved hand drew the towel swiftly out and down, masking her face.

The ambulance was rolling off. She was a prisoner, kidnaped from her own home in London. How she and Wylie had ridiculed the alleged magnitude and authority of Paula Trescott's underworld realm. Now its far-reaching might was being exposed. One nasty, foggy day, and the old woman's hooded reptiles dared to strike, and strike hard.

It was characteristic of Vivian Legrand that, even in those perilous moments, she was admiring the boldness of her enemy's thrust, and scheming how she might parry it. She hoped greatly for Adrian Wylie's aid. She was not, however, expecting him to effect her rescue.

Vivian proposed to rescue herself. She had done that very thing on more than one occasion. This could be no worse plight than hers in Constantinople, some months past, when her antagonist had been none other than the terrible Vedova Bey. She must not only confound her present captors, but also she must make old Paula pay and pay richly for such unwarranted and vengeful aspirations.

Now the ambulance, which seemed to have made good time in spite of the fog, was stopping. Vivian heard an indistinguishable murmur of voices, alien and shrill.

And now her stretcher was being lifted, even though the choking towel was not. She felt herself carried on and on, silently, quickly. She tried to count the shuffling light steps of her bearers, tried to judge what distance they were taking her.

They halted. A voice spoke a syllable or two harshly. The stretcher was roughly jolted to a creaking, uncarpeted floor.

Only a few feet away a discussion was going on. Her

captors were speaking Chinese. But, not for nothing had she spent her girlhood in her father's notorious resort in the Bubbling Well Road in Shanghai. The shrill dialect of Hanoi, with which she had once been so familiar, came back to her with a sort of stabbing comprehension. She had been right. Paula Trescott was responsible for the situation in which she found herself, and even now her captors were discussing the bargain they had struck with old Paula.

It was plain that Paula Trescott had paid a huge price to have her kidnaped. And the Chinese were disputing the nature of their further obligations in this sinister deal. There was one, who spoke loudly and harshly, and who considered that the kidnaping had been enough. Let Madam Trescott work her own vengeance upon this captive woman. Hadn't it been risky enough, making her prisoner, here in the very heart of London? And hadn't two men perished miserably in the act?

VIVIAN'S SPIRITS LIFTED. She was in a desperate plight, but if, as she now learned, one of her assailants had been mortally wounded with a sword, that must be Doc Wylie's work. Wylie would not remain idle.

And if another Chinese criminal had been burned, it only meant that their treasures were still safely hidden in their house, thanks to Wylie's cunningly improvised bank-vault protections.

The Lady from Hell strained to hear what decision her captors were reaching. The loud, harsh speaker was stilled. A low hissing voice dominated now; and Vivian sensed that her chances of surviving until Wylie and their friends might trace her and try to accomplish her rescue were growing less from minute to minute.

Yes, it had been decided. Paula Trescott must pay more, must pay for the two lost lives, pay for the promised share of treasures which the house of the red headed one had not disgorged. But the work they had bargained for must be finished. Paula Trescott was somebody worth serving.

Vivian lay with her muscles taut, resolutely in control of every nerve. She heard them arguing about how she should be tortured, tortured so that she would scream. Madam Trescott had insisted that there must be screaming. And then, after prolonged refinements of brutality, the red headed woman should be allowed horribly to die.

How long would Wylie take to find her? In the mazes of London's Chinese quarter, on a night like this, he would be doing well to catch up with her captors inside of six, eight or ten hours. Were it anybody else but Wylie it would be the wildest folly to expect him to trace her at all.

Vivian could hear the Chinese gangsters pattering into the room where she lay bound on the ambulance stretcher. Hands touched her face lightly, removing the towel. She had steeled herself, she was ready.

A whistling gasp of surprise acknowledged the sensation she had tried for; and then a shrill gabble in the Hanoi dialect broke upon her like the waves of an angry sea. For Vivian was trying to play dead, and, as in all else that she attempted with guile, she was succeeding.

Her delicately curved lips were sagging apart in a suffocating slackness. The eyes were rolled up, strained and staring. The pale face, from which her recent experience had drained all the color save the vermilion slash of the lips, was a carved ivory mask. It was, seemingly, death in a horrible form.

She knew that she could carry the thing through for only the briefest time, even in that dimly lighted room. The touch of a hand would disclose that her flesh was still warm. And if she moved even so much as an eyelid, permitted her chest to rise and fall in breathing, her trick would be exposed; her doom certain.

But it was only for a moment that the pose was necessary. Chinese feel no awe in the presence of death. Death in the crowded valley of the Yellow River is too certain and too common for it to be held in awe. She felt the stretcher on which she lay rock and tilt abruptly. She was unceremoniously rolled off onto the floor, letting herself fall slack and limp upon it.

The change was fortunate for her in more ways than one. No longer would the candle light upon her strained eyelids make the pose of death painfully unbearable. And it permitted her to lie in such a posture that her shallow breathing was even more difficult to detect.

SLOWLY SHE OPENED her eyes the merest trifle. The five men were still in the room. The fact of her apparent death had not caused them any considerable concern—possibly because they knew she was destined for death a short time later, anyway. Otherwise, any attempt to revive her would have resulted in immediate discovery of her ruse. Even as she watched, four of the men went out, leaving the fifth seated in a chair by the doorway.

This was her chance, the only chance that she was likely to have. Slim as it was, it must be made to do. A blaze of ferocity shone in the eyes of The Lady from Hell, as her eyes took in the situation, and her mouth twitched. At that moment her stony face looked as deadly as a hooded cobra, swaying for the strike. And, like the beautiful, deadly thing she resembled, she knew when to strike. And this was the time.

Near the edge of the table, above her, was the lighted candle, guttering in its saucer. Slowly, exerting every shred of her strength she managed to writhe to her knees, eyes fixed on the impassive back of the man in the chair by the door. A sound, a movement that might cause him to turn, and she was lost.

Slowly she raised her bound wrists and held the bonds that linked them over the candle flame. She had not been tightly bound, but, even so, the flame scarred her wrists as she clenched her teeth against the pain and watched the tiny flame eat into the cords. They parted without a sound, and, as soundlessly, Vivian slumped back to the floor. If the man had looked, had turned, he would have seen only the inert form of an apparently dead woman lying where it had been dumped on the floor. But he did not look, and with stealthy movements she untied the cords that bound her ankles.

Vivian knew that she must cross the space that lay between herself and the man at the door without being seen. She dared not rush him, attempt to take his gun from him. She was still weak from the experience through which she had gone, and circulation had not yet been restored to her legs, partially numb as a result of the tight cords about her ankles.

Inch by inch she crossed the space between herself and the Chinese. Once he stirred, and she stiffened. If he looked in her direction there was nothing to do save make one last desperate leap. But again he did not look and she continued her progress.

It was an error of her own that betrayed her. An error so tiny, so infinitesimal that not one person in a thousand would have thought of it, and yet an error so great, that loomed so huge that it almost spelled disaster—her shadow. She had not thought of the lighted candle on the table, and it was in horror that she glanced momentarily at the opposite wall to see her shadow, a gigantic thing, looming grotesquely on the wall, almost directly in front of the Chinese.

He saw it at almost the same instant. With a squeal of horror he sprang to his feet.

"The spirit of Yin, the Power of Darkness, is abroad," he squealed. And then, as he turned, he saw behind him a flesh and blood woman. His terror vanished immediately and his hand went toward his gun.

It was that moment of terror, that instant of hesitation that gave Vivian her chance. Without a halt in her movement, so beautifully timed that it all seemed part of the same action, she struck the man's wrist with a single chopping blow with the edge of her palm, sending his gun whirling, and then with the speed of a striking snake swept down upon the gun even as it clattered to the floor.

Before the startled Chinese had recovered from his surprise he found himself covered. And just in time. Behind him in the doorway appeared the four others, who had departed a short time since. A chorus of surprise came from them as the situation dawned on them. Slowly Vivian took a step or two backward, facing them with steady eyes, that cool, precise brain of hers functioning perfectly as she sought a way out of the dilemma, despite the weakened condition in which she found herself.

"Do not move," she said in their own Hanoi dialect. "There are five of you, and I have six shots. That will leave one in case others come to learn why I killed you…"

They halted, huddled together. They dared not rush her. That would mean death to some of them. But they knew that she dared not attempt to depart and leave them behind her.

4

WITH ONE LAST BULLET

IT WAS A stalemate with time playing heavily against The Lady from Hell.

Numbness, due to her recent bonds, had never quite left her. She had not yet taken enough exercise to restore circulation; her wrists, seared by the candle flame, smarted terribly.

And should her hand waver, her eyes disclose her agony of numbing tension, they would rush her to save themselves. She might shoot down one or two. But in that short dash of a dozen steps she could never work this unfamiliar weapon fast enough to knock over all four.

Moreover, if she miraculously did beat them off with her gunfire, the shooting would bring upon her perhaps a dozen, a score of adherents of this same underworld clan. Thus far she had been lucky, for the incident had not stirred any commotion outside in what she was sure must be the Chinese quarter. But what would come next?

They stood there, the five of them, rigid in a ghastly tableau of death or the promise of death. It was plain that they expected a corrosive rapier of flame to dart from the muzzle of her gun at any moment.

Vivian saw that they were afraid. But she also saw that

their fears would diminish as the minutes ticked away and her own sustaining domination, born of fury, spent itself upon this tense antagonism.

How to hide her mounting danger of weakness? She resolved to talk to them, in their native dialect, though all undoubtedly spoke and understood English. But just then, as she was preparing this stratagem of distraction, there came sounds of a diversion, startling to them all, since none could know what it might mean.

Steps in the passage, light, unhurried, inexorable.

"Do not move," Vivian said in Chinese, her voice cutting through the air like a metal tipped whip. Her green eyes were hard as bits of emerald. "The first who moves will find his soul mounting the Dragon Gate."

The cheap, flimsy draperies at the narrow doorway were swept aside. Two alert young Chinese, garbed in black, stepped through, each holding an automatic. Behind them came another Oriental, a Chinese. Tall, slim, almost gaunt, with features that were regular and skin of a pale bronze tint—eyes of Lucifer and face of Buddah. Once his black, beautifully shaped eyes wandered to the automatic in her hand, and a slight smile veiled his face for a moment. It was like a swift glimpse behind the serene, Buddha-like exterior.

He stared at Vivian for a long minute, then advanced into the stricken room. Behind him others entered, and among them she saw Adrian Wylie. It was a rescue, then?

"Mrs. Legrand—" the big leader began, with a bow. In his voice was scarcely a trace of foreign accent. It made him but the more sinister. He ignored her foes as so many coolies.

Vivian's iron nerve wavered a little; the strain had been so great. Hours it had seemed were dragging past. Yet actually within an hour the peerless Doc Wylie had found a key which unlocked the inmost citadel of London's Asiatic world.

And just what it was she grasped immediately when Wylie stepped forward to say: "This is the celebrated Mandarin Ko Leong Tai, good friend of our good friend, the Mandarin Hoang Fi Tut of Manila."

"Friends and allies of the great Hoang Fi Tu," said the Mandarin Ko Leong Tai, "are always safe among our people in London." An ironic gleam of mirth flashed from his black eyes. The smile did not disarm The Lady from Hell, as perhaps was intended. She knew too well that ancient evil, refined to an exquisite degree, looked at her from beneath the bronze lids. "Mrs. Legrand, you have courage, I perceive. And I am told that you are not unaccustomed to firearms.

"These sons of dogs have used you abominably. That stain must be wiped away. Shoot them! It will be a wholesome thing, a cleansing of body and mind. Shoot—my men are all around this place. There will be no one to interfere."

VIVIAN'S FLICKERING GLANCE to Wylie and back again, even as the other was speaking, informed her of Wylie's attitude. They must not seem too dependent upon the power of Ko Leong Tai. They must use him and combine with him—possibly in a second battle with the minions of old Paula Trescott—never submit to him as an inferior or beaten force.

Vivian gave the Mandarin her most radiant smile. "Since

you suggest it," she shrugged. "Though I am hardly in prac-
tise—"

Actually the long, narrow, shabby room was whirling and
dipping about her. Her five cowering targets were sometimes eight, or just a distant blur. She brushed aside a lock
of flame-tinted hair. By sheer power of will she steadied
her nerves, her vision—squeezed the trigger...

The borrowed enemy gun barked. The low voiced, hissing leader of her kidnappers, whom she had most despised,
yelped shrilly, clutching his right wrist.

"It was with that hand that he touched me," Vivian
explained to the complacent Ko Leong Tai.

"Each one of them must have taken that liberty."

The ordeal was not to be curtailed, then. She must
wound each one. Again the exquisite slender figure pressed
the trigger. But this time there was no sharp discharge, the
gun merely snapped like a toy pistol.

Vivian laughed, a brief hysterical outburst which a
great chattering of voices in the room largely suppressed.
Outnumbered five to one, The Lady from Hell had
mastered her captors with a weapon holding but a single
cartridge.

Wylie had stepped quickly forward, and was making a
show of congratulating his partner upon her game defense.

"The men who carried you off," he hastily explained, "I
traced by a bootmaker's address. Then I sought Ko Leong
Tai, used all the magic that abides in the name of our old
ally, Hoang Fi Tu, and so here we are."

Majestically the Mandarin Ko Leong Tai approached
them.

"There is yet more pleasure in store for us," said he. "A

messenger has just been taken by my men outside. He had hurried here to announce the coming of Madam Trescott. It seems, Mrs. Legrand, that the venerable one desires to hear your dying screams."

Vivian's green eyes hardened.

"We have made the message bearer and other prisoners wince over so little, and they have told us everything. Madam Trescott had expected to hear your agony under torture by means of the telephone. An ironic blending of the medieval and the modern, as we would have said at Cambridge.

"But it seems, Madam Trescott has become afraid of the telephone. She believes that her wires have been tapped. The new chief commissioner, an old acquaintance of mine in the East, Sir Mark Caywood—is not fond of Madam Trescott. And she has been warned that she is soon to be on the Caywood carpet, as one might say at Cambridge, or, in fact, anywhere else."

"The old hag is actually coming here to enjoy my expiring groans?" said Vivian. "If she had come and I had been under torture, she wouldn't have heard one sound—"

The Mandarin bowed gallantly. "I should like to believe that," said he. "But I am unfortunately familiar with my countrymen's genius for inflicting pain."

"How soon can old Trescott get here?"

"Soon, I think."

"And your men will not scare her off?"

"Hardly, Mrs. Legrand. All Chinese, I suspect, look alike to one such as this old woman, who hires the lowest of them to torture a young and beautiful enemy to death."

Wylie broke in with, "This is your special domain, Ko Leong Tai. What do you propose to do?"

"I am sure that Mrs. Legrand would enjoy teaching Paula Trescott a lesson for her declining years."

"Declining years!" snapped the much restored Lady from Hell. "I'd like to see her scared to death."

"So much the better," said Ko Leong Tai.

5

THE END OF PAULA TRESCOTT

THE VISIT OF Paula Trescott turned out much as the Mandarin had predicted. All furtive Chinese looked alike to the old queen of the underworld; and, though she came well guarded in a big black Lanchester limousine, she was quite unaware that the Orientals all around her were not of the gang she had hired, but men who took their orders from the most powerful Chinaman in the British Empire, Ko Leong Tai.

"She is being carried up to this room," came the whispered report.

"Is she in hearing?" Vivian asked.

"Yes, milady."

"Then," said Vivian, turning to Ko Leong Tai, "I had better encourage her with a scream."

His face was again the smooth blank clay-like mask, but he nodded, and portentously closed one eye. Vivian threw back her head and produced as piercing a shriek of agonized protest and pleading as ever came from the lips of a great actress, or a woman in awful pain.

Following this effect, she uttered several weak and unbearable moans. The cadence of her voice implored mercy and warned of imminent death.

"Put me down, put me down, you fools!" This cackle from Paula Trescott was plainly audible in the room. "Put me down, do you hear. I can walk. I am strong. I want to see—"

Vivian whimpered like a beaten child, groaned like a soul utterly lost.

Paula Trescott was laughing; a shrill and horribly malicious crowing triumph bubbled on her painted lips as she swept past the cheap curtains and entered the room of imagined torment. Then she halted; her face mirrored consternation.

"Madam," Vivian said, "these men of China are my friends. See!" She spoke shrilly in the Hanoi dialect. All of Ko Leong Tai's adherents having observed his small gesture of permission—bowed low to the woman with the keen, pallid face, the flame-red hair, burning, angry eyes.

"And now, Madam Trescott," said The Lady from Hell, "just what sort of Chinese torture are you most interested in—investigating?"

The old queen of vice and savage vengefulness swayed as she tried to brace herself. She had spirit, too, and in other years would have faced them out despite her dire situation. But now there was no reserve to call upon. Because he disapproved of the whole enterprise against Vivian Legrand, King Curley, her giant aid, had remained aloof from this expedition to Limehouse.

"Getting even generally costs too much," he had said. "We got troubles enough with this new head of the London police."

His words, rather than the barbed thrust of The Lady from Hell rang in old Paula's ears. She closed her eyes a moment and her hand went to her breast in a fluttering gesture. Then she collapsed on the floor, a small pitiful heap of fur and lace and brocade. That ancient heart of hers, that heart that her doctor had more than once warned her against, had been unable to stand the shock of seeing Vivian here, free, when she had expected to find her a captive.

SHE HAD, IN a way, been literally "scared to death"; but now that it was an accomplished fact, the Mandarin Ko Leong Tai was not immensely pleased. He also was troubled with the "new broom" prospects of Sir Mark Caywood, a notably able officer who would command both the uniformed police and New Scotland Yard. It would take too much explaining, this sudden death of a notorious character and very rich woman in the midst of a small army of armed Chinese.

"Has General Sir Mark Caywood ever seen Paula Trescott?" Vivian inquired abruptly.

"Few have seen her in recent years," said Ko Leong Tai. "But if he has had his men watching her night clubs—"

"You have cunning enough at your command to get rid of that body," said Vivian.

The Mandarin regarded her through narrowed eyes, although the smooth mask of his face gave not the least indication of what was going on in his brain.

"A woman such as Madam Trescott cannot simply drop out of sight," he said doubtfully. "The police, we know, are already much interested in her affairs—and then, her associates…"

"Madam Trescott will not disappear," Vivian said calmly. "I shall become Paula Trescott. I will deal with Sir Mark, tell him I am old, very old—ready to retire." Vivian made her voice a nearly perfect imitation of the shrill Trescott cackle. "I will sell out—sell out to you, Ko Leong Tai. You will take over the Trescott 'empire' in England, and though I sell what I do not own, your title to it will be good, since the British authorities will become a party to the much desired transfer of Paula Trescott's legitimate business— the police, of course, won't know of the illegitimate 'empire' that goes with the transaction."

The Chinese leader concealed what elation he must have felt. All he said was, "And can you impersonate that old woman?"

"With your protection, for a little while, yes."

"Then it is done. I can guard you from Curley and Paula's own people. Few of them lately have dealt with her directly. My spies have kept me well informed."

Vivian turned to Wylie, who was frowning. "You don't approve but it has got to be done," she said.

His frown deepened, "I think you have been through enough."

"This will merely be a vacation of theatricals. Hurry now, and make me up to look exactly like her while you still see what she was like," she added callously.

"PAULA TRESCOTT" RETURNED from her Limehouse visit in a strange mood, declined to see any of her former associates, astonished Curley by conversing with him only very briefly on a house telephone. She wanted to be alone, she said.

But when a chief inspector of police called at her club, she consented to receive him alone, and then astonished every one, even the chief inspector, by agreeing to drive with him to the office of Sir Mark Caywood. Vivian, however, insisted upon visiting Sir Mark alone.

"Madame Trescott—" began the British official.

"Look closely, Sir Mark. Don't you remember me? Think of Burma—" said the feeble, imitation Paula.

"I am quite familiar with Burma," Sir Mark said briefly. "I fail to understand what you mean. Certainly I do not remember you from Burma. I have your record here, and to the best of our knowledge you have never been in Burma."

Vivian abruptly removed her wig. "And now do you remember me?"

Sir Mark gasped. He had never forgotten the exotic, beautiful, red-haired woman with whom he had dealt in Burma, and to find her here, in the disguise of London's notorious underworld empress, was a stunning shock.

"But—but what are you doing here—like this," he asked, indicating the wig in her hand.

"Paula Trescott—the real Paula-died five years ago," Vivian lied to the head of the greatest police force on earth. "A syndicate took over her numerous affairs. It suited them to have her appear to survive. Personally I never laid eyes on the woman. But there were photographs, and her portrait by Spada. I have been assured I 'do' her very well."

Vivian went on to explain her desire to get out of the whole arrangement. She was well-to-do, the climate did not agree with her, and this pretending to be old Paula...

"Making you appear old is the worst current crime that has thus far come to my attention," Sir Mark put in gallantly. "You say you have one who will buy out your share of the Trescott enterprises? Who, may I ask?"

"Ho Leong Tai."

"My old friend Ko. He fancies that he is a law unto himself, but actually he is rather timid and always will fear deportation. England, Cambridge, his British accent and university education mean everything in the world to that Mandarin. I can handle him with or without gloves. It will be easier to keep him in line than it was Paula Trescott."

"This is really clearing up very nicely, Mrs. Legrand. Suppose I ring up Ko Leong Tai, have him come around here at once, and put the deal right through, before you, or any of your evidently undercover associates change their minds."

Vivian, hiding her satisfaction, assented.

Ko Leong Tai had helped save her life. But that had been yesterday. Today told a different tale, and the Chinese magnate should pay for his temerity in joining the Lady from Hell in any such brazen conspiracy.

The Mandarin had expected the transfer to him of the Trescott properties to be merely a matter of form, with no cash passing, since Vivian, an impostor, "sold" what she did not own.

Sir Mark Caywood's polite negotiations changed all that. Sir Mark was famous for his dealings with Asiatics, celebrated as a conciliator and as one who wrapped velvet around a hard steel fist.

Sir Mark, newly appointed, was out to make an immediate impression on both the Government and the British public. His adroit liquidation of the "Trescott Empire" would certainly launch his police administration auspiciously. He was pleased to have Vivian Legrand turn up out of his past and help him in the matter.

All unsuspicious of the trap he had helped to dig for

himself, Ko Leong Tai came with Adrian Wylie and a British solicitor to arrange the sale of the Trescott legitimate enterprises. Ko expected, of course, to take over the illegitimate ones in due course by right of eminent domain.

Vivian as Paula, having restored her disguise at the suggestion of Sir Mark himself, named a figure which sounded very moderate. Ko Leong Tai presented a check. Vivian suggested that her agent, Doctor Wylie, would take it to the bank and have it certified while they waited there. Sir Mark agreed that was business.

That made the mask which was the face of Ko Leong Tai absorb two deep, vertical creases. But what could he do with his "good friend of the East," Sir General Mark Caywood, G.C.S.L, K.C.I.E., D.S.O., chief commissioner of police, beaming upon him. Ko Leong Tai could but agree, and promised to observe the law as successor of Paula Trescott.

Vivian Legrand and her partner, Adrian Wylie, had endured an exciting and dangerous experience. But Ko Leong Tai's rage would not be so venomous as Paula's, and they were thousands richer.

THE ADVENTURE OF THE HEADLESS STATUE

The Red-headed Siren Glides Through the Sinister Alleys of Havana to Snatch the Loot of a Nation from Two Master Thieves

1

DICTATOR'S LOOT

THE LADY FROM Hell turned the corner of the Calle el Sol and stepped into another world—a world of dirt and filth and crime, crime in its nakedness as only the Latins know how to strip it of its glamour. Halting a moment, she glanced back over her shoulder at the street she had just left. It was almost deserted in the noonday heat that slashed across Havana like a naked sword. Not even a beggar, Havana's chief crop, drowsed in the sharp pools of purple shadow.

She lifted one shoulder in a slight shrug. There was no reason for her to think that she might have been followed, but the note from Antonio Gonzales had been explicit as to secrecy—had, indeed, intimated that if her errand was known she might never reach the destination for which she was bound.

Satisfied, she turned back. Here, there was relief from the sun. The overhanging galleries cast a grateful shadow, making sharp contrast between the space where she walked and the intolerable light reflected from the center of the street. In the distance the twin towers of the ancient cathedral rose above the surrounding houses.

Back in Europe, Vivian Legrand, the Lady from Hell,

had known the ruthless reputation of the man she was on her way to meet. She knew the rumors which linked him with murders from Manoas to Belize and suspected, if she did not know, that he had a finger in many of the revolutions that periodically flared up in Latin America.

But the reputation of a man, no matter how evil, did not prevent the Lady from Hell from utilizing him if the need arose. And back there in Paris he had had a part in several shady schemes she had engineered. When they were finished, Gonzales had taken his cut and disappeared, but Vivian had heard through underworld channels that he had been trapped in a robbery in Southern France, had shot a man, and, unable to claim a penny of the money which lay to his credit in Paris banks, had been compelled to flee for his life.

She had not known that Gonzales was in Havana. The

*Vivian Legrand
leaped sidewise*

note delivered to her hotel that morning, asking her to call at an address in the Calle el Sol, had come as a complete surprise. But she knew that underworld news travels fast, and realized that the news she had arrived from London with Adrian Wylie, her chief of staff, must have reached the ears of Gonzales within a few hours.

A poorly dressed white man, a Cuban by his garb, passed her with a quick glance and turned in at a fruit shop a few doors further on. As Vivian passed he was busily arguing with the proprietor and did not even glance in her direction.

She found the place she sought quite easily. First,

because of its fairly neat appearance in a street of dirt and filth, and, second, because of the door described by Gonzales in his note—a thick, iron-bound slab of teakwood inset in the black masonry front of the house. It was the only door of its kind on the street.

The Lady from Hell could see no evidence that she was being followed, but there was a queer intuitive feeling deep within her that eyes were watching her as she lifted the great iron knocker and let it drop three times against the knocking plate.

AN OLD SPANIARD opened the door, only an inch or so, and peered out. Vivian could see that the door was on a short chain.

"I want to see Antonio Gonzales. My name is Mrs. Legrand," she said.

There was a surprising ease and richness about that voice. It rose resonant and bell-like, as if it came effortlessly.

The door was opened wider as an invitation for her to enter. She ran her eye expertly over the man's figure for a sign of concealed weapons, but she could detect no suspicious bulge.

The shadowed hall into which she stepped was a typical entrance to a Havana home of the old days. Running the full length of the building, it opened in the rear into the patio, now overgrown with weeds. At one side a staircase with a wrought iron balustrade ran to an upper floor.

"*Señor Gonzales* is upstairs," the ancient Spaniard said, in his native tongue, "and is expecting you. The open door at the head of the stairs is his."

Vivian went on up the stairs and stepped through the doorway he had indicated.

Gonzales lay in a bed drawn up close to the narrow slit of a window. He passed as a white man, yet his nose was a trifle too flat, his lips a bit thickish, his skin a shade too dark. But in countries where people do not attach too much importance to these things, and to the telltale half moon at the base of the nails, he was classed as a white Spaniard.

He peered at Vivian through eyes that were still keen and crafty, despite the glaze of fever which covered them.

"I'm glad you're here. I thought you weren't coming," he said. "You're late."

"I had other things to do," she answered curtly. Then she plunged directly to the point. "What do you want to see me about?"

He did not answer directly. Instead he studied her a moment.

"I asked you to come here," he said slowly, "because you've got the reputation of never double-crossing anybody that plays square with you."

"So what?" she asked calmly, but the light that gleamed for a moment in her narrowed eyes belied the calmness of her words.

"I've got something on tap," he went on slowly, "but I'm sick... fever... I can't shake it off, and unless I hurry I'll lose my chance."

"So you want me to pull your chestnuts out of the fire for you," she shot at him. "I'm not interested."

He raised a protesting hand.

"Wait a minute," he said. "I want to offer you a partnership in it, because you're the only person I know who's got guts enough to pull it off and not double-cross me while I'm lying here unable to do anything myself."

"Well?" she said. Just the single clipped word. The Lady from Hell was playing poker and her face had slipped into an expressionless mask.

"It's big," Gonzales went on. He passed a hand across his hot brow. "Would you mind handing me a drink of water from the jug there? Thanks." He took a deep drink of the water and then lay back. "It's the biggest thing I ever tackled… got a million in it… two million, maybe… and I'm holed up here, unable to do a damn thing." He swore deeply.

"Come to the point," Vivian said crisply.

"Ever hear of Juan Cordoza?"

She pondered a moment, then shook her head.

"He was Ciprano Castro's minister of finance," Gonzales said slowly. "Does that mean anything to you?"

Enlightenment flooded Vivian. She remembered now. Cordoza, chief confidante of the dictator of Venezuela, had seen the downfall of his master coming long before the Iron Man himself had read the portents aright. He had skipped out of the country, reaching the Dutch island of Curaçao before Castro was aware of the fact that he had gone, taking a large part of the contents of the treasury with him. After leaving Curaçao his trail had vanished, and before Castro could turn his army of spies and secret agents loose on the trail of his missing treasurer the dictator himself had been compelled to follow in his treasurer's footsteps and take refuge himself in Curaçao.

"Cordoza is in Paris, isn't he?" she asked, remembering rumors now and then that, even though it had happened years before, still floated through the underworld of Europe's capitals.

Gonzales shook his head. "He never reached Paris. He chartered a boat to take him to Havana from Curaçao. He got here all right, landed secretly without anyone learning of his presence. But he never left Cuba—and neither did the stuff he looted from the treasury of Venezuela."

VIVIAN LEANED FORWARD. There was excitement in those green eyes of hers now.

"You know where the stuff is?" she queried.

"I know," he said with triumph. "If I could get out of here long enough to strike a bargain with Chang Kai I could have my hands on it in two hours. But this cursed fever won't let me. I couldn't walk a dozen feet without collapsing. And I'm not fool enough to think that if I struck a bargain with Chang Kai and wasn't there to watch after my interests that he'd play square. Oh, no. I'd whistle for my share, after he got his hands on it. One of his hatchetmen would kill me."

"Who is Chang Kai and what has he got to do with it?" the Lady from Hell asked.

Gonzales feebly raised himself on one elbow.

"Chang Kai's the head Chino in Havana. Runs a curio store in the Chinese quarter as a blind for his real activities—slipping through aliens across to the Florida Keys at a thousand a head—dope smuggling—anything that's crooked and that's got money in it. He's known about the Cordoza loot for a long time—knows it's hidden in a house here in Havana—could put his hands right on it—*if he knew the house.* But that's where he's stymied. It might be any house in the city, so far as he knows. And I know where the house is, but not where it is hidden in that house."

"I don't see why you need to bother with Chang Kai if

you have the address," Vivian said doubtfully. "Surely a million in loot cannot be hidden away like a pin, and even if it were I could find a pin, knowing it was hidden in a certain house and worth a million."

"But this is different," Gonzales told her. "I cannot gain access to the house. It is impossible. I know. I will explain it all to you later."

"Then you're stymied yourself, to a certain extent," Vivian said.

"Right," Gonzales answered. Then he looked at her keenly with his fever-bright eyes. "Do you want a cut of the stuff—if you can find it?"

There was no hesitation in Vivian's eyes as she faced the man in the bed.

"Done," she said.

"Your word," he insisted. "No double-crossing."

"My word," she told him, and the man sank back satisfied. He knew that the Lady from Hell was as ruthless as a striking snake; that she would no more hesitate to take human life than she would to step upon an insect, if that life stood in the path of one of her schemes—but he also knew that she would not double-cross a confederate who had played squarely with her.

"Here's the address," Gonzales said, reaching under his pillow and handing her a folded slip of paper. "Use your own judgment about how you go about it. Strike a bargain with Chang Kai if there's no other way, or tear the house to pieces until you find it. That's up to you."

Then he stiffened suddenly. "What's that?" he whispered.

The sound that had disturbed him could only have been heard by a man whose senses were almost abnormally developed by years of dependence upon them. It was not so much, perhaps a matter of hearing as an ability to select what was of importance in the symphony of sound that Havana is always playing. Vivian had caught the sound for a moment after he had called it to her attention. It might have been a stealthy footstep in the hall outside… it was so elusive that it defied identification.

She listened intently, wondering if her ears had not tricked her.

But all that she could hear was the strident cry of a mango seller and the faint squawk of a parrot somewhere in the distance.

"Could that man of yours be listening?" she asked, struck by a sudden thought.

"No," Gonzales said positively. "And if he were, it wouldn't do him any good. He understands no English."

"It sounded like a footstep," Vivian said, "the footstep of someone trying to walk without noise."

She got to her feet and, crossing the room, flung the door open. The corridor was deserted.

"I'm going to look on the stairs," she said.

"Want a gun?" Gonzales asked, and his hand went under the pillow.

Vivian shook her head in a negative gesture. There was a gun in the little hand bag she carried. A gun that she was seldom without—small but deadly. She went out into the corridor and descended the stairs cautiously. A faint sound of a song came from the rear of the house. She made her way in that direction. A partly opened door gave her a view of the kitchen, where the man who had admitted her stood before a table peeling potatoes. The sound she had heard had not come from him.

She made her way quickly back up the stairs toward the room on the second floor. Her suspicions had not been dispelled, but there seemed to be no one in the place save the three of them.

She reached the threshold of Gonzales' room and stopped short in amazement.

Gonzales was lying partially off the bed, face up, one arm dangling toward the floor, and a great pool of blood staining the bed covering from the gaping knife wound in his throat.

In the brief instant that Vivian had been absent from the room an assassin had struck, hoping, evidently, to silence Gonzales before he betrayed to her the hiding place of the dictator's treasure.

She smiled grimly at the thought. The assassin had been too late. In her hand bag was the slip of paper that Gonzales had given, her the slip that would lead her to a million or more in loot.

She opened it and consternation flooded her green eyes.

The slip of paper was blank.

2

BOOK AND DAGGER

VIVIAN'S FACE WAS thoughtful as she reached her hotel. She tapped on the door of Wylie's bedroom. There was no answer. He evidently had not returned from the steamship office, where he had gone to secure passage to Haiti, and she turned back toward her own bedroom. And then stopped short, her green eyes narrowed.

Brilliant sunlight poured through the high arched window and splashed in a great pool on the polished table in the center of the room. And in that pool of light a book lay open, a silver penknife fashioned in the shape of a Malay creese lying across the open page—a beautifully engraved five inch snaky blade.

That open book with the paper knife across it was a signal from Wylie—evidence that something had happened during her absence that menaced their safety. It was a prearranged signal, something that could be done with the utmost casualness without exciting suspicion.

Hurriedly she searched the room, ran through both bedrooms, but nothing had been disarranged.

She was stumped. Wylie was not there—danger threatening from an unknown quarter—and now, when she thought she had her hands on the secret of what was likely to be their greatest haul, she drew a blank. That Gonzales had been sincere enough, she had no doubt. The man undoubtedly thought that he was delivering to her the hiding place of Cordoza's loot. The only explanation was that someone had reached him first, substituting the blank piece of paper for the one with the address. But who?

The Spaniard who had admitted her to the house? She gave the thought serious consideration and then dismissed it. If the man had attempted to double-cross Gonzales, he would not have remained at the house, when, at any moment, his duplicity might be discovered. And, equally, he could not have murdered Gonzales. He had been in the kitchen, and it would have been an impossibility for him to have killed his master, and then reached the kitchen ahead of her.

Chang Kai, the Chinese Gonzales had mentioned? Her mind toyed with the thought. But if Chang Kai had stolen the slip of paper before her arrival, and substituted a blank, why return to kill Gonzales? Unless, of course, there had been delay in reaching the hiding place of the paper, and Chang Kai or his emissary had seen her entering the house and had returned and killed Gonzales to prevent his revealing the secret to her.

She took out the slip of paper and studied it carefully again, as she had done a dozen times before. There it was, mocking her impotence with its blankness.

She looked up sharply at the sound of a light tap upon the door of the sitting room. She laid the slip on the table and opened the door.

The man who stood upon the threshold was tall and dark and slim—a Cuban undoubtedly, for he had the aquiline nose of the pure bred Spaniard and the feline grace that characterizes certain Latin types. But his face was unhealthily pale.

"May I come in, Mrs. Legrand?" he asked. "I have a message for you."

Vivian opened the door wider and indicated a chair for her guest. She crossed to the table and stood there, the brilliant sunlight streaming in from outside catching her hair and turning it into a halo of flame above her exquisitely lovely profile.

Her eyes were hard as the glitter of emeralds as she studied the man before her. Something was wrong here. In her profession no one was above suspicion; no incident, however trivial, below notice. Her life had more than once depended upon being prepared for any eventuality that might arise, and her movement had brought her hand in close proximity to the little revolver that lay on the table, screened by a book.

"What do you want?" she asked after a moment.

"May I introduce myself?" inquired the man ingratiatingly. "I am Leon Ortega."

He crossed his legs comfortably and lighted a cigarette.

"What do you want?" Vivian shot at him again, her drooping lashes screening the cold calculation of her eyes.

"It's purely a matter of business, Mrs. Legrand," he said. "But before we start let me advise you that if you do anything rash you will most certainly regret it."

"What do you want?" Vivian asked.

The man leaned forward.

"Just a matter of striking a bargain with you."

"A bargain?"

The man nodded. "We've got something that you want. You've got something that we want. But we're not hoggish. We're willing to give up what we've got for half of what you've got."

Vivian's greenish eyes were narrowed and the tiny flame in them might have warned the man, had he been observant, that danger was gathering about him like a thunderstorm.

"What have you got that I want?" she queried softly.

"A certain Mr. Adrian Wylie," the man said comfortably.

"AH!" VIVIAN SAID. She knew then that this was what the sign of the open book and paper knife meant. "So Mr. Wylie is, shall we say, your guest?"

"That will do as well as any other," the man admitted. "We—er—persuaded him that it would be advisable to accompany us until such time as we could have a talk with you."

"And what have I got that you want?" Vivian queried.

"Half of the stuff that Cordoza left when he died," the man came back at her swiftly. Then, as Vivian started to speak, he went on: "I might say that it will be useless to attempt to persuade us that you do not know where it is. We know that you do. We know that you got the directions for finding it from Gonzales less than an hour ago. We saw you leave. So we immediately took what precautions we considered necessary to protect our interests."

"And why not obtain the same information from Gonzales that I obtained?" she asked. There was in her voice no intimation of her anxiety—of how much hung on the answer to that question of hers.

The man regarded her with a smile.

"My dear Mrs. Legrand, you really do not do us justice. It was only this morning that we learned of Gonzales' whereabouts. We hurried there. We saw you leave. And when we entered the house we found him murdered. The answer is obvious."

Vivian's eyes, hard as bits of emeralds, betrayed nothing of the consternation his words aroused in her. These men, then, had not killed Gonzales, and did not know that a third party had beaten them—did not know that the slip of paper Gonzales had given her was a blank piece of paper.

"Your offer then," she said slowly, "is to trade Adrian. Wylie for half of the Cordoza loot?"

"Exactly," the man said. "And I might call to your attention, Mrs. Legrand, that his life depends on your agreeing. He obviously knows nothing that will be of value to us. He is worthless to us except as a hostage. So, whether he lives or dies depends entirely upon your acceptance or refusal."

For a moment hell fires flared in Vivian's eyes. She had a strong desire to snatch the little gun from her hand bag on the table. But reason came to her rescue. She would gain nothing by violence. If this man did not return, undoubtedly Wylie would die. Strategy was called for.

"I shall have to think it over," she said slowly. "I am not alone in this, of course, and there are others that I must consult."

"Who?" he asked.

There was suspicion in his voice, but the next instant he was aware of the anxiety that lingered in the husky tones of her voice and flickered in the green depths of her eyes. The ability to dispel suspicion in a man by turning on the full force of her personality as one turns water on in a tap was always one of the greatest assets of the Lady from Hell.

"You could not expect me to tell you the names of those working with me," she said gently. "Sufficient to say that I came here for the purpose of seeing Gonzales, of obtaining information from him that I did obtain, and that I cannot make any such agreement without first consulting the people who are in on this with me. But in view of the situation I think they will agree."

The man stood up.

"Six o'clock is the deadline," he said curtly. "Let me warn you—don't try any tricks. An attempt at treachery would be fatal to the negotiations—and Mr. Wylie."

He turned with a sardonic smile and left the woman standing there beside the table in the center of the room, apparently defeated.

He did not see, as the door closed behind him, that bowed figure straighten up like a steel spring uncoiling and dash swiftly into the next room. Neither did he see, as he stepped into the car in which he had arrived, her slender figure slip through the hotel entrance.

But she did not make the mistake of letting the man she was following see her emerge. She remained just inside the arched colonnade for a moment, adjusting her hat, until his ear swung into the traffic on the Prado.

"Follow that car," she said swiftly to the driver of a taxi at the curb. "Ten dollars if you do not lose him."

3

THE HEADLESS STATUE

THE GREAT ARCHED hall of the ruined monastery of San Fernando on the road to Gibara was a purple pool of shadow, although the afternoon sunlight still struck sharply across the landscape seen through the arched opening where the great iron barred doors had been flung open. A great flame tree that stood in the doorway was dropping its blossoms in the slight breeze like a blood-red rain. In the distance El Principe Castle, once one of Havana's guardians and now a prison, stood on the top of the cliff overlooking the sea.

Just inside the doorway lounged the figure of an armed man, obviously a guard.

The great hall had, probably, at one time served as a place of worship for the monks. The ruined pile of rotted wood and carved stonework at one end might conceivably have been the altar. From narrow slitted windows, high up, three slanting beams of light fell sharply athwart the gloom, bringing into sharp relief the carved, life-sized figures that stood in niches all around the walls. Some of the figures were in an almost perfect state of preservation. Others were headless, battered, parts of their stone garments broken off. They were raised some ten feet above the floor, recessed into the enormously thick walls and each reached by three little flights of steps that led up to the pedestal upon which they stood.

Seated on a low stool almost directly beneath one of these statues, Leon Ortega faced the man he had kidnaped.

"I have just left Mrs. Legrand," Ortega said. "She is a very sensible woman. Tonight at eight o'clock she delivers to me the secret of the hiding place of the gold that I seek. When I have verified her information you are free to go."

"You have her word?" Wylie questioned.

Knowing the Lady from Hell as he did, he knew that if she did indeed have the key to the hiding place to a cache of gold she had no intention of yielding it tamely to Ortega. As a last resort, he knew that her loyalty to him would force her to yield to save his life. But he knew that she would make some effort to turn the game her way before she gave in. His mind would have been less easy, however, had he known that Vivian had nothing to barter for his safety and that the situation was causing the usually adroit Lady from Hell considerable concern.

The two had first met in Manila, where Wylie was assistant to the ancient and incredibly evil Mandarin Hoang Ti Fu, and almost immediately their partnership had come into being. It had lasted for several years now, and he had sense enough to realize that he could not have continued to be a successful crook had it not been for his association with the Lady from Hell. Among other things, he lacked the rare initiative and cold ruthlessness which distinguished her and had won for her the nickname of which she was known in the underworld of three continents. But, on the other hand, Wylie alone knew how heavily Vivian

Legrand leaned upon him in certain phases of their work;
how utterly she trusted him when she would not have
dared trust another.

"I have her word," Ortega responded satisfied. "Tonight
she yields it." He looked at Wylie. "Meanwhile, you would
prefer to remain here? It is cooler than in the room in
there." He nodded toward the narrow, iron-bound door at
the rear of the great hall that opened into the cell-like room
where Wylie had been confined until his return.

"I would prefer it," Wylie said, and his eyes flickered
toward the open gateway.

Ortega caught the glance and smiled sardonically.

"There is only one guard at the gate," he told Wylie,
"but there are others on watch above the gateway. Through
windows like those," and he indicated the embrasures
above their heads, "they command a view of the road and
the approaches. You might overpower the guard, although
I do not think it likely, but you would be shot down before
you had gone ten feet."

Normally, Ortega would have kept his captive securely
penned up until his objective had been reached. But, cleverer than most of his ilk, he was looking into the future.
There was a chance, a bare chance, that the woman might
be willing to sacrifice the life of her companion. In that
case, there was a slim chance that the man himself had
some clue to its whereabouts. If that were so, and Ortega
had been able to gain his confidence by treating him more
as a guest than a captive, he might secure that knowledge
by a bargain. Providing, of course, that Wylie knew that
the woman had been willing to sacrifice him.

With this in mind he was perfectly content to let Wylie

roam about the place, secure in the knowledge that he could not escape.

MEANWHILE, BACK IN her sitting room in the hotel, Vivian was walking up and down, that keen brain of hers seeking a solution to the problem. She had found where Wylie was being kept prisoner—that great pile of ruined masonry on a hilltop outside Havana was an ideal place. It looked strong enough to withstand the battering of artillery. But now that she had trailed Ortega to his lair, what had she gained? She had no secret to barter to Ortega in return for Wylie's safety, and Ortega would never believe her when she told him that the paper she had received from Gonzales had been blank. He would deem it but a trick on her part—and she had no doubt that Wylie's life would answer for her failure to deliver the secret.

She stopped in her stride and reached out to pick up the slip of paper again from the place where it had been on the table since Ortega's visit, an hour or more before, and gasped in astonishment.

Thin, fine lines of writing were apparent upon it now—thin lines in brown.

And then she realized what had happened. Gonzales' secret had been hidden in writing done with invisible ink. And it would have stayed truly invisible, forever lost to her, had it not been for her casual gesture in dropping it on the table. To lie in the full glare of the tropical sun! That intense heat had developed the writing upon it.

Swiftly she snatched it up, eagerly reading the two brief lines which were perceptible.

Monastery of San Fernando

That was clear enough. But then, the second line, rather blurred… some sort of odd signature, perhaps?

the Headless Saint

Yes, that final word was "Saint." A code term? Saints truly were to be associated with a monastery. The monastery of San Fernando? But, of course, here in Havana! Another gasp escaped her as the implication of what she had learned burst upon her shrewd mind.

For a moment she stood in deep thought, and then, her green eyes glowing with exultation, ran for her bedroom. Here was a situation that could not have fitted her purpose more perfectly if she had planned it.

DUSK WAS IN the offing as a tall, black-haired woman picked her way through the Chinese quarter of Havana. She was no longer young, this woman. There were lines about her mouth, lines on her forehead, and the black hair was streaked with gray here and there.

She seemed frightened as she picked her way through a maze of dim, tunneled lanes and alleys of gloom where lived the Mother of Smells. Curious eyes followed her as she moved up to the door of a store and entered, for a white woman was a rarity in that section of Havana.

Once inside the store she waved aside the clerk who came forward and asked in Spanish to see Chang Kai, the proprietor, at once. He came forward from behind the desk at the rear, his round, moonlike face wearing a look of polite inquiry.

"I wish to talk to you—to see you alone," she said with a furtive look around, "I have just come from Paris—and in

Paris I was told that if I should need help that was—difficult to obtain—to come to you."

There was a look of speculation in the eyes of Chang
Kai as he opened a door into his private apartment and
motioned her to enter. It was not often that a white
woman came to him seeking aid. Usually it was an alien
who wished to be smuggled into the United States, a drug
runner from Europe with a supply of cocaine or heroin to
dispose of.

Once inside the room the woman glanced about her
nervously.

"Can we be overheard?" she asked, in Spanish.

"We are quite alone," Chang Kai assured her. He pulled
out a curved teakwood chair and she sank into it with a
sigh, her fragile, worn hands clasped tightly in her lap.

"I am Dolores Cordoza," she said abruptly.

Chang Kai's eyes flickered slightly at sound of the name,
but otherwise he remained impassive, and she went on:

"At one time my father was Minister of Finance of
Venezuela. He foresaw that the revolution was coming,
and when it came he fled with a large amount of gold and
jewels."

"That is history, *señorita*," Chang Kai informed her
with a look of polite indifference. But a faint smile played
around the corners of his mouth, making the lips the only
living part of his features. It was almost as if he found the
irony of the situation deeply amusing.

"He reached Havana," the woman told him, "and died
here. But before he died he hid in a safe place the money
he had brought away with him."

"And," finished Chang Kai, "the money was never found.

That I know, *señorita*. The hiding place of the treasure has never been found."

"But I have found it," she declared earnestly, leaning forward. "That is why I have come to you. Looking through my father's papers a short time ago I came across something that had been hidden before—a slip of paper that told where the treasure was hidden here in Havana. I hastened here. But when I arrived I found the house where the treasure was hidden occupied by a gang of cutthroats. I can do nothing alone. That is why I seek your aid."

"Where is the treasure hidden, *señorita?*" Chang demanded. Strong as the control over his emotion was, he could not quench the blaze that came into his beady black eyes. What a fool this woman was, those eyes seemed to say; a deer walking into the jaws of the tiger.

The woman made a negative motion of her head.

"That I will not tell you," she said stubbornly, "unless you are willing to aid me. And if you are to aid me, it must be done tonight. There are others on the trail of my father's money—a woman, a Mrs. Legrand, who has obtained the secret."

"Have heard of this woman," Chang Kai admitted. "But how did she hear of the hiding place of your father's money? She arrived in Havana only this morning."

"A man named Gonzales, who had stolen the knowledge from me in Paris, sent for her. When she learned that he knew the secret she slew him."

Chang Kai's eyes flickered. Beneath the ice of his eyes fires were alive again, glowing as he stared unblinkingly at the woman.

"So Mrs. Legrand has the secret," he said, and if there

was a curious note in his voice the woman did not seem to notice it.

"Yes," came the answer, "and tomorrow morning she strikes a bargain with the man who occupies the house where the treasure is hidden—and tomorrow it will be in their hands—lost to me."

"I will aid you—for a price," Chang told her.

"I will pay, of course," the woman declared feverishly. "Twenty-five per cent of the treasure will be yours."

"I must have half," Chang Kai declared firmly, and if the gleam in his eyes meant that he had no intention of giving this woman half of the treasure, once it was in his hands, she did not see it.

"I cannot give you half," the woman said firmly. "I must make a bargain with the leader of these men who occupy this house—one Ortega, a Cuban—for twenty-five per cent of the gold. Otherwise we could not obtain it. The house is strong, almost a fortress, and his men are armed. But I dare not go there alone and reveal to him the hiding place of the treasure—I am not a fool, I know that I would not live five minutes after this scoundrel got his hands on the secret of the hiding place. That is why I wish you to go with me tonight at eight thirty, with your men, to protect me."

THE SMILE THAT flitted across the face of the Chinese was so nebulous that it might have been merely a shifting of the light and shadow effect upon his face. His voice was polite as he queried:

"Where is the treasure, *señorita?*"

"In the ruined Monastery of San Fernando, on the road to Gibara," the woman told him. "My father had purchased it, with the intention of restoring it and making it into a residence. He hid the treasure there. And then he died. The sale was never recorded, and I do not know who owns it now."

Chang Kai rose to his feet, an alert look upon his face.

"I shall make the necessary arrangements at once," he declared with satisfaction.

"But there is likely to be trouble! This man Ortega, whose headquarters it is, may not be satisfied with twenty-five per cent. He may try to seize it all," she said anxiously.

"There may be trouble," Chang Kai admitted, "but I shall be prepared for it. You need have no further cause for worry. Leave this matter to me and by tomorrow morning your share of your father's vanished treasure shall be in your hands."

He did not see the deep light, like the blaze in the heart of a fire opal, that leaped into the narrowed, greenish eyes of the woman facing him. Vivian Legrand, the Lady from Hell, had a great deal of doubt that the matter was going to turn out precisely as Chang Kai anticipated.

4

SECRET ORDERS

FOR MORE THAN an hour Wylie had been sitting on the low stool, one of the few articles of furniture in the vast room, or wandering around the place on a tour of inspection. The guard at the door apparently paid no attention to him, but Wylie knew that he was under close scrutiny.

A shout in Spanish drew his attention to the guard now—a shout that was taken up somewhere else in the great building and passed along. A moment later Ortega came into the place, buckling on a gun belt.

The guard said, in rapid Spanish, that a Chinese was approaching up the road, and Wylie's eyes flickered from the guard to Ortega. It was evident, from the thoughtful expression on the latter's face, that the visitor, whoever he was, was unexpected. Ortega turned speculative eyes upon Wylie.

"I hope," he said softly, "that you are not raising false hopes about this being your opportunity to, shall I say, desert our hospitality? I should not, if I were you, make the attempt. You may remain here, and if I find that this visitor requires to talk with me privately I shall ask you to go inside for a little time."

Wylie had not, as a matter of fact, given much thought

to the possibility of escape provided by the visitor. Ortega's warning about the guards stationed above the doorway had not left his mind.

Their visitor proved to be a young Chinese, his smooth yellow face wreathed in a bland smile beneath the wide, shadowing coolie hat of split bamboo. He might have passed for any one of the dozen market gardeners who trudge the road between their little vegetable *fincas* and the Havana markets every day in the week. Loose cotton trousers flapped above dirty feet in rope-soled sandals. The dingy cotton shirt was several sizes too large for him.

The bland smile still wreathed his face, but the eyes beneath the shadowing hat were intent as he crossed the space between doorway and Ortega.

"I bring you a message," he announced abruptly in Spanish, stepping in front of Ortega.

"From whom?" the Cuban asked.

"From Chang Kai, chief of my tong," came the answer. "Here is a paper that tells you that I speak truth when I say that I am his messenger," and he extended a slip of rice paper on which was written a sentence in Spanish, the fine spider-like letters giving evidence that the man who had written them was an artist with ink and brush.

Ortega read the sentence swiftly. Wylie's eyes were fixed intently upon the young Chinese. He was tense, waiting for any emergency that might arise, his legs pressing the stone flooring like coiled steel springs ready to hurl him to his feet at an instant's notice.

"What is the message?" the Cuban asked.

"You seek the hiding place of the gold of Cordoza," came the sing-song answer. "So does the worthy Chang Kai."

"Madre de Dios!" ejaculated Ortega, sitting up in amazement. "Does all of Havana seek this gold?"

"Of that I know nothing," the Chinese said calmly. His eyes roved about the hall, seeming to be seeking, noting, verifying, flitting from one to another of the statues in their niches on the wall. "My message is this: Today you killed a man to obtain the secret of the hiding place of the gold. If by now you have read the paper on which the secret is written you know that you have but half of the secret. The other half is in the hands of the Worthy Chang Kai. Without his half you cannot find the gold. Without your half my master is helpless. I am instructed to say to you if you are willing to join forces my master is willing to share the treasure, half and half."

For an instant silence hung over the little group. Watching Ortega, Wylie could almost read the conflicting emotions that raced through his brain. He knew that Ortega did not have the secret of the treasure and he could see that the Cuban was torn between the desire to admit the fact and a desire to bluff it out until he had obtained the secret from Vivian at eight o'clock that night.

The eyes of the Chinese youth had flitted back to the statues again. They seemed to fascinate him. His head was slightly tilted as he moved a step or two toward one of them to examine it more closely.

And so intent was Ortega upon the problem confronting him that he did not notice the interest of the young Chinese, did not see the stealthy sidewise movement that brought him in front of Wylie. Nor did he catch the movement that sent a revolver slipping from its hiding place up the loose sleeve of the Chinese and the hand that extended it to Wylie.

ORTEGA GOT TO his feet and paced up and down. And, as his back was turned, the revolver disappeared into Wylie's pocket, along with the folded paper that accompanied it.

It was the piece of paper the Lady from Hell had received from Gonzales, on which she had added a few terse instructions. Instructions so brief that to most men they would have seemed fantastic, but to Wylie, who knew from long experience the shrewd crystal-like clearness of Vivian's brain, they were simple enough.

> We're on top of treasure now. Be ready to help. Sunlight developed secret ink. Let Ortega find loot hidden in headless statue. Chink will take it from him and then *be ready.*

And, in the voice of the Lady from Hell, there came to Wylie's ears a few whispered sentences:

"Don't try getaway. Read note. I'll return tonight. Just before Chang Kai arrives tell Ortega that the loot is in the statue of Sebastian!"

Her low-voiced instructions left him with gleaming eyes. He had recognized Vivian immediately upon her arrival. That disguise and make-up of a Chinese youth was one that he himself had taught her.

He found himself perplexed as to the exact meaning of her orders. There had been so little time while Ortega's back was turned. Yet he knew the Lady from Hell well enough; hers were never idle instructions. Whatever plans she was now revolving, things she expected him to do were an integral part of them.

Besides, there was the note safe in his pocket. Her whispered, urgent words must have been rather an afterthought. Otherwise she would have written them out for him in advance, adding them to the folded paper and the welcome revolver. Obviously she was concerned about something which she could not have understood clearly before entering this very room.

Vivian's face had settled again into its smooth yellow mask and her hands were folded as Ortego turned back to her suddenly.

"You may tell Chang Kai," he said, "that I agree."

"All right," she answered. "Then I am to tell you that Chang Kai will arrive here tonight at eight thirty. He will join his knowledge with yours and together you will secure the treasure."

"Agreed," Ortega said, and with a bow the young Chinese turned away.

5

THE SHE-DEVIL'S GEMS

THAT NIGHT THE Lady from Hell slowed the car she had hired two-thirds of the way up the hill on which the ruined monastery stood and ran it behind a clump of young mango trees. A few branches snapped off and tucked here and there about the body of the car broke its outlines, gave effective camouflage. She would have need of that car in a short time, and need it badly, if her plans went according to schedule.

The pile of ruined masonry loomed on the crest of the hill above her in charred tracery against the golden globe of the rising moon, looking like some fantastic monster crouched there ready to spring. A light gleamed through one of the narrow slitted windows as she made her way up the hill, keeping carefully in the shadow of the underbrush that lined the roadway. Only the faintest of rustlings betrayed her presence. But even that, to her strained ears in the quiet of the night, was magnified to enormous proportions.

Thirty feet from her stood the black wall of the ruined monastery, and halfway between where she stood and the door a man stood sentinel by the tall undergrowth at the edge of the road. To attempt to approach the door by the road would be madness, serve only to invite a bullet from the man on guard. To even attempt a dash up the road in the moonlight, now stronger, would betray her presence. And along the side of the road it was equally dangerous.

Her only chance was to slip through the undergrowth, and she knew that her chance of getting past the man unobserved was slight. To jump him, and then make for the door, gave her only the scantiest of chances, for there was the possibility that there were others on guard that she could not see. But it was a chance that must be taken.

She might have stolen by at that, reach the door in safety, if she had not stepped on a dried twig. It snapped with an explosion of a rifle there in the stillness.

Silence... strung... pulsating... a gruelling hiatus. Minutes were eons... From the crest of a nearby palm came a querulous rasp of a parakeet, the only sound in a vast and dark silence.

Then cautious footsteps.

Vivian tensed. She was armed, but she dare not shoot, except as a last desperate expedient. The sound would bring the pack to her heels in half a minute.

And then near disaster swept upon her with sinister swiftness.

An intuition, a sudden leaping of her nerves from no visible warning, saved Vivian. She leaped sidewise under this untuitive impulse as a man behind her aimed a blow at her head with a revolver.

And then he broke into a high-pitched, choking noise as he stumbled back, clawing frantically at his eyes, writhing like a man suddenly bereft of all reason.

"Madre de Dios!" he cried in terror. "My eyes—they are burned out! I am blind—"

Concentrated ammonia does that to a man. It burns his eyes. Renders him immediately helpless.

Vivian's weapon had been a small rubber syringe filled with the stuff, and she had squirted a fine spray of it into the man's face. Then the butt of her gun fell on the head of the moaning man again and again with all the power of her strong arm—and the thing was done. The man slipped to the ground unconscious.

Without stopping to see how badly hurt the man was, Vivian slipped on quietly toward the great door of the building.

Her chief fear was that it might be locked. But it was not.

A touch, and it moved slightly on well-oiled hinges. Another touch and Vivian could peer through into the long, spacious room.

Hurricane lanterns, placed on the rude table in the center of the room, cast an irregular circle of light that barely washed the walls with a dim glow and bathed the statues in their niches in faint luminescence. Another lantern, placed on the floor, but tilted back so that its tin reflector directed a concentrated beam of light, illuminated one of the statues… a headless, battered piece of polychrome.

She caught her breath in astonishment. Here was something that she had not planned, something that startled her, made her think for a moment that her carefully-laid plans had gone wrong. Then a partial solution dawned upon her, and her tense lips parted in a slight smile as she saw how she could turn it to her own advantage.

ORTEGA, STANDING ON one of the steps a little below

the headless statue, swung a heavy hammer against it with shattering force—another and another blow. An oval portion in the statue's midsection cracked loose and fell to the floor. Behind it was a sparkle, a glitter.

Ortega shouted his triumph, and the Lady from Hell caught her breath in excitement. This was the hiding place of Cordoza's loot—a battered statue, hollow inside, standing in the ruined hall of a ruined monastery.

Ortega rained blow after blow. The statue cracked into fragments and the upper part crashed to the floor. And, like grains of corn from a ripped sack, the hoarded treasure spilled to the floor—pearls, rubies, amethysts, opals, emeralds in a glittering cascade in which the red-gold of minted coins formed dancing highlights of flame.

Dropping his hammer, Ortega leaped to the floor and scooped up a handful of the glittering gems, let them trickle through his fingers in a shining stream.

It was his last act of life. A shriek of terror burst from his lips as he glanced up from the floor just in time to see Chang Kai, standing ten feet away, raising a gun. It spat flame. A red splash appeared on his forehead. He fell over on his side, twitched once or twice, and then lay still.

"Do not stir," the Chinese snapped sharply at Ortega's astounded followers, huddled in a little knot a dozen or so feet away. The Lady from Hell could see that Chang Kai's Chinese had them covered. The Cubans saw it also. They did not move. They dared not.

Every eye in the room was fixed on Chang Kai. Softly Vivian pushed the door open a little more, slipped into the room, and closed the door behind her. None of those inside heard a sound, caught her furtive movement.

"This man," Chang Kai said with a contemptuous smile, indicating the huddled form on the floor, "was foolish enough to think that I would share Cordoza's treasure with him. He knows better now. It belongs to me."

"I'm afraid you're mistaken," Vivian said quietly from her position beside the doorway. "It belongs to me."

Chang Kai whirled, amazement upon his face, his gun held high. Then he smiled slowly as he saw that the intruder was only a woman, even though she was armed. His eyes swept her from flaming red hair beneath the trim white Panama, raked down the white silk suit and ended at the white buckskin shoes.

"What makes you believe that it belongs to you?" he said silkily. But there was deadly menace beneath the silk.

"Because I planned that it should," the Lady from Hell told him coolly. "I knew that the treasure was here, but Ortega's presence prevented my searching for it. I knew that you knew the hiding place, but did not know the house in which it was hid. So I told you the address, and arranged for you to come here,"

"You!" There was amazement in Chang Kai's eyes. "But—"

"Yes," Vivian cut him short. "I was *Señorita* Dolores Cordoza. You did exactly as I planned for you to do. You found the jewels. You removed Ortega. And now I have come for the treasure."

Chang Kai laughed. A lone woman, even though armed with a gun, to wrest a fortune from the hands of two dozen armed and desperate men. Ortega's men, he realized, had nothing to lose and everything to gain by fighting on his side, should a fight be necessary.

There was a stillness in the poise of the man opposite Vivian Legrand that told her his purpose as clearly as though the words had been spoken. Her nerves coiled like springs.

"Do not make the mistake of thinking me alone," she warned. "I would not be that foolish. You are covered by a dozen men—good shots all of them."

Chang Kai's eyes flashed about the room. It was empty save for Vivian, his own and Ortega's men. He laughed and gave a swift order in Chinese to his men.

"I warn you," Vivian said urgently, switching into staccato Cantonese, so that his men might not mistake her meaning. "Attack me and the souls of your men will leap the Dragon Gate this night, to join their ancestors!"

CHANG KAI PEERED at her appraisingly, striving to pierce the veil of shadows that filled the room, and read the expression on her face. It seemed incredible this woman should have come here single-handed in an attempt to wrest the treasure from them.

And yet there was no evidence that she was not alone.

He flung an order at his men:

"Disarm her."

As if to put a period to his words a shot rang out from somewhere behind him. Cursing shrilly, Chang Kai dropped his revolver and spun about as a bullet shattered his arm above the elbow.

"I warned you," Vivian said, her voice cutting through the sudden hubbub of chattering that had arisen from the Chinese. "Look!"

Every eye in the room followed her pointing hand.

From behind one of the statues, where he had been

hidden, Wylie stepped forth, automatic in hand. And for the first time the two opposing parties, Chang Kai's Chinese and the dead Ortega's Cubans, noticed that from behind each of the statues lining the wall behind them a slender black muzzle peered menacingly down at them.

"My men are armed with automatic rifles," Vivian said. "One movement and they can rake this place with a cross-fire that will leave not one of you alive."

After a second's pause she went on, and, had Chang Kai not been too busily occupied with the pain of his wound, he might have caught the palpable note of relief in her voice. "Drop your weapons on the floor and kick them toward me—all of you."

She raised her revolver menacingly, and again her eyes flickered toward the line of statues.

"Quick, or I fire! And the first shot will be the signal for my men to shoot."

A revolver dropped onto the stone flagging and skidded across the pavement toward her under the impetus of a hasty kick. Another—another—until the floor between Vivian and her opponents was littered with revolvers and knives.

Wylie stepped down from the niche in which he stood.

"Back, all of you," he said sternly. "Go through that doorway in the rear." He indicated the door to the room in which he had been placed.

Fear in their eyes, treading on one another's toes in their eagerness to get out of range of those deadly rifles peering menacingly down upon them, the two groups went backward and through the doorway Wylie had indicated. With a quick movement he slammed the door.

"There is no other exit?" Vivian queried.

"None," Wylie said.

"Good," Vivian said. "Now we've got work to do. I've a car hidden below and we can place this stuff in it," and she indicated the glittering heap of jewels and gold coins on the floor. Then she halted.

"But how in the world did you manage that?" and she indicated the slender, deadly muzzles that leered down at them in the half gloom.

"Oh, that!" Wylie said with a smile. "That was an inspiration. There was a pile of short lengths of pipe in my room. I thought I might as well make use of them."

THE ADVENTURE OF THE VOODOO MOON

Undaunted in the Face of Outlawed Death,
Vivian Legrand Makes Strange Magic—
and Beats a Rascal at His Own Game

1

CROOKS ON HOLIDAY

THE LADY FROM Hell was standing on the upper deck
of the little inter-island steamer as it neared the coast of
Haiti. Her crown of flaming red hair was beaten back from
her smooth forehead and her white dress modeled tightly
to her body by the strong trade wind.

She and her companion in crime, Adrian Wylie, had just
completed one of the most amazing coups in their whole
career, and were now on a vacation. The Lady from Hell
had been emphatic on that point before leaving Havana.

"Nothing is to tempt us into mingling business with
pleasure," she had told Wylie. "Not even if we stumble
across the vaults of a bank wide open and unguarded."

Now, the second day out from Havana, the sun was
just rising over the blue bubbles dreaming on the horizon
that were the mountains of Haiti, and still she could not
account for the vague sense of disquiet, the little feeling
of apprehension that had been growing in her ever since
the steamer passed between Morro Castle and its smaller
counterpart on the other side of Havana harbor.

No one on the little steamer dreamed that she was the
notorious Lady from Hell, whose fame had already filtered
even to the West Indies. And if they had, it would have

seemed incredible that this graceful, beautiful woman could have started her career by poisoning her own father; could have escaped from a Turkish prison—the only time in her career that the net of the law had closed about her; could have held up and robbed the Orient Express, a deed that had filled the press of the world, although her part in it had never even been suspected.

The daring coup in Havana that had added a large sum to the bank account of Adrian Wylie, her chief of staff, and herself had not been brought to the attention of the Cuban police. And, although the police of half a dozen European countries knew her well and swore when her name was mentioned, there was not a single thing with which she could be charged, so cleverly had her tracks been covered, so adroitly her coups planned.

She turned away and began to stride up and down the deck. More than one passenger turned to stare at her as she passed with a rippling grace of motion, a little lithe stride that told of perfect muscles and the agility of a cat.

A sound made her turn as a passenger came up behind her and fell into step with her.

"Good evening, Mrs. Legrand," he said in English, with the faintest of accents. "You are up early."

"I was eager to catch a sight of Haiti," Vivian responded with a smile. "The mountains there are lovely."

"They are lovely," he responded, "Even though Haiti is my home I never tire of seeing her mountains grow about the horizon line." Then he added, "We dock in a few hours. See that headland there," and he pointed to an amethyst bulk that thrust itself out into the sea. "That is Cap St. Feral. The port is just beyond it."

And then she saw Wylie. He was tied to a post in the clearing

THERE WAS AN impression of power, perfectly controlled, about Carlos Benedetti that was perfectly evident to Vivian Legrand as she surveyed him for a fleeting instant through narrowed eyes. His face was unhealthily pale, the nose slightly crooked, the black eyes very sharp and alert beneath the close-cropped and sleek black hair. He had the air of one to whom the world had been kind, and from it he had learned assurance and a kind of affability.

But behind his assurance—this affability—the Lady from Hell sensed something that was foreign to the face he presented to the world, something that made her cautious.

"Do we dock?" she queried. "I thought that we landed in small boats."

"The word was incorrectly used," he admitted. "I should have said that we arrive. Cap St. Feral is not modern enough to possess a dock for a ship of this size, small as the vessel is." He hesitated a moment. "I assume that you are not familiar with Cap St. Feral."

"No," Vivian said. "This is my first visit to Haiti."

The man's oblique stare was annoying her. Not that she was unaccustomed to the bold stare that men give beautiful women. But this was different. Had the man been wiser he might have taken warning at the hard light that lay in the depths of her greenish eyes.

But he went on suavely:

"To those of us who know the island it offers little in the way of entertainment," he said, "but to a stranger it might be interesting. If you care to have me, I should be glad to offer my services as a guide while you are in port."

A casual enough courtesy offered to a stranger by a native of a place. Vivian thanked him and watched, with a calculating eye, as he bowed and walked on down the deck. The man was sleek, well groomed and obviously wealthy. His spotless Panama was of the type that cannot, ordinarily, even be bought in Equador, where they are woven. A hat so fine and silky that usually they are reserved as gifts to persons in high position. And the white suit that he wore had not come from an ordinary tailor.

It was made of heavy white silk—Habatui silk that in the East sells for its weight in gold, literally.

Adrian Wylie found Vivian on deck. In a few swift words she told him of the invitation and of the intuitive warning she had felt.

Wylie nodded slowly. "That explains something that had been puzzling me," he said. "For an hour last night the purser insisted on buying me drinks in the smoking room and casually asking questions about the two of us. And hardly five minutes after he left me I saw him talking earnestly to Benedetti at the door of the purser's office.

Evidently the man hunted you up for the first thing this morning, after his talk with the purser."

Benedetti, they knew from the ship's gossip, was an exceedingly wealthy sugar planter, who owned the whole of an exceedingly fertile island called Ile de Feral, not far from the port of Cap St. Feral. The Haitian Sugar Centrals—actually the sugar trust, so ship gossip ran—had attempted to drive him out of business, and failed miserably. Despite a price war, he had managed to undersell the trust and still make a profit. Then he had been offered a staggering sum for the island, and had refused. The offer was still open, so she had been told, and any time he cared to sell the sugar trust would be only too eager to buy him out.

A little smile formed on Vivian's lips. Benedetti, she suspected, was accustomed to having his own way where women were concerned. And the Lady from Hell knew full well her own attractiveness as a woman.

But even the Lady from Hell, astute as she was, could not have fathomed the dark reason that lay behind Benedetti's advances.

2

DANGER'S WARNING

THE FAINT SOUND of drums somewhere in the distance; a regular, rhythmic beat, as though a gigantic heart, the heart of Black Haiti, were beating in the stillness of the blazing noon, hung over the little city of Cap St. Feral as the Lady from Hell, Wylie and Benedetti rode through the sun-washed streets.

The heat that hung about them like a tangible thing seemed to be intensified and crystallized by the monotonous beating of the lonely drums.

The Lady from Hell turned to Benedetti with a question, the brilliant sunlight through the trees overarching the road catching her hair and turning it into a halo of flame about her exquisitely lovely face.

"Voodoo drums," he said. "The night of the Voodoo Moon is approaching. The drums will keep on sounding until the climax of the Snake Dance. They're beating like this all over the island, even in Port-au-Prince. Worshipers in the cathedral can hear the sound of the drums from the hills outside the city drifting through the intoning of the mass. Then, almost as if they had been silenced by a gigantic hand, they will all stop at the same moment—the climax of the Snake Dance."

Vivian stole another glance at the people along the road-side as their car passed. Voodoo. It was something out of a book to her, something a little unsettling to come so closely in contact with. And it seemed difficult to believe that the happy, smiling faces were the faces of people who had run mad through the streets of Port-au-Prince, so history said, tearing President Guillaume Sam to bloody bits while he still lived.

Benedetti caught the thought in her mind.

"You have not lived here, Mrs. Legrand," he said quietly. "You cannot understand the place that Voodoo holds in these people's lives; the grip it has upon them. And you are not familiar with the effect of rhythms upon the nerve centers. It does strange things to blacks, and to whites things stranger still."

He leaned forward and flung a few words in Creole French at the driver—words that Vivian Legrand, fluent as her French was, could barely follow. The car stopped before a long, rambling structure, of gleaming white *coquina*, half hidden behind crimson hibiscus bushes.

"I brought you here for lunch," he said. "It would be unbearably hot on the ship and there is no hotel at which you would want to eat, even if you could, in the town itself. This is a little house that I maintain, so that I may have a comfortable place to stay when necessity or business compels me to be in town. I took the liberty of assuming that Dr. Wylie and yourself would have lunch with me here."

Vivian looked about her curiously as their host opened the little gate and ushered them into the flower garden that surrounded the house.

From the whitewashed, angular, stone walls of the old house, almost smothered in pink Flor de Amour, her eyes went to the table set beneath a flowering Y'lang-y'lang tree in the center of the close-cropped lawn. An old woman stood beside it, an ancient crone with more than a trace of white blood in her, one of those incredibly ancient people that only primitive races can produce. Her face was a myriad of tiny wrinkles and her parchment skin had the dull, leathery hue and look that is common in the aged of the Negro race.

THE WOMAN TURNED slowly as the trio approached and her eyes fastened on Vivian. In her cold, yellow eyes was a look almost of fear. Something that was like lurking terror coiled in the depths of those alert, flashing eyes and rendered them stony, glassy, shallow.

And then, as Benedetti and Wylie went on past her she made a gesture, an unmistakable gesture for Vivian to halt, and her voice, lowered until it was barely a sibilant whisper, came to Vivian's ears in French.

"Do not stay here," she said. "You must not stay."

There was definite horror in her eyes, and fear also, as her glance flitted from Vivian toward Benedetti. Despite the whisper to which her voice had been lowered there was fear to be distinguished in her tones also.

Her face was impassive as she turned away. Only her eyes seemed alive. They were cold, deadly bits of emerald. The Lady from Hell abhorred the unknown. All through her criminal career the unsolved riddle, the unsolved personality, the unexplained situation, inflamed her imagination. She would worry over it as a dog worries a bone.

And how her mind hovered over this problem with

relentless tenacity, her brain working swiftly, with smooth precision. Her intuition had been right, after all. The feeling of danger, of disquiet, of apprehension that had haunted her ever since the coast line of Haiti came in sight over the horizon had not been wrong. She knew now, beyond a shadow of doubt, that danger hovered over her like a vulture.

The fear that she had glimpsed in the old woman's eyes, Vivian reasoned, was fear for herself should she be caught warning the white woman. But what was the danger against which she was warned, and why should this old woman, who had never seen her before, take what was obviously a risk to warn her against it?

Luncheon was just over when a long hoot sounded from the steamer.

"The warning whistle," Benedetti told her. "A signal to the passengers that the steamer will sail in an hour."

He turned to Vivian.

"My roses," he said, "are so lovely that I took the liberty of requesting Lucilla to cut an armful of them for you to take back to the ship as a remembrance."

THERE WAS A distinct warning in the old woman's veiled eyes as Vivian stretched out her hands for the big bunch of pale yellow roses that Lucilla brought; not only warning, but that same terror and fear that had stood starkly in them a short time before. Instinctively Vivian stiffened and looked about her, her nerves tense. Was the danger, whatever it was, ready to spring? But the scene seemed peaceful enough.

"How lovely they are!" she exclaimed, and wondered if it could be her imagination that made the old woman seem reluctant to part with the flowers. Then she gave a little exclamation of pain as she took them from Lucilla. "Like many other lovely things, there are thorns," she said ruefully, gazing at the long, thorny stems, still slightly damp from standing in water.

"That is true," Benedetti said, and there seemed to be an expression of relief in his eyes. "Our Haitian roses are lovely, but there have longer and sharper thorns than any other roses I know."

"Don't you think we had better be leaving?" Vivian queried, glancing at her watch. The shimmering heat haze that covered everything seemed to have blurred her vision, and she had to peer closely at the little jewelled trinket to make out the time. "It's a long drive back to the ship."

"There is still plenty of time," Benedetti assured her. "The warning whistle is supposed to sound an hour before sailing time, but it always is nearer two hours." Then he gave a little exclamation of concern. "But you are ill," he said as Vivian swayed a little.

"Just the heat," she said. "I am not yet accustomed to it."

The flowers she had been holding tumbled to the table and thence to the ground. The long-stemmed yellow blossoms gave no hint of the fact that from the moment Benedetti's message had been delivered to the old woman until the moment before they had been placed in Vivian's hands their stems and thorns had been soaking in a scum-covered fluid brewed by Lucilla herself.

"You must go inside for a few moments. You must rest," Benedetti said sharply. "I should have realized that you were not accustomed to heat. It might be fatal for you to drive back to the ship in this sun without a rest."

Wylie, a look of concern on his face, took Vivian's arm and helped her to her feet. Even then, with her vision blurred and an overpowering drowsiness creeping over her, the Lady from Hell did not realize that she had been drugged. It was not until she reached the threshold of the room to which she had been guided that the truth burst upon her dulled senses with the force of a thunderbolt.

Stacked neatly against the whitewashed walls of the room was the baggage she had left in her cabin on the steamer!

Dizzily, clutching at the door for support, she turned… just in time to see a short heavy club descend with stunning force on Wylie's head. And then, even as her companion crumpled to the stone flooring, blackness flooded her brain.

3

VIVIAN LEGRAND TRAPPED

DUSK HAD FALLEN with tropic swiftness before Vivian awoke. She had not been conscious of her journey, wrapped in coco fiber matting from the house where she had been drugged, to Benedetti's launch, nor of the subsequent trip to the man's home on the Ille de Feral.

Now, anger smoldering in her greenish eyes, she faced him across the dining room table. In the dim room the table floated in a sea of amber candlelight. Barefooted black girls passed in and out, their voices keyed to the soft stillness, a thing of pauses and low voices. The whole thing, to Vivian, seemed to take on a character of unreality—a dream in which anything might happen.

She waited for Benedetti to speak after the slender black girl drew out her chair for her. But the man did not, so finally she broke the silence herself.

"What do you hope to gain by this?" she queried.

"Won't you try your soup?" he said bitterly. "I am sure that you will find it very good."

He halted as one of the girls stopped beside his chair and said something in Creole in a low voice. He rose to his feet.

"Will you pardon me?" he said. "There is someone outside, with a message. I shall be gone only a moment."

He disappeared through the door beside the staircase, the door that Vivian imagined led to the rear of the house.

Swiftly she beckoned the black maid to her, slipped the glittering diamond from her finger, and folded the girl's hand about it.

"Come to my room tonight," she whispered tensely, "when it is safe. No one will ever know. And in Port-au-Prince or Cap St. Feral you can sell that ring for sufficient to live like a *blanc* millionaire for the rest of your days."

The girl's face paled to a dusky brown, she glanced furtively from the glittering jewel in her hand to the pale face of the woman who had given it to her. Vivian caught the hesitation.

"I have others in my room," she urged desperately. "You shall choose from them what you want—two—three— when you sell them there will never have been another girl in Haiti as rich as you will be."

"I will come," the girl said in a whisper and stepped back against the wall. A moment later Benedetti returned.

"I regret to have been so poor a host as to leave you alone for even so short a time," he said.

"Please," Vivian said shortly, and there was in her manner no indication of the triumph that filled her breast. "Why dissemble. You've brought me here for a purpose. Why not tell me what it is?"

Already a scheme was forming in that agile mind of hers. When the girl came to her room that night she would persuade her to find weapons—guide Wylie and herself to a boat so that they might escape. But was Wylie still alive?

Benedetti's answer interrupted her thoughts.

"It is not so much what I hope to gain, as what I hope

to keep," he said smoothly. He paused, and through the silence there came to her ears that queer rise and fall of notes from drums that had followed her ever since she arrived in Haiti—the drums of the Voodoo Moon, Benedetti had called it. He leaned forward.

"You might as well know now," he said abruptly. "You have until tomorrow midnight to live."

"Unless?" Vivian queried meaningly. She was very sure that she knew what the man meant.

BENEDETTI CALMLY PLACED the spoon in his plate and pushed it aside.

"There is no proviso. I know nothing of your personal life—of your finances. They are no concern of mine. You may be extremely rich, or completely poor—that does not enter into the matter at all. You have nothing that I care to buy. All I know is that you are young and extremely beautiful." He studied her with a cold dispassionate interest, then sighed, a bit regretfully, it seemed. "That is the reason you must die tomorrow night."

The thing was utterly fantastic. Vivian listened in amazed fascination. She could hardly bring herself to believe that she had heard correctly. So sure had she been that the man's interest in her rose from the fact that he was attracted to her that the thought there might be another, more sinister motive behind the drugging and kidnaping had not occurred to her.

Her green eyes narrowed a trifle—only that, but there was the impression of a steel spring tightening. Then she said quietly:

"Why must I die?"

"Because," he answered, "tomorrow night is the night of

the Voodoo Moon—the night when the Papaloi and the Mamaloi present Ogoun Badagri, the Bloody One, with the Goat Without Horns."

"The Goat Without Horns?" Vivian repeated, uncomprehendingly. "What is that?"

"You," the man said tersely. "Tomorrow at midnight, when the Voodoo Moon is fullest, you will be offered as a sacrifice to Ogoun Badagri, the snake god."

For a moment the Lady from Hell stared at him, a chill feeling clutching at her breast. Then an alert look came into her eyes, a look that she quickly veiled. She was listening intently.

"You're not actually in earnest?" she asked quietly. Every nerve was strained to catch that sound again—the drone of an airplane engine that had come faintly to her ears. It was louder now. "You are trying to frighten me, to trap me into something. You will find that I am not easily frightened or trapped."

The sound of the plane was louder now. She shot a furtive glance at Benedetti. Could aid be on the way? Could Benedetti's plans have gone wrong, and a search be underway for them?

"I am very much in earnest," the man opposite her said. "You see, that is the secret of my successful defiance of the sugar trust, the secret of why my laborers never leave me, the secret of why I can manufacture sugar at a cost that the sugar trust cannot possibly equal and still make a profit. Once a year I present the Papaloi and the Mamaloi, the high priest and priestess of Voodoo, with a human sacrifice—a white man or woman—and in turn these two guardians of the great snake see to it that my laborers do not leave, and are kept content with the lowest pay scale in the island of Haiti."

He broke off and smiled.

"You may relax, Mrs. Legrand," he said. "That plane that you hear will not land here. It is the marine mail plane that passes over the island every night between eleven thirty and twelve o'clock."

Vivian looked at him blankly. "Plane?" she said vaguely. "Oh, yes, that is a plane, isn't it? Quite honestly, I had not noticed the sound before you spoke."

IT WAS SO well done that it fooled him. She picked up the slender silver fruit knife that lay on the table in front of her, twisting it so that it shone in her fingers, a pale, metallic splinter of light. She regarded him with eyes that had turned mysteriously dark, and leaned forward a little. Her voice, when she spoke, was very soft, and it held a quality of poignancy.

"You seem to live alone here," she said, and her eyes regarded him warmly. "Don't you ever become—lonely?"

There was a world of promise and invitation in the soft tone, in the alluring lips.

He looked at her and tightened his lips.

"That is useless," he said. "You are beautiful, one of the most beautiful women that I have ever seen, but a dozen such women as you could not make up to me for the loss of my plantation. No, my dear, your charm is useless."

"But you wouldn't dare," she said. "A woman cannot simply disappear from a steamer without inquiries being made. This is not the Haiti of twenty years ago. The Americans are in control—they are the police…"

Benedetti shook his head. "Do not raise false hopes.

You sent the purser of the steamer a note saying that you had unexpectedly found friends in Cap St. Feral and were breaking your voyage here. The same man who brought the note took yours and your companion's baggage off the ship. By now he has probably forgotten your existence.

"There is nothing to connect you with me, and if inquiries should be made it will simply be assumed that you either left the island or were murdered by a wandering *caco*. And as for an Haitian, who might know something of your disappearance, aside from the fact that the secrets of Voodoo are something that are never discussed, there is an island saying: '*Z affaires negres, pas z'z affaires blancs.*' And you will find that the affairs of the Negroes are not the affairs of the whites. And then," his voice was bland as he made the significant statement, "there is rarely any proof— left—when the great green snake god has completed his sacrifice."

"And my companion—Dr. Wylie—what have you done with him?" Vivian queried steadily. A bright spark glowed in her narrowed green eyes for a moment. It died slowly.

"He is safe, quite safe," Benedetti assured her, "for the time being. He also will be a sacrifice to Ogoun Badagri."

He said it with simple, sincere ruthlessness; undisguised, but neither vindictive nor cruel.

"You are quite sure of yourself," Vivian said softly, and had Wylie been there he would have recognized the meaning of that tone; the threat of that greenish glow at the back of her eyes. He had seen that cold light in her eyes before. But Benedetti, even had he glimpsed it, would not have known that it was like the warning rattle of a snake before it strikes.

Now, with a swift movement she flung the silver fruit knife she held at the gleaming shirt front of the man opposite her. Her aim was deadly, for few people could throw a knife with the skill and precision of the Lady from Hell.

BUT BENEDETTI HAD caught the glitter of the candlelight on the metal a split second before she launched the knife. His agile mind perceived her intention and he flung himself to one side just in time. The knife thudded into the high back of the chair in which he had been sitting and rested there, quivering.

"You are a fool," the man commented curtly. Striding to the French windows he flung them wide, letting moonlight stream into the room. The sound of the drums came in louder, a barbaric rhythm beating in strange tempo with the pulse in her wrist.

"Look at that," he said, flinging out an arm.

At the edge of the veranda, which ran along the front of the house, lounged a white cotton-clad Haitian, a three-foot cane knife clasped in his fist. Further along, at the edge of the beach, another man leaned against the bole of a coconut tree, and the glitter of the moonlight on steel betrayed the fact that he also was armed with a cane knife.

"Even if you had killed me," he said quietly, "you would have been no better off. You could not escape from the island. There are no boats here. Even the launch on which you arrived has been sent away and will not return until after the ceremony. And if you had attempted to swim, the sea swarms with sharks."

It was after midnight when Vivian went upstairs to her room again. Benedetti escorted her to the door.

"I am locking you in," he told her. "It is really quite

useless to do so. You could not escape. There is absolutely
no possibility of success. But it is a precaution I always take
with my annual—visitors."

Then he drew from his pocket the diamond ring that
Vivian had, earlier in the evening, given to the little black
maid.

"You will find," he said with a smile, "that it is useless to
attempt to bribe my servants. The fear of the Voodoo in
them is greater than the greed for money."

With a slight bow he closed the door, leaving her staring at the blank panels with a sinking feeling in her heart.
She was a prisoner in a prison without walls, and yet
the sea that girdled the land was a barrier as effective as
stone ramparts and iron bars. Instead of one jailer she had
dozens—perhaps hundreds—for she realized that every
laborer on the island was a potential guard, alert to halt any
attempt to escape. She did not attempt to deceive herself
by thinking that every native of the place did not know of
her presence and the fate for which she was destined.

She wondered what prompted the old woman—Benedetti's servant—to take her life in hand and warn her, back
there in Cap St. Feral? The woman had, of course, realized
Benedetti's purpose in bringing her here, since it had been
she who had prepared the drugged rose stems. It was not
for a long time, and then only by accident, that Vivian
was to discover that in a Haitian the desire for revenge
can transcend even the fear of Voodoo, and that it was to
avenge what she considered a wrong that the old woman
had warned her.

Vivian turned her thoughts back to her position. She
believed she knew where Wylie was being held. On her way

down to the dining room a little earlier she had encoun-
tered one of the black maids with a tray; had noted the
door through which the girl had passed. That, she reasoned,
must be the room in which Wylie was held prisoner, unless
there were other prisoners in the house of whom she knew
nothing.

SHE SMILED A trifle grimly at the thought of being locked
in her room. If Benedetti only knew of how little importance a lock—particularly an old-fashioned one such as
this—was to her. Opening her suitcase she took out a hand
mirror with a long handle. Unscrewing the handle, she
removed from the hollow interior a long slender rod of thin
steel. This she forced slowly into the thin opening between
door and jamb. The rod scraped on metal. She worked it up
and down, slowly pressing inward. Bit by bit the sloping
tongue of the lock was forced back into its sheath, until
the blade slipped through. A twist of the door handle and
Vivian was peering out into the corridor.

Darkness hung before her eyes. It was as if a curtain
of some impenetrable texture hung before her. She knew
nothing of the floor plan of the big, rambling house, but
she knew that the room she had seen the girl entering was
the last on her side of the corridor, and accordingly she
made her way cautiously in that direction, feeling her way,
finger-tips trailing the wall, listening intently every step
or so for some sound that might warn her of the presence
of another person.

Her hand trailing along the wall touched a door—the
fifth one she had passed. This was the door she sought.
Gently she tried the knob. It was locked. A few minutes'
work with the thin steel rod and the door swung inward

with only the faintest of sounds. But even that was sufficient to betray her presence to Wylie's alert ears.

"Who is it?" he queried.

"Shhh," she whispered warningly, and, closing the door, crossed swiftly toward the chair where he sat beside the window.

In low, tense whispers she told him of her conversation with Benedetti and of the fate that was in store for both of them.

"We've got to get away tonight," she finished. "It's our only chance. There must be some way—perhaps we can make a raft. At least we can try."

4

THE FIRST VICTIM

WITH WYLIE BY her side she made her way to the door; peered cautiously outside. By diligent practice the Lady from Hell had long ago acquired the chatoyant eye—the cat's—good for prowling about and seeing things in the dark, but here in the corridor the blackness was intense, with a tangible quality that was numbing to the senses. The utter opacity was tactile, half fluid, like fog. She crept down the hallway with feline assurance, passing her fingers delicately over objects that came into her path with a touch light enough to stroke a butterfly's wing. The house was a sea of silence, and on its waves the slightest noise made long and screeching journeys.

To Vivian's hearing, sandpapered by suspense, the slight give of the polished boards of the staircase beneath their slow steps produced a terrific noise. By making each step a thing of infinite slowness, they crept forward safely. Each downward step was a desperate and long-drawn-out achievement, involving an exactly calculated expenditure of muscular energy, an unceasing, muscular alertness.

Once, as they reached the bottom of the stairs, there came from the dining room in which they stood the rattle of a clock preparing to ring out a quarter hour. It struck

Vivian's tense nerves as a thing of abominable violence—
like countless, swift hammer strokes on the innumerable frayed ends of her nerves. She had the sensation of
being driven into the woodwork of the floor upon which
she stood, of being crushed under an immense and light-
ning-like pressure.

After what seemed an eternity they reached the further
side of the dining room. Under her careful manipulation
the latch of the door slipped slowly back. The door moved
silently, slowly. A brilliant line of moonlight appeared.
Vivian caught her breath sharply.

Standing there in the open ground in front of the
veranda stood a Haitian, alert, watchful, armed with a
machete.

There was no escape that way. Weaponless, they were
helpless before the menace of that shining three-foot
length of steel, even if they could cross the moonlit space
that lay between the veranda and the man without being
detected.

"The back of the house," Vivian whispered to Wylie, her
voice barely perceptible.

She knew that the door to the kitchen was beside the
staircase they had descended. That much she had observed
during her interview with Benedetti earlier in the evening.
By locating the staircase first in the blackness, she found
the door she sought and opened it. A passageway opened
before them, dimly illuminated by a shaft of silver that
poured through a half opened door at its further end.

Silently they made their way down the passage and
cautiously peered through the partly opened door. Another
disappointment.

It was a small room, one wall covered with shelves, boxes and bags stacked high on the other side with a single window, half way up the wall, through which moonlight poured. A storeroom of some sort.

Vivian reached out and caught Wylie's arm, drew him silently into the little room and closed the door.

"There may be weapons here," she said. But she was mistaken. The nearest approach was a broken kitchen knife used, probably, to slash open the burlap bags which stood against the wall.

IT WAS A poor substitute for a weapon, but Vivian took it thankfully. And then she gave a gasp. Her hand, exploring a shelf, had come in contact with something clammy and sticky that clung and would not be shaken off. Her first thought was that it was some monstrous tropical insect. It seemed alive, it clung so persistently, despite her efforts to shake it loose.

Then, as Wylie snapped his cigarette lighter into flame, the tiny glow illuminated an oblong of sticky fly paper fastened to her hand. There was a pile of the sheets upon the shelf. Despite the tenseness of the situation she almost laughed at the uncanny feeling the thing had given her there in the darkness.

In the dim flame of Wylie's lighter they searched again for anything that might prove of assistance to them in their predicament. Bags of flour. Bags of potatoes. Kegs of pig tails and pig snouts in brine—evidently food for the laborers. A half-emptied case of bacale—dried codfish, a staple article of diet in the West Indies—and a can of phosphorescent paint. Also row after row of canned food. But nothing that might be of assistance to them.

Climbing upon a box Vivian peered through the window, then turned back to Wylie, excitement in her voice.

"We can get out this way," she whispered. "There is the limb of a tree almost against the window and shrubbery around the tree."

"Anybody in sight?" Wylie queried.

"No one," Vivian said, and pried the latch of the window with her broken knife blade. It came open with a tearing shriek that sounded like thunder in the silence. Disregarding the noise Vivian slipped through the window and swung on to the limb of the tree. Wylie followed her, and in a moment they stood on the ground in the midst of dense shrubbery.

"We will have to keep in the shadow," she said as they crept silently through the bushes, only an occasional rustling leaf marking their passage. "The moment we step in the moonlight we'll be seen, if anyone is watching."

Even there in the bushes the brilliant moonlight illuminated the ground about them. A faint drumming ebbed to them through the brilliance, faintly touching the dark membrane of the night as they emerged on what seemed to be a well-defined path leading toward the beach.

A sudden opening in the trail, a burst of moonlight, and they stood on a strip of white sand with breakers creaming softly in front of them.

"There," Vivian said, still keeping her voice low. "See that pile of driftwood. We'll make a raft of that. Drag it to the water's edge while I cut vines to lash it together."

Feverishly they worked, Wylie dragging the heavy logs into position, lashing them firmly together with the vines that Vivian cut from the jungle's edge, until at last a crazy-looking affair bobbed up and down in the ripple at the edge of the beach. Makeshift, clumsy, but it would float and it was an avenue of escape, the only avenue that had presented itself.

Vivian returned from a final trip to the jungle, dragging behind her three bamboo poles.

"We can use two of these to shove the thing with, until we get into deep water," she said. "The other we can lash upright as a mast and use my dress as a sail."

At that instant, from the path behind them, came the sound of voices. Vivian flashed a frantic glance at the jungle rearing up behind them, and then leaped on board the raft. Wylie followed. It dipped and swayed, but held their weight. The voices came nearer. Desperately Vivian braced her pole against the sandy bottom and shoved. Wylie followed suit. Sluggishly the clumsy craft moved away from the shore—five feet—ten feet—and then half a dozen men poured through the opening in the jungle and raced across the sand, splashed through the shallow water and surrounded the little craft, gleaming machetes raised threateningly.

VIVIAN DID NOT see Benedetti when they returned to the house with their captors that night, nor was he visible when she awoke the next morning after a night spent in futile speculation and planning, and descended to the dining room.

A black girl served them breakfast. Golden sunlight poured through the wide French windows, beyond which they could see the beach and the green cove. Nowhere was there evidence of the fate that hung over them. But both knew, and the fact of that knowledge was evident in their eyes, in their short jerky words, that Death's wings were already casting their shadows across them.

The sun was well up when they went on to the veranda. There should have been the click of machetes in the cane fields and the low, lazy laughter of the workers. But everything was still, and that stillness held an ominous meaning.

Wylie was frankly without hope—more so as the day wore on, and Vivian, although she had never admitted defeat, admitted to herself that she saw no way out of the impasse. Benedetti, she saw now, had made no mistake when he told her that escape was impossible.

The day wore on, and still Benedetti did not put in an appearance. Once Vivian asked one of the maids where he could be found and received in answer a queer jumble of Creole French that held no meaning. Later, they essayed a walk to the Sugar Central, whose smokestacks rose on the other side of the cane fields, but one of the ever-present natives stepped slowly in their path, his machete openly in evidence. From the corner of her eyes Vivian could see others, alert, ready, at the edge of the jungle. Their captors were taking no chances.

On the far side of the cleared space Vivian could see a break in the jungle where a path ended. From this path men kept coming and going, and this, she surmised, must lead to the place where they were scheduled to die that night.

It was after dinner when Benedetti made his appearance, and with him stalked tragedy.

Vivian and Wylie were on the broad veranda, walking up and down. Something—some sixth sense—warned Vivian of danger, even before she heard the quick, catlike tread behind her. She made an attempt to swing around an instant too late. Someone leapt on her. A strong arm was locked about her throat. A hand was clamped over her mouth. A knee dug into the small of her back. She wrenched, tore at the gripping hands, even as she saw other hands seizing Wylie; she was aware of Benedetti's face, his features hard as stone. In the same second something dropped over her head and blotted the world into darkness.

How long she was held there motionless on the veranda she did not know. Then came a quick gabble of Creole in Benedetti's voice and the smothering hand was removed. **SHE FLASHED A** glance around. The place was deserted save for herself, Benedetti and one tall native who stood beside the veranda steps, the ever-present machete in evidence. Obviously a guard.

The man interpreted her look.

"Your companion is gone. You will never see him again," he said, and his voice was indifferent. He might have been speaking of some trivial object that had disappeared. He turned back toward the dining room, where candlelight made a soft glow. Vivian followed. The house seemed curiously still, as if all life had departed from it save these two.

"Gone—you mean—" She could not finish the sentence.

Benedetti nodded and selected a cigarette from a box on a little side table; lit it at one of the candles.

"He will be the first sacrifice to Ogoun Badagri. When the great green snake god has finished with him they will come for you. You will be the climax of the ceremony," he told her brutally.

"You mean that you—a white man—will actually permit these men to make a sacrifice of us?" she queried. She knew, before she said it, that any appeal to him would be useless, but her mind was going around frantically, seeking a method of warding off the death that was imminent.

"What is your life and that of your companion to me?" he asked. "Nothing—not so much as the ash from the cigarette—compared with the fact that your death means that I keep my plantation a year longer. I refused close to half a million dollars from the sugar trust for the island. Do you think, then, that I would permit a little thing like your life to rob me of it?"

5

VOODOO DEATH

VIVIAN DID NOT answer. Her eyes roamed around the room, although already every article in it had been photographed indelibly on her retina. A fly had alighted on the border of the sticky fly paper that lay in the center of the mahogany table. It tugged and buzzed, but the sticky mess held it too firmly.

"You may comfort yourself with the thought," Benedetti went on, "if the fact is any comfort, that you are not the first. There have been others. The little dancing girl from the Port-au-Prince cabaret, a Spanish girl from Santo Domingo…"

He was not boastful, purely meditative as he sat there and smoked and talked, telling Vivian of the victims whose lives had paid for his hold on his sugar plantation. Vivian's eyes were fastened on the feebly fluttering fly on the sticky paper. They, too, were caught like flies in a trap, and unless she could do something immediately—she faced the fact calmly—it would be the end.

Abruptly she leaned forward. There was a stillness in her pose, a stillness in her opaque eyes. Her hands coiled like springs. She found it difficult to keep her detached poise as the scheme began to unfold and take shape in her brain.

She smiled thinly. The air was suddenly electrical, filled with the portent of danger. Benedetti caught the feel of it, and peered at her suspiciously for a moment. The Lady from Hell knew that it was a thousand to one that she would lose. But, if her scheme worked, she could save Wylie's life and her own, and Benedetti might be made to pay for the thing he had attempted—pay as he had never dreamed that he would have to pay.

Reaching out one hand she moved the candle in front of her, so that its glow fell more on Benedetti's face than her own. Her voice, as she spoke, was quiet, almost meditative. But her eyes told a different story.

"How much time have I to live?" she said.

The man glanced at his watch.

"Roughly, two hours," he said. He might have been estimating the departure time of a steamer, his voice was so calm. "It might be a trifle more or less—the time of my workers is not accurate. When the drums stop they will come for you. And when they start again—well, you will be there then."

She rose to her feet, leaning lightly on the table.

"If I am to die," she said hysterically, "I will die beautiful." Then she added as an explanation, "My makeup is in my room."

But he was on his feet too, alert, wary. "You must not leave my presence," he said. "I cannot permit it. The sacrifice must go to the arms of Ogoun Badagri alive, not a corpse."

His dark eyes held no recognition of the fact that she was a very beautiful woman. Vivian sensed, and rightly, that to him she was merely a woman who might thwart his plans. But she caught the implication in his last sentence.

"I shall not take poison," she said. "You may come with me—watch me, if you wish."

SHE TOOK A step or two and groped blindly at the table for support. Instinctively he stretched out a hand to steady her.

That was the moment for which she had planned, the instant for which she had been waiting. Benedetti made the fatal mistake that many men had made with the Lady from Hell as an opponent—of underestimating her as an adversary.

Like a striking snake her hand darted to the table, seized one of the heavy candlesticks. Before Benedetti could interfere, had even divined her purpose, the heavy metal fell across his forehead with stunning force. He crumpled to the floor without a murmur.

Leaving him where he had fallen, Vivian ran to the door and peered out. The gigantic black on guard at the veranda steps had heard nothing. He was still standing there, unaware of the drama being enacted within the dining room.

Swiftly she turned back and her slender fingers searched the drawers of the carved mahogany sideboard against the wall until she found what she sought—a heavy, sharp carving knife. She balanced it speculatively in her hand. It would do, she decided.

The man was still standing there when she peered out the door again. He never saw the slender blade as it flew through the air, sped by a hand that had learned its cunning from the most expert knife thrower in Shanghai. The blade went through, sinking into the flesh at the base of his throat as though it had been butter. He died without an outcry.

Now she must work fast, if she were to escape and save Wylie too. Benedetti she bound and gagged and rolled against the sideboard where he was out of the way. But first she had taken his revolver from his side pocket.

Trip after trip she made, first to the flat tin roof of the house, and then to the front of the house. Finally she was satisfied with what she had done, and, snatching up a flashlight from the sideboard, fled toward the path in the jungle that she knew led to the place of sacrifice.

A tropical squall was rising out of the sea beyond the little cove. A cloud, black in the light of the moon, was rising above the horizon. She glanced at it anxiously. Then she plunged into the jungle.

The valences of the palms were motionless against the moonlit sky. The atmosphere, as she pushed her way along, seemed saturated with mystery, dew dripping, bars of green moonlight between the trunks of the trees; the cry of night birds, the patter of something in the dark mystery of the tree roof overhead, the thudding of the drums that had never ceased. Out of that familiar hollow rhythm of drums that had begun to emerge a thread of actual melody—an untraditional rise and fall of notes—a tentative attack, as it were, on the chromatic scale of the beat. A tentative abandonment of Africa. It was a night of abandonment, anyhow, a night of betrayal and the peeling off of blanketing layers down to the raw.

Once she stopped short with a sudden emptiness in her chest at sight of what she thought was a man in the path ahead. But it was only a paint-daubed, grinning skull on a bamboo stake planted in the ground—a voodoo *ouanga*. Then she went ahead again. Evidently there were no guards posted. With every inhabitant of the island concerned in the ceremony in one way or another there would be no need for guards to be posted now.

THE RAPID SEQUENCE of events had edged Vivian's nerves, and the boom of the drums—heavy, maddening, relentless—did nothing to soothe them. That passage through the jungle was galling, fraying the nerve ends like an approaching execution.

A red glow came to her through the trees, and seemed to spread and spread until it included the whole world about her in its malignancy. The drums, with that queer rise and fall of notes that it seemed impossible to achieve with taut skins stretched over drum heads, beat upon her senses, pounded until the air was filled with sounds that seemed to come from the earth, the sky, the forest; dominated the flow of blood with strange excitations.

She had formulated no plan for rescuing Wylie. She could not, until she reached the spot and saw what she had to contend with. She had the gun she had taken from Benedetti, but six cartridges against a horde of drum-maddened blacks—that was only a last resort.

And then she stood on the edge of a clearing that seemed sunk to the bottom of a translucent sea of opalescent flame.

Something that was age-old was happening in that crimson-bathed clearing, something old and dark, buried so deeply under the subtleties of civilization that most men go through life without ever knowing it is there, was blossoming and flowering under the stark madness of those thudding drums.

Coconut fiber torches, soaked in palm oil, flaring red in the blackness of the night lit up the space in front of her like a stage, the torchlight weaving strange scarlet and mauve shadows. Tall trees, lining the clearing opposite her, seemed to shelter masses of people, darker shadows against the red glow of the burning torches.

Two enormous drums, taut skins booming under the frenzied pounding of the palms of two drummers, stood on one side. A dozen, two dozen dancing black figures, male and female, spun and danced in the center of the clearing, movements graceful and obscene—animal gestures that were identical with similar dances of their ancestors hundreds of years before in Moko or the Congo.

And then she saw Wylie. He was tied to a post in the center of the clearing, and the dancers were milling about him. Beside him stood a woman whom Vivian instinctively knew must be the Mamaloi, the priestess of whom Benedetti had spoken.

Now and then the priestess gave vent to a sound that seemed to stir the dancers to greater activity—to spur the slowly humming throng of watchers to a point of frenzy; a sound such as Vivian had never heard before and hoped never to hear again. When she stopped, it would hang, incredibly high-pitched, small, like a black thrill in the shadow. It was shocking and upsetting out of that ancient thin figure.

Her eyes shifted from the aged figure to the sky line above the trees. The black cloud that, a short time before had been no larger than the palm of her hand on the horizon, was visible through the branches of the trees now.

Even as she looked a faint flicker of heat lightning laced through it.

And then, as if at a conductor's signal, more torches flowered on the edge of the clearing, and in their light the Lady from Hell saw half a dozen men staggering forward with an enormous thing of bamboo—a cage—and in that cage was a great snake; a boa constrictor, perhaps, or a python, although neither of them, she seemed to remember, was native to Haiti.

6

WHITE MAN'S VOODOO

THEY PLACED THE cage in the center of the clearing, and Vivian saw that it had been placed so that a small door in the cage was directly opposite Wylie's bound figure. The significance of that fact went through her like a breath of cold wind. If she failed, she also would be bound to that stake. Mentally she could see the little door in the cage opening, the great triangular head of the snake gliding slowly...

Swiftly she bent over and caught up a handful of the black leaf mold underfoot, smeared it over her face, her arms, her neck, her shoulders. A section of the dress she was wearing was ripped off and made into a turban that hid the flaming crown of her hair. More earth was rubbed onto the white of her dress.

Then, with swift leaps, she was on the outer fringe of the dancers, and the chaos of moving arms and legs caught her up and swallowed her as a breaking wave on the beach swallows a grain of sand.

It was a mad thing to do, a desperate thing. She knew that, normally, her crude disguise would not have fooled the natives. The Haitian black seems to have the ability to almost smell the presence of a *blanc,* much as an animal can smell the presence of another. But, in that flickering torchlight, the crudeness of disguise would not be so apparent, and in that unceasing madness of drums that went on like a black echo of something reborn, she hoped that her alien presence would pass unnoticed long enough for her to accomplish her object.

Slowly she worked her way through the writhing, dancing mass of figures toward the center. She knew that her time was short—that the lesser ceremony was approaching its height. Even as she reached the inner ring of dancers she saw the ancient Mamaloi joining in the dance, while the others kept a respectful distance from her. Monotonously, maddeningly, the priestess twisted and turned and shivered, holding aloft a protesting fowl. Faster and faster she went, and while all eyes were fastened on that whirling figure Vivian managed to reach Wylie's bound figure.

A swift slash with the knife she had hidden beneath her dress and his hands were free.

"Keep still… don't let them see that you're not bound," she whispered. Another motion and the bonds that fastened his ankles to the post were free.

Vivian moved about Wylie with graceful motions, imitating the movements of the blacks about her, and her voice came to him in broken, desperate whispers:

"Signal… you'll recognize it… don't move until then… dead tree by the edge of the clearing… that's the path… I'll be waiting there… it's only chance…"

Then she was gone, breasting her way through the black figures that danced like dead souls come back from Hell in the evil glow of the sputtering torches. And then came a great shout as the Mamaloi caught the chicken she held by the head and whirled it around and around.

Throom... throom... throom. The drums were like coalescing madness. A moan went up from the onlookers and a chill went through Vivian.

SHE KNEW FROM what Benedetti had told her that the chicken was the prelude of what would happen to Wylie. Next, the old woman would slash Wylie's throat... let his life blood spurt into a bowl with which the dancers would be sprinkled. Then would come the lesser ceremony, while the guard at the house would start with her for the ceremony that would end with the door in the great snake's cage being opened...

Vivian snatched a torch from the hands of one of the dancers. The man did not even seem to be aware of the fact that it had been taken away. From beneath her dress she took a stick of dynamite with fuse attached—part of her loot from the storeroom—and touched the fuse to the flame of the torch.

It sputtered and she hurled it with all her strength at her command toward the overhanging tree beneath which the drummers sat, then fled for the bare naked branches of the dead tree that stood where the path entered the clearing— the spot where she had told Wylie she would meet him.

She had barely reached the spot when there came a tremendous concussion that shook the earth, and a gush of flame. The thing was as startling, as hideously unexpected to the drum-maddened Haitians as a striking snake. Scream after scream—long, jagged screams that ripped red gashes through the dark, were followed by a swift clacking of tongues, a terrified roar as dancers and onlookers milled about, black bodies writhing in the light of the remaining torches. A black tide, rising, filled the clearing with terrified clamor. A moment later there was the sound of running feet and Wylie was at her side.

"This way," she whispered, and guided him into the path.

Both of them knew that it would be only a moment before the startled natives recovered their wits and discovered that their victim was gone. Then they would take up their trail again immediately.

"Where are we going?" Wylie asked her as he ran behind her along the winding jungle trail.

"The house," she answered tersely.

"The house?" He almost halted in his amazement. "But Vivian—that's the first place they'll make for. Even if you've found weapons we can't hold them off forever."

"Wait," she said. "No time to explain now... But if things work out, we'll be off this island before morning, safe and sound."

From behind them a quavering yell rose on the air and the two fugitives knew that Wylie's escape had been discovered. It was a matter of yards and of minutes now. Then they burst from the shadow of the jungle into the moonlit clearing.

"Follow me," she said quickly. "Don't take the path," and he followed her footsteps as she twisted and twined about the space toward the steps.

At the steps he halted a moment in wonder at what he saw there, and then, in spite of the gravity of the situation, a chuckle broke from his panting lips.

"So that's it," he said, and Vivian nodded.

"That's it. Be careful. It's a slim enough chance, but there is just a chance it'll work—the only chance we've got."

"But even that," he said, a thought striking him, as he threaded his way carefully up the steps to the veranda, "will only be temporary. Even if it holds them at bay until dawn—when daylight comes…"

"I know," she said a trifle impatiently, "but long before then—" She broke off suddenly as their pursuers appeared, breaking out from under the palms, just as a flash of lightning came.

"They're here," he whispered. "If the scheme won't work, then it's all up with us."

"It will work," Vivian said confidently.

But, although her tone was cool, confident, there was anxiety in her eyes as she watched the black figures pouring out of the jungle. Vivian knew that her own and Wylie's lives were hanging by the slenderest margin in their criminal career.

THE PAPALOI, THE giant Negro with the white lines and scar ridges criss-crossing his muscular torso, was the first to see them as another flash of lightning illuminated the veranda where they stood. He uttered a single bellow, a stentorian cry, which seemed to shake the house, and bounded toward the stairs. Behind him came part of his followers, while others rushed for the other pair of stairs.

The Papaloi leaped for the steps, his men close behind him. His feet landed in something that slid quickly under him, that clung to his soles. He lost his balance, fell asprawl, his followers in a momentary confusion that quickly increased to panic—the panic of the primitive mind confronted with something unseen that it cannot understand.

The hands of the gigantic black Papaloi were glued now to squares of sticky fly paper that he could not shake off—the fly paper that the Lady from Hell had taken from the storeroom and spent so much precious time placing upon the steps and around the veranda without encountering it, save along the narrow, tortuous trail along which Vivian had led Wylie.

There was a square of fly paper on the Papaloi's face now, clinging there, flapping a little as if alive, persistent as a vampire bat. There were more on the side of his body where he had slipped. He struck at them and accumulated more.

The Mamaloi, that ancient crone, was in trouble also. She had slipped and, in falling, had a sheet of fly paper plastered squarely across her eyes. She was uttering shrill cries of distress as she pawed at her face with hands that were covered with sticky fly paper and glue. All about the two, men and women were struggling, shouting in alarm. The silent attack had materialized out of nothing with such appalling swiftness, and continued with such devastating persistence that it robbed them of every thought save alarm.

Robbed of their spiritual leaders, terror was striking at the hearts of the voodoo worshipers. At the edge of the veranda, black men writhed in horror, snatching at one another for support, tearing at the horrible things that clung as if with a million tiny sucking mouths. Their machetes, covered with glue and flapping fly paper, had been dropped, forgotten in the confusion. Torches had dropped underfoot, forgotten, so that the struggle was in darkness, illuminated only by the light of the moon through the clouds and the flashes of lightning. Fly paper in their hair, across their eyes, clinging, hampering, maddening them with the knowledge that some frightful voodoo, stronger than their Papaloi or Mamaloi, had laid hands upon them.

A flare of lightning slashed from the very center of the storm cloud that was now hanging overhead. Its brilliance illuminated, for a moment, the figure of the Lady from Hell, standing at the edge of the veranda, her arms uplifted as if calling down the wrath of the heavens upon them. A shattering blast of thunder followed and a gust of wind swept across the clearing.

That gust of wind was the crowning touch, the straw that was needed to break the camel's back of resistance in that struggling, milling black throng. It set all the loose ends of the fly paper fluttering, where it was not fastened to bodies. And, more than that, it caught up the sticky squares that were still unattached and sent them dancing through the air.

THERE ROSE A howl of fear. The demons of these *blancs*, not content with lying in wait and springing out upon them, were now flying through the air; attacking them from the heavens, sucking from their bodies all their strength.

What use to resist when even the magic of the Papaloi and the Mamaloi was not sufficient to fight off the demons.

They bolted headlong, fly paper sticking to every part of their anatomy. They fell, scaled with the awful things, and promptly acquired more. Women fell and shrieked as they were trampled upon, not from the pain of the trampling feet, but from the fear that they might be left behind at the mercy of the demons. Men, blinded by the sticky things, ran in circles and clutched at whatever they came in contact with.

Then came the low drone of an airplane engine in the distance, flying low because of the storm. Turning, Vivian ran back into the dining room, where Benedetti still lay, bound upon the floor, his eyes glaring hatred at her. Calmly she sat down and wrote upon one of his letterheads which she found in the desk there. Then she snatched off the gag that muffled his mouth.

"The danger is all over," she told the man, "for us. But for you trouble is just beginning."

"You can't escape," he raved at her viciously. "I don't know what you've done, but you won't be able to leave the island. In an hour, two hours—by daylight at least—they will return, and what they will do to you won't be pleasant."

Vivian smiled. The invisible plane seemed to be circling the house now. She waved the paper she had written to dry the ink.

"What the American authorities in Port-au-Prince do to you will not be pleasant, either," she told Benedetti. "Voodoo is forbidden by law. You have not only aided and abetted voodoo ceremonies, but you have also procured human sacrifices for the ceremonial. There was the little French girl from the Port-au-Prince cabaret, and the girl from Santo Domingo—you should not have boasted. For you murdered them as surely as if you had driven a knife in their hearts, and the law will agree with me."

"You'll never live to tell the Americans, even if they believed the tale," he scoffed.

"Oh, yes I will," she mocked. Her voice was as dry and keen as a new ground sword. "Within an hour I shall be on my way to Cape Hatien. Hear that," and she raised an admonitory hand. In the silence the plane could be heard. She threw open the French windows. From where he lay Benedetti could see a Marine plane slanting down toward the comparatively sheltered waters of the little cove.

"In less than ten minutes," she said, "the plane will have taxied up to the beach and the Marine pilot and his observer will be in this room, asking if we need aid. You see," and her smile was completely mocking and scornful now, "you yourself brought about your own downfall— planted the idea in my brain when you told me that the plane passed overhead every night at about this time. There was a can of luminous paint in your storeroom. I saw it, and there he is coming to see what it's all about—and to take you to Cape Hatien—unless…"

"Unless what?" he queried eagerly.

"Unless you sign this memorandum. It deposes that I have purchased this plantation from you—that you have received the purchase price—and that proper legal transfer to it will be made later."

There was a calculating gleam in the man's eyes as he made assent. His gaze flickered out through the open door to where the plane had already landed on the surface of the cove.

Vivian had caught that gleam. "Of course," she went on smoothly, "we will have the Marine officers sign it as witnesses in your presence. Then you can accompany us back to Cape Hatien in the plane, and the lawyers of the Haitian Sugar Central will be glad to see that memorandum is put in proper legal form before I, in turn, resell the plantation to them. I shall not refuse the price they are willing to pay—and it will not matter to the sugar trust whether you or I are the owner." She gazed at him for a moment. "Well, do you agree?—or do you go to Cape Hatien a prisoner?"

Benedetti shot a glance at the trim, uniformed figure coming cautiously up from the beach. Feverishly he scribbled his name at the bottom of the memorandum.

THE ADVENTURE OF THE
CAYENNE FUGITIVES

*They Were Five Desperate Men in an Open
Boat Drifting across the Tropic Sea—into the
Clutches of the Arch-Villainess, Vivian Legrand*

1

THE DANGEROUS FUGITIVE

THE LADY FROM Hell wasn't looking for trouble, and did not guess that she was finding it. She swept the horizon with powerful binoculars, focusing momentarily on a distant, as yet indistinguishable speck on the water and then continued to gaze until she had described a casual arc. Her eyes, as they came to rest again on Adrian Wylie, seated in the stern of the boat, were thoughtful.

"Today," she said, "is the fourteenth."

Wylie was fishing. He glanced up with a smile.

"And tomorrow," he observed, "will be the fifteenth."

Vivian Legrand did not smile. "Things happen to me on the fourteenth," she said seriously. "It was the fourteenth of September when I walked into that house on the Plaza Goiti in Manila—the house of the Mandarin Hoang Fi Tu—and met you for the first time. It was the fourteenth when I first met Sir Mark Caywood in Burma. It was the fourteenth when we first collided with Vedova Bey—"

She raised her binoculars again, watching the distant, blurred speck bobbing upon the sea which was moving with a leaden, sultry calm in which there seemed a lifeless and sinister oppression. Wylie watched her, his own face thoughtful. Although she was in the shadow of the awning

*Vivian Legrand
lifted the gun*

overhead, an aura of brilliance from the shimmering sea silhouetted her delicate, exotic face; her curved red lips, the wind-stirred crest of her red hair.

He had a great deal of respect for the intuitive powers of this forceful woman who had been the guiding genius in all of their criminal activities, and it was quite evident that something was troubling her now. A scent of trouble. It hung in the heavy, overheated air. It seemed to breathe an uncertainty into her actions. It was nothing—but he could see that it had infected her with an unnatural tension, a psychic awareness of impending evil.

Vivian Legrand, whom the underworld of three continents had nicknamed The Lady from Hell because of her daring exploits, was on a vacation from her career of crime. With Adrian Wylie, her chief of staff and companion in all her schemes, she had sailed from London. Havana, through chance, had brought a considerable amount of money to swell the bank account of the two criminals, and in Port-au-Prince a week before the two had blackmailed a planter of his sugar plantation and resold it to the sugar trust. Now, they were cruising among the lower islands on a yacht they had chartered.

"Is it just the fact that today is the fourteenth, Vivian," Wylie queried, "or is there something else in the wind?"

She shrugged and raised her glasses again.

"I don't know," she confessed.

Her glasses were riveted now on that queer horizon dot, which had gradually come within range of her strong lenses.

She saw a peculiar sort of boat, with a small, ragged sail. There were men in the boat—she counted three—but even as she watched one of the figures slumped down out of sight. Only two huddled forms to be seen. Then but a lone man....

The little craft had no cabin or deck and no cover of any description. The men, as she coolly studied them, appeared to be dying.

FOR SEVENTY-TWO HOURS past the fugitives in the dugout canoe had scarcely dared to change position. They were cramped and numb and miserable. But in that time, so it seemed, they had voyaged a long, long way. From a world of concentrated horror to a world of vague despair.

They had been all but overwhelmed by two terrific thunderstorms. They had skirted treacherous mud banks, survived whirling currents and heat and hurricane gusts. Lately they had not dared to steer toward shore to land and forage and obtain fresh water, because of suspected pursuit and quicksands as well as habitations known to be hostile. Failing onward almost helplessly, without prayer or a compass, they had come to the final hazards of the surging tropic sea. They were becalmed.

The wind which had braced them and swept them madly along had died down to a fitful breeze, capricious as their own turbulent destiny. It flirted with them for a while, puffed them ahead, then retarded them, winning the applause or bracing the abuse of criminals condemned for life and fluently profane in five languages.

Waves slapped the sides of their clumsy little craft, drenching them with spray. When they had to bail they used the tin food basins which were not so much dread reminders of the prison from which they fled as painful reminders of their own overmastering hunger and thirst. The water jars empty half a day! The last of the fruit and frugal supplies eaten hours ago!

They were feverish with longing for drink, for food and unstirring sleep. They were sick with anxiety, tortured by hope, feeble from days of fugitive ordeal.

The canoe that held them was a roughly carpentered log some eighteen feet in length, with strips of *moca-moca*—a much lighter wood, buoyant as cork—lashed on either side. There was a crudely improvised rudder and keel to it, and a stumpy mast with a draggled, lateen-rigged sail. And in this curious blend of coffin and argosy they tossed beneath a blistering sun.

There were five men in the boat, one of whom was bound and gagged in the bow. The four escapers looked much alike; scorched, bearded, cruelly emaciated. And they were equally uniform in their fierce resolve to get beyond the reach of French law. They wore grimy white blouses and cotton trousers. On their backs were stenciled numbers. Three of them had wide-crowned, flatbrimmed limp straw hats. The fourth had his head bandaged with a piece of cotton cloth, soiled and stained with blood.

The man aft, who steered and seemed the least inert, was Tristan Malliard, a notorious murderer.

Suddenly he raised a sun cracked hand.

"There," he croaked. "Land! Land!"

"Again?" One of them spoke as the others strained bloodshot eyes to see the dim line at which Malliard was pointing. "Not Surinam or Demerara?"

There was no relief awaiting them in Dutch or British Guiana. Fugitives from Cayenne were taken in those neighboring colonies by whites and blacks alike—returned to the convict cantonments at two hundred francs a head.

"Trinidad, I think—or perhaps Tobago," Malliard responded. "We're far off the mainland. A low flat coast, Courelle always described it. And he should know. They dragged him back from Trinidad."

"But Tristan," one of the others said slowly, "the English, they were different there today."

"Yes," their leader responded. "We will be safe there—if they have not heard of the escape."

"But what about him?"

Lerulot, anarchist and would-be assassin of a premier of France, pointed to the tumbled heap of rags, sail cloth and rope which covered their prisoner.

Most Cayenne prison breaks are furtive affairs in which the convicts await an unguarded moment and steal away from one of the labor camps, making for a river or a jungle retreat. But Malliard and his comrades, originally seven in number, made their dash for freedom as part of a minor convict uprising. Two warders and a convict had been killed. The shrewd leadership of Malliard had directed that they protect their flight, if possible, with a hostage. And largely by chance they had been able to seize the man they hated most.

The reputation of Pedro de Martinque is still seared in the minds of decent residents of French Guiana. No convict, young or old, who had the misfortune to have him as a warder, ever forgets what terror he was able to inspire in the bravest convict. His name was really not Martinque. It was Pedro de Gorot. But, because he had come from Martinque, where his brother lived, he had been given the nickname by the convicts.

Now bound and helpless, gagged most of the time, until his lips and tongue had become so swollen that it did not matter, this hated chief warder of the road building camp whence Malliard and the others had fled, lay in the bow of the boat, blistered, practically insensible—and yet refusing to die.

So long as they feared pursuers overtaking them, the fugitives counted upon the presence of their captive to save them from being killed upon the spot—their canoe riddled by rifle fire and allowed to sink under them in a shark-infested sea! But now land, distinctly visible, made the situation different.

PEDRO DE MARTINQUE, as a hostage or a corpse, was a dangerous liability. He must be tossed overboard.

Urged on by the vindictive Lerulot, they tried to lift him and dump him over the side. But they had all become too weak. Groaning, cursing and heaving, they nearly capsized their craft. It was no use.

Pedro hung about their necks like a millstone. When they could afford to abandon the canoe, they might dispose of him—but not before.

The exertions of their attempt only weakened them all the more. And the rough handling given the man seemed to revive him. He looked up at them for a moment, and it seemed that his glance was mocking. Actually he was too close to madness to have any rational thought. But he had mocked and tormented them so often. Lerulot, cursing, struck the warder feebly.

There was still that sultry calm, and the canoe was making no headway under a sky into which a faint yellow glaze had crept; a glaze that was almost the color of sulphur. Yet with land in sight, inspiring their hopes again, the four convicts decided to paddle toward the haven. And here again strength failed them.

In bitter realization of their exhausted state they had just stopped paddling when Vivian Legrand first saw their craft.

Dropping her glasses, Vivian gave a swift curt order to the master of the *Esmeralda*. Wylie looked up quickly, then got to his feet and came to her side. He gazed long through her glasses and then turned to her.

"Better be careful, Vivian, there's something queer about that boat."

"I know," she responded. "But this is the fourteenth!"

"There's no profit in a canoe filled with dead or dying men," he argued. "It's obviously not a ship's boat. No chance of it being the millionaire owner of a wrecked yacht."

She raised her glasses again. The *Esmeralda* was close enough now to the dugout canoe for her to see clearly the slack forms of its castaway crew.

She gave a little exclamation. "They are escaped convicts, Doc," she said. "Probably from Cayenne. The one on the bow has a number stenciled on the back of his blouse. There is profit in convicts," she added, her tone reminiscent "There was profit in Stavinsky, you remember."

"Stavinsky was a secret service man whom we rescued from a penal colony," Wylie reminded her. "I don't like the smell of this." There was uneasiness in his voice.

"I always like the smell of profits," The Lady from Hell said crisply. "Besides, don't forget it's the fourteenth."

She turned to issue sharp orders to Matteo and his sons, who manned the *Esmeralda*. In a few minutes five limp forms were lifted from the wallowing canoe and laid beneath the awning on the after deck. The canoe was turned adrift again.

Wylie, assisted by Matteo, worked over the five they had curiously rescued. It was Tristan Malliard who first opened his eyes, tried to sit up and could not. Only by terrific exertion of will was he able to force a few words through swollen lips.

"Water," was the only word they could distinguish.

Pedro de Martinque revived next. But there were only his bloodshot eyes to report upon his flickering consciousness. His tongue and lips were too swollen to permit an articulate sound.

LATER IN THE day the five had partially recovered. Malliard and Brune were quiet, seemingly content to enjoy whatever brief blessings of fortune came their way. Their comrade, Despard, was weak and ill, having less than a fifty-fifty chance, Wylie said, to pull through. Lerulot, perhaps because he had been most intellectually active, was quite out of his head. The sun had boiled that fiery and fanatic brain to a tempest of delirium. Wylie improvised a straitjacket of rope and canvas.

Pedro de Martinque lay silent, watchful, apparently wondering to find himself still among the living.

Lerulot grew calmer, and by pleading murmurs and rolling of the eyes, implored them to release him from his bonds.

"Go ahead—let him loose. He's had shackles enough in his time," Vivian said.

"But the delirium will return," Wylie protested.

"Take a chance on that," she said.

Of course it did return just at dusk. Raving and gesticulating, the man who had fixed his mind on escape from Cayenne madly struggled with Matteo and one of his sons, easily brushed Wylie aside, leaped to the rail and plunged overboard with a hideous yell.

Matteo signalled to come about with the yacht, which was cruising at only five knots, using her engine. There was no wind for the sails, and the sea was long, oily rollers that seemed to have taken on something of the yellow tint of the sky.

"Who is he, that delirious one?" Vivian bent over Tristan Malliard to ask in French.

"Andre Lerulot, the great anarchist. A lifer at Cayenne. He shot and badly wounded Premier Phillippe—"

"The man is a fool. It is good riddance," she turned and crisply shouted an order to Matteo.

"But he is swimming—I can see him plainly, *Señora* Legrand," protested the master of the yacht. "A sudden plunge into the water has cleared his head. We can put about and pick him up with ease in this light—"

"Let him swim." Her voice held the ring of steel.

"But *Señora*, I cannot," Matteo protested. "It would be murder." He turned and shouted an order to one of his sons.

"I wouldn't, Matteo," The Lady from Hell said smoothly. Something in her tone made him turn to glance at her. The tiny but deadly little gun that she was rarely without had appeared in her hand as if from the empty air, and was covering him. "If your son tosses Lerulot a rope…" she said significantly, and lifted the gun just the slightest fraction.

The man stared at her. "You wish him to die?" he queried slowly.

"He has chosen," The Lady from Hell said crisply. "Let him swim. If he reaches land, so much the better for him."

"Yes, *Señora*," Matteo said. He turned away with a helpless shrug and shot a swift order at his son. The coil of rope was dropped to the deck again, and the boat drew away from the struggling man.

"An anarchist," The Lady from Hell said to Wylie. There was in her manner, her voice, not the slightest shadow of the callous thing she had just done. "I want nothing to do with politics—and fanatics of his sort are especially bad. Give that Lerulot two days of good treatment on board, and we'd have had a trouble-maker to deal with."

"So you figure the others as gentle as lambs?" Wylie smiled.

"I can handle the others," Vivian assured him confidently.

2

A FLOATING FORTUNE

MURDER, UNLIKE SOME other crimes, does not necessarily put its mark upon those who have been fated to kill a fellow being. And later that day Tristan Malliard, shaved and bathed and decently dressed, proved to be a decidedly presentable, if worn and emaciated, young man.

He had belonged to a gang responsible for the death of several French policemen. Tristan's youth had seemed to his judges a mitigating circumstance, and at sixteen he had been saved from the chopper, while being condemned to the "dry guillotine" of Guiana for the rest of his life. Tristan was now twenty-nine, with a keenness and quality of leadership that showed what first rate material had gone to waste when the slums enlisted him with the most reckless *apache* gang of Paris.

Late that afternoon, briefly and modestly, without carping affectations of reform or remorse, he told his own story. Brune, he continued, had been a robber. Despard, whose life was still in danger, had been a pal of Brune's. Their depredations in Marseilles had been a nine days' wonder. But at length the police cordon—the Assizes—and a sentence of transportation, carrying life exile from their native France.

Malliard tactfully passed over the career of the lost Andre Lerulot.

"We are, I'm afraid, unable to thank you or repay you," he went on. "Even if you choose to return us to Cayenne and collect a triple reward, we are worth 'on the hoof' precisely two hundred francs each."

"That's a lie," Pedro broke in. "Thousands of francs reward will be offered for them. If you had not let Lerulot drown, at least ten thousand would have been collected on him alone."

Vivian turned quickly to Malliard before Pedro could continue. "Tell me, why did you choose to carry Pedro alive through waters thick with hungry sharks? Why didn't you get rid of him?"

He told her of their ultimate attempt to rid themselves of their hostage, and how all the puny strength they could exert was not enough to tip him out without overturning the dugout canoe. He finished with:

"Pedro was chief overseer at the road-building camp near Kou-Rou. His cruelties were endless. He would bury a man in sand to his chin, and let ants crawl into his mouth, ears and eyes. He was a killer only by accident. He preferred that the convicts should live to be disciplined by his tortures. He would even steal their food and clothes and sell them."

"You lie!" Pedro cried out.

Vivian stared hard at the snarling warder from Cayenne. "I believe you," she said to Malliard. Then she turned to Pedro. "Let's get this straight. You were, I understand, a thief—in league with bigger thieves. That means you know where money is hidden. You can afford to ransom yourself. You two," she turned to Malliard and Brune, "are not beaten. You are free. There's life in you. Think, consider your situation—tell me how we may turn your being pursued to account?"

"And if we can't think so quickly—if the sun has cooked what brains we ever had?" Malliard queried.

"Then, when a patrol boat sights us and hails us, perhaps I may have no ideas either. Get busy and think of some way to pay your passage, my friends, or I'll have to give you up."

Pedro smirked and quite audibly chuckled.

The Lady from Hell turned on him. "As for you—if we are chased by a patrol boat, start in praying. I know your kind of prison bully. There's no reward being posted for your return to Cayenne, I'll bet on that. And I don't think you ever will return—a dose of salt water will cure all your ailments."

THE *ESMERALDA* WITH its ill-assorted human freight sailed on, and was now on the course of larger vessels bound to or from Brazilian ports.

Tristan Malliard approached Vivian Legrand, and spoke in an even, half-apologetic tone.

"We can think of no way of paying you," he confessed. "And you had better toss us overboard soon, Madame—the three of us—and Pedro."

"Why?" Vivian snapped.

"I'm afraid the pursuit is on," he said simply.

Vivian wheeled and stared off in the direction that he indicated. Sure enough, a distant smudge of smoke on the horizon revealed the approach of a vessel apparently traveling at full speed. The Lady from Hell brought her powerful binoculars to bear upon it, and could make out a slim, rakish white craft that might very well be a French gunboat.

She handed Malliard the glasses and watched him studying the oncoming ship. His hands were steady; his nonchalance was a quality she admired.

"I suspect we're in for it," he said. "Luck's against us—"

"It's odd they'd overlook you those days you were drifting or becalmed in that rotten log, but now find you when you get aboard this yacht."

"The answer is, Madame Legrand, your power yacht has not drifted but cut squarely across a ship lane. And the question is—what are you going to do?"

Vivian's eyes sparkled. "I'm not going to throw a valuable cargo overboard. Whoever it is, we'll fool 'em. Call Brune."

Wylie did not object to her latest whim, for a warning beacon of fire blazed in her eyes. She was absorbed in her plot, and meant to see it through.

Matteo and his sons she cowed and suppressed. Pedro de Martinque she ordered bound and gagged, and saw to it herself that the bonds cut savagely and the gag was secure and cruel. Brune and Malliard she disguised with deft, sure strokes—one a master of the *Esmeralda,* clad in a yachting outfit borrowed from Wylie—the other a guest, with Wylie again the outfitter.

Presently all was arranged as she had planned it, and the *Esmeralda* was shipshape, ready for an encounter with the French naval craft.

Wylie trained his glass upon it. "Say—" He stared hard again, then whistled softly. "Maybe you win after all, Vi."

"What is it?" she said quickly.

"That's no French gunboat—hell, I ought to have known

it first glance. Look at the slope of her stack and those rakish masts. Has wireless—everything up to date. Vi, my dear, unless there's two of them, that's the *Iroquois*—finest pleasure craft afloat, the latest toy of Myron T. Granville, magnate of steel, magnate of oil, magnate—"

Vivian had heard enough. "Stop the engine," she ordered.

"Good Lord, why? That yacht's making eighteen knots. She'll overhaul us fast enough."

"But we're in distress, Doc. Off our course—drifting—a lady in distress, small crew, one guest. Malliard—no, come to think of it, he'll have to switch to the crew with Brune. Can your wardrobe manage it?"

"If you say so, it'll have to. What'll all this make me, a tattooed man?"

"No, you'll be on your dignity. Get busy—gray hair, eyeglasses, wide black ribbon and all the rest of it. With your South'n Kunnel accent, Adrian. You're playing my father."

He consented, laughing. "And with just what object in view?" he said.

"The rich, majestic Mr. Myron T. Granville."

"Suppose he's not aboard, after all this planning?"

Vivian waved the suggestion aside. "I'm playing a hunch. Myron will be aboard. Else why would that gorgeous floating mansion be churning through these waters?"

"And our being in distress," said Wylie as the *Esmeralda* lost headway and began to drift, "you think it will win us an invitation aboard the *Iroquois*? They say Granville's worth a cool hundred million. And I've heard he's susceptible to beautiful women."

She flashed him a dazzling smile.

THE SPLENDID *IROQUOIS* steamed up alongside of the bobbing little *Esmeralda* with a long halyard of bright signal flags whipping in the breeze. Wylie was able to interpret the code message.

"Asks us if we need help."

"Tell him yes."

The two vessels were now close enough for a hail. Wylie, who had deftly added twenty years to his age and an austere dignity to his manner, cupped his hands and called an answer across the water.

In no time a small boat, smartly manned by four seamen in immaculate uniforms, put off from the *Iroquois*. It was a Vivian Legrand of untold enchantment and charm who presently received the florid, robust Granville.

"My daughter, suh—Mrs. Legrand," said Wylie, having introduced himself as "Colonel Mortimer Wylie." He assured the multi-millionaire that it was "an honor, suh, a great honor" to have so famous a compatriot come to their aid.

"Lucky I sighted you," Granville boomed. "My old tub"—he gestured toward the shining *Iroquois* as though he'd found it abandoned on some American inland canal—" my old tub there has wireless, just like the newest liners. And my operator picked up a call in French. Speak French like a native, myself. I translated it. And it means danger—serious danger for a boat the size of this one. The French are warning all ships to be on the lookout for a dangerous band of criminals—"

"Criminals, suh?" Wylie gasped. "On the high seas!"

Vivian spoke gently. "Do you mean pirates, Mr. Granville?"

"Ma'am, I mean French convicts—escaped from that hell hole"—he stopped short and apologized to The Lady from Hell—"that penal colony at Cayenne."

"They were heading this way, suh?" Wylie exclaimed with dignified dismay.

"That's just it, nobody knows where they're heading, Colonel. But they've got a boat they stole—"Vivian gasped.

Granville turned toward her, his voice softened. "Very sorry to frighten you like this, Mrs. Legrand," he said, "but it's best you folks should be on your guard. Having no wireless—"

"I am not frightened, Mr. Granville," said Vivian. "Not a bit frightened while your great ship is near. It's so superb, so perfect—like a man-of-war. What could harm it?"

"Right you are," the millionaire boomed proudly. "We rode out a hurricane in the West Indies. And rather than stand here, may I not have the honor of your company at dinner? I'll send my second engineer over to you, meanwhile, and he'll have your motor going before we get to coffee and liqueurs."

"Most hospitable, suh," Wylie replied, waiting for Vivian to give him his cue.

"I'm afraid our accident is worse than engine trouble, Mr. Granville," she put in quickly. "We seem to have struck a floating log and sheared off a propeller blade. Very difficult to repair, our mate says." Her small, graceful gesture indicated Malliard, standing at a respectful distance, as the mate.

"Propeller, eh? Can't be fixed this side of a dockyard. Well," said Granville, now completely subjugated, "I guess your trouble's my good fortune. You, Colonel, and your daughter are my guests. The *Iroquois* 'll take you in tow. Speed's no object at present."

He returned Vivian's electrifying smile with interest. "In fact, speaking as a lonely widower, just cruising about and bored to death—I won't mind how long it takes to get you safe to port."

3

MILLION DOLLAR INTRIGUE

MALLIARD SOUGHT THE first opportunity to speak with Vivian alone. "I have been long shut away, Madame. But I still have an eye for men. That Granville is no fool, beware of him."

"I'm not underestimating him. He understands French. Nobody else on board does, according to him. Make an excuse to address him in French, Tristan. He'll want you with us. And I shall need you with us."

"Command me," Malliard said quickly.

"When I need you most, be sure you are ready for anything, Tristan," she said earnestly. "And meanwhile, we can't risk them catching me in a lie about the *Esmeralda,* can we? Matteo mustn't know. See that the *Esmeralda's* propeller is really damaged. Be sure Brune watches over Pedro. Say nothing of what you do to anyone."

Granville suddenly came in sight along the deck. It was time to return to the *Iroquois.* Malliard saluted Vivian respectfully.

THE VIVACITY OF The Lady from Hell at dinner stirred Wylie's admiration even as it obviously quickened the pulse beat of Myron T. Granville. None could have imagined, observing her, that she was virtually in a trap of her own designing, and that neither she nor Wylie—nor Malliard when furtively consulted—could discern any way of shortening their cruise with, and now utter dependence upon, the multi-millionaire.

Wireless code flashes were still coming in, proving the French, as Pedro had predicted, were not going to lose a Lerulot, a Malliard or a Brune without searching far and wide to run them down or determine their fate. The wireless reported that the dugout canoe had been found, afloat and empty, leading to the latest warning that the convicts must have gained control of a swifter and more seaworthy craft.

The *Iroquois*, with the power yacht in tow, was cruising at a comfortable eight knots. Granville was gallantly evasive when Vivian asked their destination. She noticed that he drank rather heavily, and showed it not at all. Truly a man armed for contest; masterful, wary—and now as fascinated as any callow youth.

She held all his interest and his attention, while Wylie was left to converse with the master of the yacht, Captain McNeal, or roam about as he pleased. Vivian knew that if there were valuables in the safe, her partner would need time to discover it. And if any other prize—or any unforeseen peril—lurked on board the *Iroquois*, Adrian Wylie, most invaluable of subordinates, would straightway find it out.

Pleading exhaustion from the varied events of the day, Vivian retired to her stateroom about ten. It was as roomy as all the cabins of the *Esmeralda* combined. And for a moment, as on more than one previous occasion when she had deliberately set about attracting a rich or influential

man, Vivian thought of how this luxury and lifelong security might be hers, if only she chose to play out the hand
in a different fashion.

But then all the past crowded in, the excitement and
tension of the present, a restless forward glance at the
possibilities of the future. A swift attack, a quick profit, a
sudden and conclusive getaway—that had been her favor-
ite strategy always, and so it would remain. It had enriched
and amused her and she asked no more.

Myron Granville might be persuaded to lay his millions
at her feet. And, catching him off guard, she would pick
his pocket generously, and vanish—another example of
her art as a criminal.

Tonight, however, she felt a curious foreboding. With a
touch of dismay, she recognized that she and Wylie were
proceeding for once without teamwork, and obviously
without a plan. Dangerous—foolhardy—she must think
of some way out. And thinking, she fell asleep.

IT MUST HAVE been close to dawn when she awoke,
instantly conscious of the presence of someone else in her
cabin.

She could feel an alien presence as she had often done
in times past. Long ago Wylie had said that she had "not
less than five sixth-senses." This instantaneous alertness
after sound sleep was one of them.

Vivian lay very still, one hand thrust under her pillow.
With groping finger tips she felt for the revolver. Then with
a start of chilling alarm she discovered it was not there.
What stupidity! She had kept it with her every minute
since accepting their complement of strange ocean guests.
She had never trusted the fugitive convicts. Why be such

a fool as to grow careless on board the yacht of a Myron T. Granville? She realized she had forgotten to slip the gun out of the pocket of the white serge jacket she had been wearing before she changed to a dinner gown.

Having no weapon handy, she acted at once. Speed and surprise were always her emergency arsenal.

She drew her knees up slowly, rested her weight on one elbow, and turned slightly out of the berth. Her catlike quickness had never been more pronounced.

Her outstretched hand barely brushed the intruder, then on to the cabin wall, the door, the wall again. In split-seconds she had circled the small compartment, reached a dressing table. Her fingers dropped familiarly upon a metal tube. Up swung the electric torch. *Click!* Its blinding white beam fell upon the hesitant, ape-poised figure of a man leaning near the berth she had vacated.

It was the ex-warder, the formerly notorious monster of tropic discipline, Pedro de Martinque. But how had he escaped from the *Esmeralda?* He was dripping wet, she observed. And now she missed the vibration of the yacht's engines. They were not under way. What might that signify?

Vivian held the torch with grim steadiness.

But where had she left the white serge jacket? An enforced habit of traveling light and, almost constantly, of spendthrift haste, made her careful in choosing her wardrobe, but utterly careless about preserving it. That jacket— the revolver? And who was going to be the first to move?

Pedro, his badly inflamed eyelids in agony from the torch glare, moved first. He shifted his feet, bobbed his head.

"Well?" said Vivian.

"I have come to warn you," Pedro gulped.

"That, like Lerulot, you prefer to go overboard and swim for your life?" Vivian's French was a rapid snarl; her tone mocking, defiant. "Speak!"

Pedro dropped to his knees, head lowered, beaten.

Not many days ago the most hated and dangerous man in South America, outcast from humanity, outlawed from Africa, that broiling journey while cruelly bound in the dugout canoe had sapped all his overbearing volcanic impulses.

HE HAD BEEN half menacing, half grotesque as he stood there, sodden and sun-scorched, with bulging muscles straining the cotton shirt and white drill trousers, sizes too small, which Matteo had lent him. Now in this unexpected, cowering pose, he was not merely animal and abject, he was revolting.

"I came to warn you," he insisted.

"Then go ahead!"

"Those convict rats—"

"Begin by telling me how you escaped."

"Brune left Matteo to guard me, Matteo is afraid of you since you threatened him and his sons and let Lerulot drown. Matteo feared what Malliard and Brune were plotting, and I persuaded him to cut me free."

"You couldn't swim from the *Esmeralda* to this boat."

"I did swim it. They're now almost side by side."

"Go ahead, tell the rest," she urged, the torch still as steady as a rock.

"Malliard and Brune, as you'd expect if you knew such scum as I know 'em," he whined, "plotted to seize the *Iroquois*."

"Don't lie," Vivian snapped, but her pulse had leaped at his words. Somehow she knew it was true.

"I'm not lying," said Pedro. "Matteo told me. He's scared to death, and no wonder. Piracy's one thing no country stands for—"

"Piracy!" exclaimed The Lady from Hell. Even the torch wavered perceptibly. Her green eyes flashed fire. After weeks of comparative inactivity, to land in a vortex of such mad, such stimulating excitement. "Go on—tell what you know—"

"Malliard first signalled the *Iroquois* that the tow-line had fouled. That stopped their engines. They sent back a boat and three men to fix it. The men were unarmed, of course. Malliard had a gun he'd stolen from Matteo's locker.

"Nothing was wrong with the towline. But he made one of the *Iroquois* men yell something—I couldn't hear what—but that got them to maneuver the big yacht, so the two were close together.

"Malliard bound everybody, but Matteo not tight enough. The men from this boat were knocked out cold. Malliard, Brune and Despard—who's not so done in as he's been pretending—took the yacht seamen's uniforms, came aboard the *Iroquois* easy enough and took control. As soon as they could arm themselves, the odds didn't matter."

"How did they know where to find the arms on this vessel?"

"Malliard, posing as your mate on the *Esmeralda*, got it all out of one of the seamen who brought Granville aboard."

Vivian stabbed him suddenly with a telling question.

"And how did you know which cabin was mine?"

Pedro gulped, swallowed painfully, did not answer.

"I thought so," said The Lady from Hell. "You'd better find your tongue, man. Just where do you come in on this?"

"Matteo was scared half to death. He's no pirate. I'm no pirate. Somebody had to warn you people on the yacht. It's Malliard's plan to load all who won't join him—which would be most everybody—on the *Esmeralda,* then tow it far off the ship lanes, wait for a storm and cut the tow-line.

"With propeller out of commission—and I think he's smashed the steering gear—you can see what would happen. Not to you, of course. Malliard's only doing this to get you away from all the others."

"A likely yarn," said Vivian, but again some instinct told her Pedro could not have invented any of it. "You came to warn me, eh? Repaying me for saving your life?"

"Yes—yes, that was it," he said eagerly.

"Just luck brought you to my cabin?"

"I crept about till I found you. Malliard and the others didn't hear me climb aboard."

VIVIAN WAS TENSE. The smallest sound, the least movement was always enough to warn or to inform her. Now, in a twinkling, she understood what the situation really was. Coolly she turned her back on Pedro, a calculated act of contemptuous indifference. He had thought she was armed with more than the torch. She deliberately switched on her cabin light and put the torch aside.

Pedro, still grovelling, loudly sucked in his breath. She was the most entrancing creature he had ever seen; and her easy mastery only added fascination for him. A brute, informer and bully, he had always abused any powers he had, while fawning upon superiors who had more.

Vivian's body was erect and slender in a cobweb thin gown; a tube of sheerest emerald green. Her flame-colored hair was an angry, molten cloud. The web-like embroidery over her breasts rose and fell evenly, unexcitedly, with her breathing. She was like a goddess, insolent, unhurried. She took two steps, picked up a foamy negligee—was about to slip it on—

And her eyes fell on the white serge jacket, flung over the back of a chair. It had been under the negligee.

It was characteristic of her that she picked up the jacket, rather than drop the revolver from its pocket, permitting her adversary the notion that she might be weak or afraid. And it was equally characteristic that, armed, Vivian Legrand was no more confident, commanding, or composed, than she had been all along, while mentally groping to locate the jacket and resolve the odd situation confronting her.

She held jacket and negligee easily, so that they made a billowy rampart from behind which she faced Pedro and the cabin door, standing ajar. Her voice lifted slightly.

"Come in, Mr. Granville," she said, "and rid me of your spy."

Myron Granville, still pompous looking, but taut, his face less florid, with white serge trousers belted over a blue silk pajama coat, blocked the doorway. He held—rather awkwardly—a blue steel automatic of heavy caliber.

She left the burden of speech to him, and he fumbled for sarcasm. "How nice! The Southern colonel and his fair daughter not precisely what they seem, eh? Harboring convicts, letting lunatics drown—dodging the police, perhaps?"

Vivian cut him sharply where she knew it would hurt. "You handle that gun, my dear, like the last surviving veteran of the War of 1812. May I call you Granny hereafter? Put it down," she snapped, "before you bump yourself on the back of the head."

Granville's face reddened slightly.

"I don't advise you to presume on my seeming awkwardness," he said. "Naturally I am not accustomed to shooting guests aboard the *Iroquois*—"

"But I've heard you've never missed your aim shooting a corporation out from underneath its stockholders, Granny."

"You'll spare yourself nothing, Mrs. Legrand, by abusing me."

Vivian, when she spoke again, raised her voice. "Then you are inclined to offer terms?" she asked.

"I shall dictate terms!" barked the true Myron T. Granville. He came into the cabin, holding the gun now very firmly.

Vivian, as if startled, suddenly dropped the garments she had held gathered in a cloud before her. Cowering, she presented an exquisite imitation of Beauty overcome by fear. Granville, in his ignorance, saw nothing incredible in that Pedro, who knew her better, gaped.

THEN SUDDENLY FROM the corridor came a *pop*, a blinding flash of white light, and the eddying drift of flashlight smoke, as quickly swept away by the perfect ventilating system of the yacht.

Adrian Wylie stood framed in the cabin doorway. In his left hand he held a camera of the finest foreign make, and pocketing the flashlight gun with his right hand, he snapped out a serviceable Colt.

Vivian Legrand laughed lightly, stooped and snatched the jacket and negligee. She donned the latter; and from the jacket drew her own ugly-looking little gun.

"Terms," she told her confederate, "were just about to be dictated."

"Fine," Wylie said. "Let's go right ahead. Whose bid is it? His?" Wylie taunted.

Granville could only snarl at them. "You—you crooks—"

"Take it easy, Granny," Vivian said, and though her tone was mocking, her eyes were hard and menacing. "No use fooling with your blood pressure." She turned to Wylie. "Doc, how do you figure Pedro being here? Just who is running—or not running—this yacht?"

"I've been on deck," said Wylie. "Malliard and Brune seem to have everything very well in hand."

"You pirates," Granville stormed. "I'll see you all swing for this—yes, if it costs me every dollar—"

"—that we leave you, Granny," The Lady from Hell put in. "And just to correct an error and relieve the monotony of your recent conversation—*threats with us are never cheap!*"

Granville was not easily cowed, not a craven thing like the sun-blackened Pedro who, dazed and fearful, still crouched on the cabin floor. But as the millionaire started to retort, Vivian checked him.

"Every word you speak will cost you something. We have no knowledge of what the French escapers may have done. You aren't likely to believe that, but it happens to be true."

"About this camera film, Granville," said Wylie. "I daresay you're an art collector? Any picture of Mrs. Legrand is rare art, and this one is peculiarly rare because of her—ah—informal attire, her intimate pose—and you."

"Blackmail as well as piracy?" Granville snapped.

Vivian interrupted. "Doc, let me handle this," she said. "Granville, we have a photograph by a master of amateur photography—my friend here couldn't fumble a shot like that. I am in it, as you know, with you, clad as you are, threatening me with a revolver. The picture is priceless. Your many Wall Street enemies would agree. As we don't collect pictures, traveling as much as we do, this snapshot, though priceless, can be bought. Here's an auction, and you are the sole bidder. Well?"

"I won't submit to blackmail."

"I know three rich men in New York alone who would bid against each other—very privately, to be sure to get this tiny bit of film," said Wylie, "and have it enlarged."

Granville winced.

"To be made ridiculous, even quietly among your coterie of business associates and rivals," Wylie pursued, "would cost you millions, Granville."

"The price of the picture," said Vivian, "is now one million dollars."

"Cash, I suppose," said the rich man, sneering.

"This yacht is worth a million and we accept it. Where can we put you ashore, my dear Myron?" she said quickly.

Even Wylie looked a bit stunned by her proposal.

4

WEALTH AGAINST DEATH

GRANVILLE OPENED HIS mouth to speak, thought better of it, and shut his bulldog jaws fiercely, his lips making a thin, purple line.

There they stood for a minute or two, deadlocked.

Tristan Malliard, looking as immaculate and striking as a musical comedy juvenile, walked briskly into the cabin. He had borrowed an officer's new white uniform, cap and white shoes. One would have needed an X-ray to discern the fugitive convict and murderer in this trim, debonair French mariner.

He glanced admiringly at Vivian Legrand, ignored Pedro, and turned upon Granville and Wylie. He addressed the millionaire owner of the *Iroquois*, but in rapid French which Granville either did not or would not understand.

"He says," Wylie translated slyly, "that your officers, who have resigned to him the command of the yacht, are afraid to tell him what orders you gave them."

"What have *my* orders to do with a gang of crooks, blackmailers and pirates?"

"That costs you another hundred thousand, Myron," said Vivian. "Price of the photograph now one million one hundred thousand dollars."

"One of the mates hinted," said Malliard, "that this man wanted to sail on and on, keeping out of the way of other ships—on your account, Madame," he told Vivian.

"Was that why you would have prolonged our voyage, Myron, with the *Esmeralda* in tow?" she asked. "How gallant!"

"You forget, I mistook you for decent Americans," he shot back.

"The film in your camera, Wylie, will now cost him a cool million and a quarter," said The Lady from Hell.

Malliard asked about the picture they were mentioning, and was told what had occurred while he and his companions, under cover of night, were gaining control of the yacht. That brought the silent, cringing Pedro to his attention. Malliard drew his revolver.

"Get up—come along with me!" he ordered, and then turned to explain to Vivian.

"We saw him sneaking aboard. I knew Matteo would be against us. He has no nerve at all. And it seemed to me safer to have Pedro here with us. He could do us no harm, as Brune and I already had seized all the firearms—"

"Except this!" Granville's voice was high pitched and metallic. He sounded deranged.

A man used to giving orders, to dominating those around him, inspiring fear and awe, a man who always bought his way, who was not able to endure opposition, who had stopped at nothing in gaining wealth and power—the tormenting events of the night had brought him now close to the breaking point.

So little had they heeded him as an adversary that Wylie, gun in hand, and Vivian likewise ready, had not troubled to disarm their angry host. Malliard also was equipped to shoot. And against such odds Myron Granville undertook to assert himself.

His right arm was swinging up. He took hasty, awkward aim. There was a flash, a sharp, jarring report that echoed loudly in the confined space. Pedro de Martinque, eager to serve so much money, at once leaped to Granville's assistance.

THE BULLET GRAZED the scalp of Malliard, and blood streamed down upon his spotless uniform coat.

Vivian fired, a tardy shot because so carefully aimed. She knocked the gun out of Granville's hand. It was numbed, and he clasped it anxiously; but the impact of the bullet on the weapon had made no mark upon his flesh.

Pedro, true to a treacherous nature, lurched at Wylie, striking at the precious camera he held tucked under one arm. Malliard, though handicapped by the blood that half blinded him, fired at Pedro. Wylie, taking one quick backward step, fired also and at such close range the discharge scorched Pedro's damp cotton shirt.

Hit in the mouth by Malliard, and in the chest by Wylie, the ex-warder of Cayenne cried out hoarsely and spun around, once, twice, with an odd, demented velocity. On the third turn he suddenly went limp and crashed to the floor of the cabin.

Vivian stood over him, callously gestured with her gun.

"Stone dead," she said to Wylie. "You'd better look after Tristan. I'll keep my eye on Granny here—he's pinched his finger."

The millionaire grew purple with fury and frustration.

"Pedro was your faithful dog, and on very short acquaintance. Strange what would draw you two together," she added, eyeing Granville contemptuously. "He was as low a specimen as I ever saw in human form. When he came sneaking to you tonight, told you who he was, and about the escaping convicts added to our crew, you believed him at once. And your first thought was to send him prowling into my cabin while I slept. I'd locked that door, Granville. You gave the beast a duplicate key you'd been saving, eh?"

He meant to keep silent, to ignore her scorn. But those burning eyes of hers extorted a feeble self-defense.

"You and this man were deceiving me, betraying my hospitality in a contemptible fashion," he said. "I took any advantage that offered. I had to know whether you were imposed upon—intimidated by the fugitives—or were in league with them in their scheme of piracy. Using that fellow as a spy, hearing you talk to him, gave me my answer right enough."

"Which was, that we are pirates?"

"A crime you'll swing for, so help me!"

"You only keep boosting the price you'll pay for that postage stamp of film. It's small, but it will enlarge, and then you'll have to resign from your clubs—the American newspapers will make it a nine days' wonder and you a laughing stock!"

His hand had stopped aching from the bullet's shock, and his temper was a furnace of molten hate. He started to answer her hotly, but stopped short. He was listening. Vivian also listened. Wylie, improvising an emergency dressing for Malliard, paused.

Granville broke the silence, laughing harshly, mirthlessly. Malliard sprang to his feet, his wound only half bandaged.

Elsewhere aboard the *Iroquois* a vague stir of commotion spread and resounded. Running feet along the decks, a shot, voices shouting, the sound of heavy blows, a wild cry in the night, then a splash. More shouting, more shots, a crackling broken volley, a fusillade.

Malliard dashed out to join his evidently hard-pressed comrades. But he was already too late.

Brune and Despard were not his equal as strategists, combatants or ordinary sentries. Those shots fired in Vivian's cabin—two, and then two more, close together—had signalled the imprisoned officers to attempt to overthrow the opposition. Their captors' strength was, of course, unknown, or they would have hazarded the break much sooner.

DESPARD WAS STILL weak, and badly hurt in the first surprise. Driven back against the rail, overpowered, beaten, he still fought savagely and was finally tossed, half conscious, into the sea. Brune tried to keep the attackers away from the store of arms. But as they increased their number by liberating other members of the *Iroquois* crew, he could not stay their rush.

Shouting to Malliard, he was backing toward the cabin, when a burst of gunfire caught him in its tornado path.

Uncertain as to the actual connection between the men who had briefly dominated the yacht and the guests of its owner, a selected group of armed men stole toward Granville's suite, to set him free if necessary, or receive his orders.

Malliard just at that moment dashed out of Vivian's stateroom and turned aside in the corridor by which they were approaching. He saw them dimly, recognized them as foes, for they were too many to be his accomplices.

Recklessly he opened fire. They returned his fire, a withering deadly blast. He was barely agile enough to dodge back in time.

Acrid powder smoke clouded the corridor, drifted into Vivian's stateroom. Hearing the fusillade so near, Vivian and Wylie looked at each other with a kind of consternation, rare indeed in all their past campaigns of triumphant offensive. They had not planned this mad piracy. That was young Milliard's handiwork.

Yet Myron Granville accounted them pirates-in-chief. Pedro had talked, had probably lied. He now lay dead. Malliard might already have perished. Vivian and Wylie stood to suffer for the foolhardiness of others. Granville would be vengeful, merciless, they knew.

And where, for that matter, was the furious yacht owner?

He had vanished. Smoke of battle had camouflaged his flight. Their perfect hostage was now out of their sight. Malliard, stained with blood and stalled by the accurate shooting of his foes, crept back to the shelter of Vivian's cabin. He had suffered two more superficial wounds. And his welcome from the pair who had thought him already slain was the opposite of cordial.

"Does every Frenchman think he was born to play Napoleon?" Vivian raged at him. "We should have left the pack of you to rot in that canoe."

"I know," said Malliard abjectly. "I have got you into bad trouble—"

"We've begun to notice it!" The Lady from Hell turned to her partner. "Doc, we'd better hide that camera film.

Granville's vanity is bigger than his bank account. That flashlight picture is all we'll have to strike a bargain with."

Wylie pointed to the camera he had put aside out of the way on a chair. It was shattered. The film roll was undoubtedly damaged, if not hopelessly exposed and perforated. A ricochetting bullet from a revolver of heavy caliber had crashed into it, working this final ruin.

"Then," said Vivian Legrand, always at her best in leading a forlorn hope, "we'll have to use something else." She fiercely swept Malliard into her plans. "Both of you do exactly as I say.

"I had Granville right where we wanted him till Pedro was allowed to escape and somebody started playing pirates—"

"All my fault," Malliard admitted.

"Shut up! Now our one chance is to maneuver Granville back to where I had him. Quick now—lock and barricade that door. They'll be creeping up on us. Drag Pedro's carcass somewhere out of sight. I'll not want it till later.

"You, Tristan, you're bleeding like a stuck pig. I've got to be made up to look fatally wounded. Get busy, both of you, daub and decorate me."

SHE CAST ASIDE the negligée, standing before them in vivid, slender magnificence. And now she posed herself for sudden death, motioned Tristan to hurry. The Frenchman was weak and unsteady from his wounds, but obediently he knelt and daubed the ivory flesh of her throat and shoulders with his blood.

"Not my face!" Uncertain of the effect, she improved upon it, moving over without a qualm to lie among the dark stains marking the spot where Pedro had expired.

"Hide that camera, anyhow, Doc. Tristan, you have two guns? Both loaded?"

"Yes."

"Put them here under me. Can they be seen?"

"Not now."

"Good! Doc, give him my gun. You have yours. Those two you'll surrender. I'm the emergency arsenal." She issued further orders, then closed her eyes and by an artful trick of will composed her form and features to an utterly convincing replica of the insensible lassitude heralding death.

Following her plan the men thrust aside some of the furniture barricade, opened the cabin door a few inches, and commenced shooting wildly. Myron Granville's shrill anger could be heard between the shots, ordering his crew to return to the attack.

A volley crashed, and another, then sporadic firing. Wylie and Malliard hugged the walls, careful of angles as Vivian had commanded. She alone was dangerously exposed to a ricochet. By a miracle no glancing slug seared her.

Wylie and Malliard, having each discharged five shots, were now curiously silent. They left the door ajar. This was the crisis—the great moment of multiple perils.

Would Myron Granville so inflame his men, who must have suffered casualties, that they would charge in and massacre the trio? Or had Vivian Legrand judged his temperament as accurately as in the past she had judged other men of wealth and consequence?

Granville presently boomed, "Have you had enough, you crooks?" That didn't sound promising. "Do you surrender?"

"Make him come nearer," Vivian whispered.

But Granville approached them cautiously, fearing a trap. "I say—do you surrender?" he thundered, with a snarl.

"Yes—yes," Wylie groaned weakly. "Hurry—"

Granville did not hurry. But after a bit the door was pushed open slowly. A heavily armed seaman peered in. Then the burly owner of the *Iroquois* thrust him aside and started into the battle-scarred compartment.

"Throw down your arms!" he commanded from the doorway. The "Napoleon" that lurks in many masterful men of affairs had, as Vivian expected, come to the fore in him as he sniffed the smoke of gunpowder.

Malliard crouched as one half dying beside the arrow-straight stricken form of Vivian. Wylie anxiously bent over her, seeming to work upon a ghastly throat wound with fingers that trembled with anguish.

Granville stepped closer.

"Good heavens!" he said, startled.

He saw her more beautiful now then he had discerned heretofore, or even had imagined. And now she was lost—dying, or already dead.

She had fascinated him, and even when Pedro de Martinque came with his tale of deception and plotting, the thought had soared in Granville's self-centered brain that Vivian being a criminal rather than the daughter of a well-to-do gentleman only gave him more power over her. But now, though he had never denied himself what he wanted, his wealth would not weigh against death.

5

VIVIAN MAKES A SALE

WYLIE AND MALLIARD had cast their revolvers aside. Both perfectly feigned their concentration upon the ebbing life of Vivian. Granville was influenced by their pacific attitude. Here was surrender—and more.

He waved back his men who were following him on tiptoe.

"There's a chance, I think," Wylie suddenly exclaimed. "Dim the lights a little. She mustn't be moved. We can make her comfortable right here. Send for whatever medical supplies you have on board."

"But—" Granville started to object.

"Let's forget what's past for a moment. I'm a qualified doctor, no matter what else you may think me."

Granville began issuing orders, dispersing his men. A new worry had come to him. Criminals or not, to have a woman shot to death on his yacht meant an inevitable leak into the American press, then the exaggerations of his enemies—scandal with a big S. Who would listen to his honest explanations? ·

"We must try to save her. Full speed ahead. We'll make for the nearest good sized port," he said.

"Hurry that first-aid kit!" Wylie urged.

Granville repeated his order. He had returned to stand close beside the two men crouching over Vivian. This was the closest he had been to them, yet was not quite close enough. He bent lower, worried, admiring, suddenly suspicious.

"Where is the wound?"

"Glancing bullet, just below the ear—internal hemorrhage," said Wylie, and then the signal Vivian had planned, in order that she might be warned when he was really near. "Look! She's coming to!"

The eyelids trembled, opened. Vivian's eyes were actually misty with pain, troubled, wondering.

She sighed faintly.

"Send for brandy, quick!" said Wylie.

The yacht owner nodded to a seaman, who hurried out, leaving only one man remaining on guard by the door.

Vivian sat up. "But you must not—" Granville started protesting.

Wylie and Malliard reached for the two hidden guns. But Malliard was weak and fumbled his. Vivian herself, by a lightning twist of her supple form, snatched it up. Wylie had Granville covered.

The armed guard at the doorway was staring, aghast. The combined shock of Vivian's resurrection and her revelation of loveliness was too much for his wits.

"Get out. Quick, drop that gun, or we'll kill Mr. Granville," she snapped at the seaman. And the man obeyed; let his weapon fall, and turned and ran.

"Tristan, pull yourself together!" She swept with feline grace to the door, slammed it shut, began rebuilding the furniture barricade. Malliard hurriedly helped her.

GRANVILLE, STRANGELY SILENT, unprotesting, stood in the center of the stateroom. He ignored Wylie's revolver close to his ribs, and seemed absorbed in the spectacle of Vivian's intense leadership.

She resumed her negligee and turned toward him, saying:

"The fortunes of war!"

"For the second time I trusted you. No wonder you take me for a fool," said the millionaire.

"I take you for a smart man who wants no scandal and knows when he's had enough." It was just before sunrise. She switched off the cabin lights and fiery glints of the new day coming were reflected by her cloud of hair.

"You've got me prisoner," said Granville, "but you'll have to deal with the master of this yacht, McNeal. He's a hard man."

"But loyal to you?"

"Naturally."

"Very well." She turned back to her companions. "We'll have to bind and gag him, so that he can't make a move or sound. Also I want that signet ring—"

"Don't be cheap," said Granville. "A gold ring, only valued as an heirloom. What is it worth to you?"

"We'll return it. You can have it sterilized if you like." Her cryptic remark puzzled Granville and worried him. He was no longer bellowing and masterful. What troubles would overtake him next? And so he offered no resistance to their gag and bonds.

"Now, Doc," said The Lady from Hell. "A touch of surgery. Look at Granville's fingers, then pick one of Pedro's that can be made to resemble it and chop it off.

We'll slip on the ring as further disguise—" She saw that even Wylie, hardened to her stratagems, was aghast. "Have I got to attend to this, too?" she demanded. "How else can we bring McNeal to terms? If he sights another ship, or resorts to his wireless—"

Wylie nodded and turned away with a grimace to Granville, whose eyes above the gag were saucers of amazement. What a woman!—they seemed to say. And what a lucky escape! To think that he had wanted to have her in his power!

Outside in the corridor all remained quiet. Officers and crew must be conferring on the rescue of their employer.

Calling through the battered door panel, Vivian insisted on treating with none but the yacht's captain. McNeal was obdurate. She then warned him to wait and listen. She signed to Milliard, who had been rehearsed, and he uttered a terrible groaning outcry.

"Just a bit of amputation, Scotty," she jeered. And Pedro's finger, bearing the signet ring of Granville, was tossed out through a crack of the door.

"You—you foul monsters!" McNeal was beside himself. "I'm master on my own deck—power of life and death. And by God, I'll string you up—"

"Ears and nose will follow, unless you do as you're told."

After a minute's thought, Granville's chief retainer capitulated.

The terms were, first, surrender of all available firearms. Milliard knew what weapons were on board. Protected from a rush by the barricade, he could see what revolvers and rifles the seamen brought and piled at the threshold of Vivian's stateroom.

Then Milliard gathered them all in, protected by Wylie and Vivian with guns ready.

THE ODDS WERE still great, but disarmed men were not likely to attack unless Granville urged it. His gag was removed, so that he could reassure the baffled McNeal about the apparent mutilation of his hand.

"Save that signet ring, but toss the finger overboard," Vivian called, still capitalizing her display of extreme callousness by means of which she had been able to dominate every man on board. "Send two men in with a sheet of canvas, to dispose of what goes with the finger. And tell the chef to hurry along a hearty breakfast *for four.*"

She went to the adjoining bathroom and changed to sports attire. Granville was still bound and closely guarded, but a kind of exhausted amity had taken possession of the antagonists aboard the *Iroquois*.

"You'll land the three of us at Tobago," The Lady from Hell dictated as they sat down to breakfast, still heavily armed. "And no questions asked. You don't trust us, and I can't blame you, so you may have our clothing, all our baggage, everything we take with us searched—"

"Why?" Granville questioned.

"To make sure we sell you every scrap of camera film that Wylie or I brought on board your yacht."

"And the price?"

"How much cash in the safe when you looked?" she asked Wylie.

"Forty thousand and some odd hundreds—"

"You broke into my safe last evening while—"

"Yes—while you were discussing I know not what with my 'daughter.' I left everything just as I found it."

"We never steal, you see, Granville," Vivian explained. "We only sell useful and necessary things—in this case, camera film. The price was once very much higher, you remember. But forty thousand cash will be accepted. We rebate the rest for a safe passage to Tobago and a letter signed by you inviting Wylie and Milliard and me to take this short cruise as your guests aboard the *Iroquois*. That'll take care of any future charge of piracy."

THE ADVENTURE OF THE DYING DICTATOR

*Up the Marble Stairs of a Guarded Palace
Steals the Red-Headed Siren to Snatch Power
from a Dictator, and Millions from Thieves*

1

REVOLUTION IN TRUJILLO

A SINGLE SHOT was the first intimation to the Lady from Hell that she was in danger. The bullet whined past her automobile, crashed into the window of a shop and sent a shower of glass tinkling to the narrow sidewalk.

Instantly the heat-struck quiet of Trujillo's siesta hour was shattered. It was as if the sound of the shot had been a signal. Doors closed quickly. The thick iron shutters that are almost universal in Latin America were slammed shut over windows. Indian women, squatting at the edge of the plaza to nurse their babies, with their bare feet sticking out from innumerable full length skirts, fled soundlessly. A porter dropped the baggage he was carrying and ducked into a doorway. A priest picked up his robes and vanished around a corner. Even a slumbering dog in the gutter seemed to recognize the danger and fled, with a yelp, toward the protection of a cobbled *calle*.

The driver of the automobile in which Vivian Legrand and Adrian Wylie, her companion in crime, had that morning driven up the steep mountain road from Monteverde, the chief port, to Trujillo, the capital, recognized the danger also and stepped on the gas.

And not a moment too soon. A second later a shout-

The officer froze
in his tracks

ing, yelling group of men and boys burst from a street that
opened onto the cathedral square, and almost immediately
a machine gun hidden in an alley began to sing its song of
death. The Lady from Hell glanced over her shoulder and
a little icy wind brushed her neck. Had their driver been
a fraction of an instant slower their car would have been
directly in the line of fire from the machine gun.

Firing broke out ahead of them as snipers behind the
shuttered windows searched for the machine gunner
with staccato bursts of rifle fire. More men, some of them
armed with rifles, others with machetes, poured out into
the square, from the side streets, Windows crashed out and
wood splintered as the sleet of bullets spattered the fronts
of the houses. An Indian boy stiffened in the recess of a
stone doorway where he had taken refuge and crumpled
to the street, the basket of scarlet cactus flowers spilling
over the cobbles like a blood-red rain.

Through it all flashed the car, the driver, white-faced, sending it for the haven of a side street at full speed.

Adrian Wylie, who occupied the rear seat with the Lady from Hell, leaned forward.

"Is it a revolution?" he queried in Spanish as fluent as the man's own.

"*Si, señor,*" the driver flung over his shoulder. A frantic jerk of the wheel was his answer to a ringing "*ting*" as a bullet struck the hood in front of him. The side window shattered as a stray shot passed through the car, missing Vivian Legrand by inches.

Ahead of them yawned a narrow street, wide enough for the car. They were a bare two hundred feet away when the first of a troop of cavalry, swords drawn, began clattering out into the plaza from the narrow opening. Instinctively the driver slowed the car.

The Lady from Hell threw a swift glance behind her. Already some of the rebels were prone on the flagging of the plaza, firing at the oncoming troop of cavalry. It would be death to remain there, she knew. In another moment they would be enveloped in a hail of bullets.

From the hand bag in her lap she snatched a small automatic. Leaning forward she shoved it into the back of the driver. Her voice, when she spoke, was full of menace.

"Drive on," she ordered in Spanish.

"But, *señora,* the soldiers," protested the man.

"Drive into them," she ordered, and the man recognized that death for him lay behind those biting words if he did not obey.

There was no choice for the driver. He sent the car speeding ahead straight for the oncoming cavalry. Their

leader snatched an automatic from his belt and raised it
to fire, but caught sight of a woman in the rear seat of the
car just in time. A shouted order and the detachment split
in two and the car sped toward the safety of the street
between two lanes of lively horses that closed in behind
them like a living wall.

Mounted men were still pouring from the street, and
Vivian ordered the car stopped. They could not enter that
narrow opening as long as it was filled from wall to wall
with men and horses, and the men behind them formed a
protection against bullets.

A young officer stopped his horse by the side of the car.
"THE STREET WILL be clear in a moment or two, *señora*,"
he said, flicking an admiring glance at the exquisite, exotic
face beneath its crown of red hair. "It will be wise, once you
are able, to drive straight to your hotel and remain there.
The revolt is not serious; it will be over shortly, but in the
meanwhile it is not safe to be on the streets."

"I did not know that there was a revolution in prospect,"
Vivian said.

The officer shrugged. "Fools have been spreading the
report that His Excellency, the President, is dead." He
looked at Vivian boldly. "May I present myself? I am Lieutenant Sanchez. When this trouble is over, may I have the
honor of inquiring at your hotel as to your safety?"

"With pleasure," Vivian told him. "Mrs. Legrand is the
name, at the Hotel Montebelle."

The last of the cavalry out of the street ahead of them, the
young officer saluted and waved them on and in another
moment the car was in the shadowed coolness of the street.

"If President Rajas is really dead," Wylie said slowly,

"this will be a wise city to stay out of. There will be hell popping when his iron grip is relaxed."

Vivian glanced out at the shuttered windows, the closed shop fronts of the narrow street through which they were passing.

"There will be trouble," she agreed. Her voice, despite the slight trace of excitement that had crept into it, was low and rich and marked by a huskiness that was rare because it was musical. "For nearly thirty years Rajas has been dictator—has had the entire country under his thumb—and for thirty years the spirit of revolt has been simmering. And yet, under his rule this has been one of the most prosperous countries in Latin America."

"It is really the wealthiest country in South America," Wylie agreed, "and the treasury is so full that it's probably on the point of bursting. Which makes it all the more reason that the outs should want to be in, if Rajas dies."

"He's an old man, isn't he?" Vivian queried thoughtfully.

"Nearly seventy, I believe," Wylie responded curiously. "Why?"

"No reason," Vivian responded, but Wylie knew from the little flame that came and went in her green eyes that there had been a reason, a very definite one, for the query. "I wonder, if the dictator were dead, if the men around him, the officials, would not let it be known until they'd had a chance to loot the treasury and flee?"

"They'd probably try to loot it," Wylie responded easily. "What gave you the idea?"

"Do you remember the big white yacht tied up at the dock at Monteverde alongside our steamer?" Vivian Legrand queried. "I happened to hear, before we left the steamer, that her captain had been ordered to keep steam up and be ready to sail on an instant's notice. The yacht belongs to General Miguel Mignerra, head of the army, and most trusted adviser of the dictator."

"Oh," Wylie said softly, "then in all probability the contents of the treasury are about to take wings to Europe."

Their car drew up at the facade of the Hotel Montebelle.

"Possibly," Vivian Legrand admitted thoughtfully. "And then again, the contents of the national treasury might stay right here—but in different hands."

2

BONDS OF FEAR

AN AIR OF electric tension hung over the sitting room on the third floor of the Hotel Montebelle a few days later.

"You are sure, absolutely sure, Sebastian?" the Lady from Hell queried.

Angele Sebastian shrugged. "I am not infallible. I have guessed wrong before," he said dryly. "But I believe that what I have told you is correct."

"How many others know this?"

He shook his head. "No one, for a certainty. No one told it to me as a fact. But I have fitted what I have heard to what I know and it has added up to what I have told you."

The Lady from Hell was lost in thought for a moment. Angele Sebastian, she knew, missed little of the subtle undercurrents that made up the shifting political life of the republic. From the mountain highlands that stood back of Trujillo, from the almost impenetrable reaches of the jungle up the mighty river that pierced the republic, from the steaming lowlands of the coast, bits of information drifted to him.

Presumably conducting an import and export business, he had a finger in nearly every secret affair in the country, whether it was smuggling arms, slipping a man who had earned the disfavor of the dictator quietly out of the country, or as quietly slipping another who had been banished back into the country again.

"And the army—the police?" she queried after a moment.

There was nothing about her as she sat there, elbows on the table, smoke from her cigarette in front of her inscrutable green eyes, to indicate that she was as deadly—and as merciless—as a striking snake, or that she was planning the most daring coup in the entire annals of Latin America. The reflected light from the balcony outside caught her red hair and caused it to take on something of the nature of a quivering flame above the exquisitely molded face that was a mask for a nature that had no mercy, no conscience, no passion.

"The army," Sebastian said, "is loyal to the dictator as long as he lives. Once he is dead,"—he shrugged—"it is any man's army, and I should not like to be in the shoes of General Miguel Mignerra, their commander, when that happens. The police?" He became thoughtful. "Colonel Moreno, the head of the national police force, can answer for his men, whichever way the cat may jump. They might not be loyal to the dictator, but they are to him, I believe."

"This is Moreno?" The Lady from Hell picked up a photograph from a pile on the table.

"That is Moreno," Sebastian told her.

"And these rebel leaders?" She glanced at the names she had scribbled on the slip of paper in front of her. "This Don Diego, Gabriel Zalas and Ansele Palemar—you are sure that you can reach them on short notice if occasion demands?"

Sebastian smiled grimly. "Since I smuggled them into

the country and provided a hiding place there need be no doubt in your mind."

"Good," Vivian said. Her eyes were hard, as emeralds are hard. "Now listen: Whatever happens is likely to happen tonight. Have everything in readiness as I have outlined it to you. When you receive a message from me, go ahead according to schedule. Until you do hear—sit tight and do nothing."

"And—?" questioned Sebastian gently.

"When you have done what is necessary, you will receive the money I promised."

She stood up to signify that the interview was at an end, just as a light tap came upon the door to the hallway. A swift gesture of caution silenced any remark.

"It is Lieutenant Sanchez," she whispered. "He must not know that you were here, yet. This way," and she flung open the door that led to the veranda. Like a gliding ghost Sebastian slid through it and disappeared.

LIEUTENANT SANCHEZ DID not suspect, as he greeted the Lady from Hell, that in the few brief days that he had known her she had learned more about him than even his most intimate friends knew. To him she was simply a very lovely woman, whose eyes held a promise that her lips had not yet made good.

Vivian's smile was gracious, but in her heart was not the slightest particle of pity for the terrific shock that was in store for this slender, black-haired, black-eyed officer. Such luxuries as pity or compassion she had eliminated from her makeup early in her career.

"A drink?" queried the Lady from Hell casually, motioning to the little table on which stood a bottle and glasses.

She knew the dramatic value of a sudden attack, and she counted on it in this instance to play in her favor. As Sanchez turned toward the table she said, with rapier smoothness:

"I sent for you, Lieutenant, to ask what provisions for escape you have made when the order for your arrest is issued tomorrow."

The man whirled like a cat. He gasped as the realization of her meaning burst over him, and for an instant his black eyes flashed from the woman toward the door as if expecting to see a soldier with the order for his arrest.

"What did you say?" he asked.

At the bottom of the eyes of the Lady from Hell a light flamed and went out. It was a warning signal that came into her eyes when she had the game in her hands. It was a little flicker of triumph that she could not control. Sebastian had been right, then. The man had embezzled funds entrusted to his care. The story of his impending arrest was an invention of her own; but in view of the man's guilty conscience an exceedingly plausible one.

"You heard correctly," she assured him coolly. "You know, of course, that the order for your arrest will be issued tomorrow morning at ten o'clock."

"How do you know that?" he demanded hoarsely. His face had gone white and there was a hunted look in his eyes. "Are you sure?"

"Quite sure," she told him calmly. "You are to be arrested tomorrow morning for having embezzled palace funds entrusted to your care. An hour later you will be facing a firing squad—unless I intervene."

"What can you do?" the man queried.

"I can save you," she told him. "Arrange the matter so that there will be no further trouble. *If* you are reasonable."

"I have no money. I cannot pay you." He looked suddenly much older than his years. He was in a trap, and there are few men who can face the prospect of a trap closing upon them with any degree of calmness. Then he glanced at her sharply. "I do not know how you knew this, but I do not believe that you have sufficient influence with His Excellency to do as you say. You have never even seen him."

"True enough," she agreed. "The nearest I have come to seeing President Rajas is his autographed picture there. But if you will perform one or two little services for me you will find that you need have no further fear of arrest."

"What is it that you wish?" Lieutenant Sanchez queried suspiciously.

Lowering her voice the Lady from Hell talked to him rapidly for a few minutes. The man sprang to his feet, consternation upon his face.

"It is impossible. It cannot be done. I will not be implicated in such a thing as that," he said rapidly.

"A man is dead a long time," Vivian Legrand said, and her voice crackled like the snap of a whip. The light from the windows touched her face—glinted on the iciness of her eyes.

The lieutenant found drops of perspiration on his brow. The incredible and merciless savagery of this woman was; for the first time, evident to him.

"Do you prefer to be led before a firing squad like a sheep—or save yourself from death and disgrace?" she went on.

"I would do anything you asked, within reason. But this, it cannot be done," the officer repeated doggedly.

"It can be done!" the Lady from Hell flung back at him. "It is planned, down to the last minute detail, and it will be done, regardless of whether you work with me or not! But"—and her voice was deadly suave—"if you are not willing to work with me, I done not think it will be necessary for you to wait for tomorrow's firing squad."

The implication was starkly evident and the man got it. He was trapped, and he knew it. He surrendered.

"I will try to do it," he said, "but I warn you, it will not be successful. Why, it will shake the country to its foundations—and we will all face a firing squad."

"It *would* shake the country," Vivian corrected him dryly, "if it were discovered. But I do not think that it will be. And if it is successful…."

She did not go on. There was no need. The lieutenant knew, fully as well as Vivian, the almost incredible future that lay before them if her scheme worked.

FOR A MOMENT neither of them spoke. Vivian walked quietly back and forth in the room. Audacious as her criminal career had been, she knew that the thing she was planning was the crowning touch to a career that had made her the most glamorous and resourceful criminal of her age. There was a cold glow in the back of her eyes that, had Lieutenant Sanchez but known it, was like the warning that a rattlesnake gives before it strikes.

And then suddenly, with the swiftness of a snake, she struck. Before her companion knew what was happening she jerked open the communicating door between the sitting room and the bedroom. The man whose ear had been plastered to the keyhole literally tumbled into the room, to find himself covered with a revolver in the hand of the Lady from Hell.

The lieutenant whirled in startled astonishment at the sound.

"What are you doing here?" Vivian demanded in Spanish.

"Your pardon, *señora*," whined the man. "I was seeking the room of the distinguished Señor Madrigules, and I thought—"

"Do not trouble to lie," Vivian cut in harshly. "Who sent you here?"

"But, *señora*," whined the man, raising an imploring hand. His unkempt hair was dotted with patches of gray. He was unshaven and his clothes, although clean, were old and patched. "No one sent me."

"There are means of making you talk," Vivian warned him curtly. "Such as slivers of burning wood thrust beneath the finger nails, or strips of skin carefully, oh, so carefully, peeled off your back... Who sent you here?"

The man's face was ridden with fear—a sickening fear that gave the face a greenish tinge and left his hands trembling and unsteady.

"Who sent you?" her relentless voice slashed at him.

"The police," he said finally in an unsteady voice.

"A police spy," Lieutenant Sanchez muttered, and his own face, which had recovered some of its color, went pale again.

The Lady from Hell silenced him with a gesture.

"Why should the police spy on me?" she wanted to know.

"Because," the man said slowly, "you have been doing

things that tourists do not do. You have talked with Angele Sebastian, and he is suspect. You have asked questions that tourists do not ask. So Colonel Moreno sent me to spy upon you."

"And you heard, what?" Vivian demanded.

"Everything," the man said slowly, the words seeming to be dragged from him by some irresistible force. "I heard what Sebastian said to you—and the plans you made with the lieutenant here."

For a moment none of the three spoke, and the seconds ticked by in such a silence that Vivian thought that she could almost count the pulsing of her own heart.

Then Lieutenant Sanchez said unsteadily, "He has heard too much. Shall I kill him for you?"

"He has heard too much," Vivian agreed, "but we shall not kill him—yet. You must leave. Find Angele Sebastian—you know the place of business—and tell him that I will see him within an hour to make final plans for tonight. Meanwhile, I will call Dr. Wylie and we will give this man a hypodermic that will prevent him betraying us. He can be locked in the clothes closet there until tomorrow. You are to return here as soon as you have seen Sebastian."

The lieutenant nodded agitated agreement. The Lady from Hell kept her cowering victim covered with her gun until the last sound of the lieutenant's footsteps had died away on the polished boards of the corridor. Then she tossed the gun onto a chair with a laugh.

"Quite well done, Adrian," she said.

Adrian Wylie, the companion in crime of the Lady from Hell, pulled off his mottled gray wig. He smiled as he crossed to the table and extracted a cigarette from the silver box there.

"It will hold him, I think," Wylie responded leisurely. "It was a good idea, Vivian. There was a bare chance that he might not have returned once he got from under the power of your engaging personality. But now that he believes a police spy has heard him plot against the dictator he will not dare to stay away."

Vivian studied her chief of staff in crime speculatively. She had seen him play many parts, but never one that was quite as far removed from his normal, alert self as this. She was forced to admit that there was nothing in his face, his bearing or his expression which reminded her in the least of the Wylie who had worked with her in many a criminal scheme. He had stepped into the identity of the down-at-the-heels Spanish police spy with a facility that was perfectly marvelous.

"He will come back," Vivian said with assurance in her voice. "But before he does we have work to do. Because tonight we strike."

3

GUARDED GATES

TEN O'CLOCK RANG out from the clock in the tower of the cathedral. And almost on the stroke, a car sped past the parked automobile in which the Lady from Hell, Lieutenant Sanchez and Wylie sat. They watched until it passed through the gates of the palace grounds on the opposite side of the plaza.

"That was Carlos Pillar, His Excellency's financial adviser," Sanchez said. His face was pale, but his eyes were very bright. "That was the fifth. They are all inside the palace now."

The Lady from Hell nodded. "Good. We will wait fifteen minutes to give Secretary Pillar time to join the others. Then we will start."

Silence fell across the little group. Vivian Legrand was keenly aware of the tremendous magnitude of the thing she had set out to do, and even now, when she was ready to take the first step of her audacious scheme, that keen brain of hers was planning, sorting, analyzing, seeking any loophole that she might have left unguarded. Finally she glanced at the luminous dial of her wrist watch.

"Let's go," she said simply.

Her nerves were tense as their car rolled slowly across

the plaza and stopped before the heavy iron gate of the palace grounds. The headlights ran along the graveled drive inside, along banks of darkly gleaming foliage and stopped full upon the ornate marble facade of the palace. The two guards beside the gate brought their rifles to "ready," and two more inside the gates stood in readiness.

For one of the few times in his career, Adrian Wylie was nervous. There was nothing about Wylie to hint that for years he had been a consummate crook. He gave the impression of a man of affairs, a banker perhaps. But this was the biggest part that the Lady from Hell had ever called upon him to play in the whole of their criminal association, a part that would call for every shred of nerve and cunning that he possessed.

Lieutenant Sanchez leaned out of the car.

"You know me, do you not?" he said to the guard.

"*Si, señor,*" the man said.

"Then let me pass."

"But, I have orders—"

"Our business will not wait, and your orders do not instruct you to prevent the passage of persons properly vouched for by an officer of the palace guard."

"I do not prevent your passage," Lieutenant," the guard said desperately. "It is only these orders—"

"They go with me," the lieutenant cut in swiftly. "It is an order."

The man saluted and stepped back. The gates were flung open and the big car went slowly up the driveway between hedges of spiky cactus with waxen blossoms of white and scarlet. A whole squad of soldiers came to attention at the doorway and a straight-backed and capable lieutenant hurried up to them.

He flung a word of greeting to Sanchez and then turned to Wylie and Vivian.

"I must ask you not to come any further," he said formally. "It is not permitted for visitors to even come this far. Lieutenant Sanchez has exceeded his authority in passing you through the gates."

Vivian stepped forward.

"Lieutenant Sanchez is not to blame," she said quietly. "He merely acted as our escort because we were not familiar with the palace. As a matter of fact we are here at the express request of His Excellency."

The officer shook his head.

"I am afraid that you have made a mistake. His Excellency sees no one."

"He will see us," Vivian said confidently. "Here is his own signature," and she thrust under the officer's nose a request for their presence at the palace bearing the scrawled and well-known signature of the dictator himself. It had taken a great deal of care on Wylie's part to reproduce that signature.

The officer looked puzzled. "I have not been notified of this," he said, "and my orders are to permit no one to enter the palace unless passed through by Colonel Moreno himself."

"Then," Lieutenant Sanchez said, "you will take the responsibility for refusing to admit these people."

"I will not," the officer said stiffly. "I will place the matter before Colonel Moreno as my superior officer."

He turned to go and Vivian cut in swiftly. It was no part of her scheme that they be forced to wait outside.

"Surely, Lieutenant, you will not force us to wait outside in the night until you consult your superior officer. It can certainly do no harm for us to wait comfortably inside the door."

THE OFFICER HESITATED. Vivian could almost see the thoughts that flitted through his mind. If these people were on a legitimate errand it could do no harm to show them a slight courtesy. And if there should be something wrong what harm could there be in their waiting in the foyer while he sent a servant to Colonel Moreno? He shot a glance at the briefcase Wylie carried.

"I must examine that before I permit you to enter the palace," he said.

"That is impossible," Wylie said firmly. "The papers that it contains are for the eyes of His Excellency alone. I will not answer for the consequences if anyone else sees them. In fact, I will refuse to enter before I permit them to be examined."

The officer hesitated. Then Wylie's bluff won. The officer bowed.

"If you will come with me," he said.

They entered the spacious foyer where a wall fountain dripped on green-gray tiles and yellow *capa de Ora* and scarlet hibiscus slashed in the shadows with color and birds fluttered in and out among the tree ferns.

The officer turned to close the door—and then froze in his tracks, his hand still upon the knob. The feel of the gun in his ribs was unmistakable.

"Turn around," Vivian said gently. "But do not make a false move. I will not hesitate to shoot."

The officer turned slowly, his eyes taking in the fact that both Wylie and his fellow-officer, in addition to Vivian, were armed, and that their weapons were covering him. A man of more than usual acumen, he realized at once that his life was nothing to these three if it stood between them and whatever it was that they planned. But his eyes were bitter as they rested upon Lieutenant Sanchez.

"Colonel Moreno and the rest of His Excellency's cabinet. Where are they?" the Lady from Hell demanded tersely. There was a tigerish threat in her voice and the officer answered instantly, instinctively lowering his voice to hers as if realizing that it would not be safe to speak more loudly.

"In the council room."

"Lead the way," Vivian told him. "But don't try anything. There is a plot on foot against His Excellency and we are here to thwart it."

He started across the foyer, toward the stairway. Vivian Legrand nodded slightly to Wylie.

The officer never knew what hit him. Wylie's gun butt caught him just above the ear and he crumpled to the floor without a sound. Silently Wylie and Sanchez worked, tying him up with the thin strong line that Wylie had taken from his pocket. Then, together, the two men carried him to a small closet, dumped him inside and locked the door on him. Wylie pocketed the key.

"His Excellency's room is at the head of the stairs, on the right," Sanchez whispered. "There will be a guard outside the door. I will attend to him."

Silently he strode up the wide white marble stairs, their footfalls inaudible on the red velvet carpet that covered it. At the head of the stairs he motioned them to halt while he went forward alone toward the guard on duty outside one of the doors. The man came to attention and saluted.

Lieutenant Sanchez returned the salute negligently. "Colonel Moreno wishes you to report to him in the council chamber at once," he said. "I am to remain outside His Excellency's door until you return."

The man saluted again in acknowledgment and turned away.

And it was then that catastrophe almost overtook them.

Lieutenant Sanchez leaped for the man's throat—and missed. His clutching hand closed about the soldier's shoulder. Startled, the man jerked away from the officer's grip, leaped to one side.

In that instant it would have taken but the merest straw in the wind to wreck the entire scheme that Vivian Legrand had so carefully built up, Although the three of them were armed, they dared not use their revolvers. The sound of a shot would bring the whole palace staff swarming upon them.

It was the soldier himself who turned the scales against himself. He retreated slowly down the hallway, away from Lieutenant Sanchez, his gun held in readiness for another attack, his eyes fixed suspiciously on the officer.

And as he neared the head of the stairs where the Lady from Hell and Wylie lurked, Wylie leaped and struck him with the edge of his palm across the back of his neck. A deadly, paralyzing blow, the product of jujutsu that can be used to fell the strongest of men. Just one blow. The man dropped his gun as the exquisite, paralyzing pain of the blow ran through every nerve of his body, rocked for an instant, then crumpled.

In a moment the man's hands and feet were tightly lashed and Wylie was working intently at the lock of the door the soldier had been guarding. There was a tiny click as the bolt was shoved back and the way was open.

4

SECRET OF THE DEAD

THE LADY FROM Hell opened the door herself, an inch or two at first, and then wide as a careful survey through the crack showed her that the room was deserted—or almost deserted.

There was a silent figure lying on the tumbled bed.

It took only an instant's survey at the white hair, the bushy eyebrows, the white mustache and beard to show them it was His Excellency President Rajas, cold in death.

Angele Sebastian had been right when he told her that the dictator was already dead, and that the five members of his cabinet were hiding the fact until they could make their getaway. The one thing was the pivotal fact upon which her scheme had rested. If the dictator had been alive—well, there had been another scheme in her mind which necessity might have compelled her to put into operation.

"Dead for nearly twenty-four hours," Wylie said, examining the body with practiced hands.

"We've no time to lose," Vivian snapped. "Adrian, you and the lieutenant know exactly what you have to do?"

"We know," Wylie assured her.

The Lady from Hell nodded and slipped out of the room. Her part in the scheme had already been mapped out, and she knew that she must so time her own actions as to dovetail precisely with the events that were scheduled.

She gave a swift glance from a hallway window that overlooked the plaza outside the palace, and nodded with satisfaction. It was dotted with half a dozen little groups of men, and even as she looked others straggled in from the side streets, converging on the palace. There was no hitch here. Angele Sebastian's agents were doing their work well.

Quietly she tapped on the door that Sanchez had pointed out as the door to the council chamber. The man who opened it she knew, from his photograph, to be Colonel Moreno. Before the man had time to recover himself from his astonishment at seeing a woman standing outside the door, she had stepped inside and closed it.

Colonel Moreno found himself staring into the muzzle of a small, but exceedingly businesslike pistol.

"If you will be so kind as to return to your companions," Vivian suggested sweetly.

The man backed away, still staring in amazement at the Lady from Hell.

"What does this mean? Who is this woman, Moreno?" demanded one of the men impatiently.

The man backed away across the room whose walls were lined with mirrors sparkling into brilliant day from the light of the glittering crystal chandeliers. His eyes were fixed in smoldering amazement upon the Lady from Hell.

She moved quietly across the room and sank into a chair with the catlike grace that characterized every movement. Her hand, still grasping the gun, rested carelessly upon the table top.

It was Colonel Moreno who recovered from his astonishment and spoke first.

"What does this mean?" he demanded.

For a moment she studied him speculatively, with the unreadable, faintly slant-eyed gaze that was one of the attributes of her beauty. He was a slender, grimly-built man, perhaps forty-five years old, tanned, with watchful eyes that were faintly sardonic and lips that were thin and inclined to be both cruel and a trifle self-indulgent.

She was matching her wits against those of men she did not know—men whose attributes were an unknown quality. True, she had gathered what information concerning them she could in the scant time at her disposal. Angele Sebastian had furnished her other facts, and a careful study of their photographs had placed her in possession of information that would, perhaps, have startled them had they known it.

But, at her best, knowledge of these men was fragmentary, and in the minutes to come she would have to play them as an angler plays a fish—and her fish was a stake so tremendous as to exceed any for which she had ever played.

"I wished to see you gentlemen on a matter of importance," she said simply. "So I am here."

"How did you get in here?" demanded General Miguerra.

"Does it matter?" she asked.

She leaned back and smiled… and had these five men known what was in her mind at the moment, the smile would have pleased them a great deal less than it did. She leaned back in silence in the big, leather-upholstered chair, quite at ease. The pistol had disappeared. Her hands were clasped on the table in front of her, chin tilted, eyes looking upon them as a cat's eyes look upon the mouse it is about to play with.

"LET ME SEE," she said musingly after a moment. "This is Colonel Moreno, is it not? The officer in command of the national police. And this," indicating the tall, silver-haired man at the head of the table, "is Señor Rodriquez, His Excellency's Minister of Foreign Affairs. General Miguel Miguerra, head of the army, is the gentleman nearest to me, and next to him is Carlos Pillar, His Excellency's adviser on all matters of finance. But the fifth gentleman I do not seem to recognize."

Colonel Moreno stood up.

"Madame," he said sternly, "I do not know by what method you managed to force your way into a conference of His Excellency's council, but I must ask you to leave at once."

"This is most extraordinary," Secretary Pillar thrust in.

"It is extraordinary," Vivian agreed sympathetically. "Almost as extraordinary as what happened last night."

Sudden tension settled upon the little group. It was the kind of tension that falls over a quivering wolf pack that sees its prey menaced, or that strange, quivering alertness that blankets a regiment as it waits for an attack. The Lady from Hell watched them warily. She was setting in motion the wheels of an intricate scheme—a scheme that would take every particle of her skill and cunning to carry through to completion. She waited quietly to let the full significance of her remark sink into the consciousness of the five men.

It was the Secretary for Foreign Affairs—a dark, taciturn man, with cruel devils in his black eyes and an ugly twist to his lips—who spoke first. He leaned forward and his voice was slow and dangerous:

"Perhaps madame will be good enough to explain?"

"Are you sure," Vivian shot at him, "that you want me to explain?" She glanced ostentatiously at the door through which she had come. "The guards—are they also in the secret? Do they know that His Excellency—"

"Wait!" The imperative demand from Colonel Moreno was almost a shout. "Such things are better discussed by inference. Suppose, for the sake of argument, that we admit that—er—certain occurrences did take place last night. What is your interest in the matter?"

Vivian laughed. She said swiftly, stabbing each word at him as if it were a weapon:

"My interest, Colonel Moreno, is precisely the same as yours and that of these other gentlemen."

"I am afraid that I do not understand," he said with a frown. For a moment they looked at each other. The woman's face was alight with a smile and in his face—not disbelief, but an inability to accept the answer that had begun to creep into his mind. "You are not a citizen of the country. You have no possible interest in what took place last night."

"Money has no citizenship, Colonel Moreno," she told him.

He looked at her with dawning uneasiness in his manner and she watched the changing play of expression on his face through narrowed eyes. After all, success in crime, as in crime detection, is largely knowledge of humanity, and the Lady from Hell could deduce pretty shrewdly what was going on in the man's mind. The knowledge that she knew what he thought only the five of them knew had been a staggering blow, and his mind was still groping through a mass of conjectures as to her project.

"Please explain," he said finally.

She shrugged. "If you wish, I should imagine that it would be quite clear. You five gentlemen expect to benefit financially by what took place last night before departing for Europe on General Miguerra's yacht."

This was another blow below the belt for the five conspirators, and she paused at the gasp of consternation that came from them. And then she went on smoothly: "It seems to me that there are better ways of handling the situation than by simply dividing up the contents of the treasury and living the balance of one's life in Paris."

Colonel Moreno stared at her a moment in silence. It seemed incredible that this beautiful woman should be sitting here calmly blackmailing him and the four other most prominent men in the republic... pitting herself against the five men who held the country in the hollow of their hands.

"I take it," he said suddenly, "that your proposition might be called blackmail?"

"Not at all," she said smoothly. "Simply an arrangement that is likely to be much more lucrative financially than the one you have mapped out. You see, gentlemen, you are men of the moment, men who seem able to grasp only the present and immediate future. But I am a business woman, and I have my eyes on not only the present, the immediate future, but the far distant future as well."

"And I suppose," Colonel Moreno went on, his tone matching hers for smoothness, "that your proposition is that unless we agree to whatever proposition you may have in mind, that you will—er—talk?"

"Talk is an exceedingly useful thing, sometimes," she said calmly.

Secretary Pillar got to his feet.

"Stop all this nonsense," he said angrily, "all this beating around the bush. The woman knows something. She is dangerous. But His Excellency knew how to deal with people who might be dangerous to him, and we can do no better than follow his example."

"You mean—the cells beneath the palace?" queried Rodriquez.

"Precisely," Secretary Pillar said grimly. He laughed silently with an unpleasant twist of his thin mouth. The smoke from a half-smoked cigarette crawled slowly up in the hot, lifeless air and wreathed his face. "Send the guard away. If we five men cannot handle one woman we do not deserve to be called men. Let her talk all she wants to after we are gone—if she is ever found."

Coldly, implacably, Secretary Pillar pronounced the death warrant of the beautiful woman standing there before him. And her answer was a low, rippling laugh.

5

HELL'S MASTER STROKE

"DO YOU THINK that you are dealing with a fool?" she demanded. "Do you think I would be idiot enough to come here without having made provisions to insure my safety? The body of the President of the Republic has been removed from the palace—ah, you did not know that, did you? If I fail to give the proper signal at the proper time that body will be displayed in the city… and not only will you utterly fail in your plan to loot the treasury, but not one of you will leave this room alive. You see, you are trapped in the palace. You can leave it alive only if I wish it."

The low murmur outside had grown now until it was distinctly audible inside the room. With a reckless disregard for whatever action the men might take the Lady from Hell strode across the room and flung aside the heavy draperies.

"Look out there," she said.

The huge square was packed with people, a tightly-wedged throng that filled the open space and overflowed down the side street. Even the branches of the trees were black with men and boys.

Secretary Pillar's face blanched as he caught sight of that packed mass of humanity.

"It is a revolution," he stammered.

General Miguerra laughed.

"What of it?" he asked with a sneer. "They are sheep. Give my men ten minutes' work with machine guns and I will guarantee that those that are left will go away from here faster than they arrived."

Suddenly the Lady from Hell seemed to draw herself together like the slow curl of a steel spring. There were men in Manila, in France, in Turkey who knew that there was trouble brewing when the Lady from Hell looked like that. Her alert ears had caught something that none of the five men had heard.

"But," she queried, with pointed suavity, "will your men use machine guns when they know that the dictator is dead?"

For a moment General Miguerra looked at Vivian with dawning respect in his eyes.

"So this is your work, madame? The ace in the hole, as I believe the Americans say, on which you have been counting? It was clever. But not clever enough." He turned to the head of the national police, "Colonel Moreno, order your men to take this woman to the cells beneath the palace." His gaze shifted to Vivian. "And, madame, it would be most regrettable if one of the colonel's men should be forced to—er—injure you."

The Lady from Hell watched in silence as Colonel Moreno strode to the great double doors and flung them open. A gasp of consternation came from the five men at the sight that met their eyes.

There were no guards on duty outside the door. Instead three men stood on the threshold—three grim-faced men whom all five of the dictator's officials knew quite well and believed to be far away—the leaders of the parties who had fought desperately against the dictator's rule.

Death glittered in the colonel's eyes, narrowed to slits. A gun appeared from nowhere in his hand. But quick as he was, the Lady from Hell was quicker. Her own hand flashed forward like lightning, and Colonel Moreno felt the sharp jar of a gun muzzle as it came to rest against, his body.

"You'll live a lot longer if you drop that gun," she murmured. Her tone carried immediate and devastating menace, so that Colonel Moreno retired a pace, looking about him wildly with unmistakable fear in his eyes. For a second he stared at the red-haired woman, his free hand clenching and unclenching as though he would like to strangle her with his bare hands. Vivian's gaze shifted to the door.

"Come in, gentlemen," she said quietly.

When the door was once more closed behind the three men, Vivian said, in a businesslike voice:

"These three men, as you are aware, are here at the express request of His Excellency, President Rajas, and under his safe personal conduct."

For a moment the silence in the room was like a tangible thing as the five men stared at one another. They knew, all of them, that President Rajas was dead, and not one of them could divine what diabolical scheme lay behind the words of this clever woman.

"His Excellency, the President," Vivian went on smoothly, "wishes to talk to these gentlemen, and has, I believe, instructed you five men to remain here until this conference is over."

Then she switched into swift English, which all of them understood, but which the three newcomers did not.

"These three men," she said, "are emissaries of the mob outside. They bear a safe conduct signed by you, Colonel Moreno—your signature was not difficult to imitate— and an order from the dictator himself requesting their presence at the palace and pledging that their lives would be safe. Do not attempt to harm them, or you will be torn limb from limb by that crowd outside. Because if they have not returned within a certain time, the body of His Excellency, President Rajas, will be shown to the crowd by my confederates—and you, better than anyone, know what will happen once the people are sure that His Excellency is dead."

She turned back to the three with a charming smile.

"You will pardon my speaking in English," she said, "but there were certain instructions from His Excellency that it was necessary to convey to His Excellency's counselors. As you know, His Excellency has sent for you to request you to convey to the people news of certain reforms that he has in mind."

As she spoke her hand went out behind her and closed about the handle of the door that led into the adjoining room. Slowly she turned it, and then, with a swift movement, flung the door open.

"His Excellency will tell you himself," she said dramatically.

ON A LOW couch beside a table lay His Excellency, President Rajas, clad in a brilliant uniform with a row of medals across his chest. The lids, beneath the bushy white eyebrows, were closed, and the hands were folded across the chest in the immemorial gesture of death. The erect figure of Lieutenant Sanchez stood behind the head of the couch.

And then, a gasp of horror burst from the five conspirators. *For the figure of the dead dictator was moving.*

Slowly, ever so slowly, one of the folded hands moved down to the side of the still form. Slowly the eyes opened and the dictator raised himself slowly into a sitting position.

"Colonel Moreno," came from the thin, bloodless lips, "come here."

Slowly, unwillingly, unable to credit his eyes, the head of the national police advanced into the room. His gaze was fixed on the old man, gaunt, immobile with a face the color of old ivory, who sat there on the couch.

The aged man fumbled in a dispatch case, which lay beside him on the couch and produced three papers.

"These are pardons for the three rebels with you," he said in his tired voice. "They are to be permitted to return to their places in the republic as citizens. Their estates, once confiscated by the government, are to be restored to them."

"But Your Excellency—" stammered the colonel.

"I know, Colonel," the dictator said, "that the estate of one of these gentlemen was bestowed upon you. You will return it to him in as good a condition as when it came into your possession." He raised a feeble white hand to still any further protest from Colonel Moreno. "Now request the three gentlemen whose pardons you hold to come forward."

Wordlessly Colonel Moreno gestured to the three rebel leaders to advance into the room.

"Gentlemen," President Rajas said, "I have been quite ill—so ill that at one time, I am told, my people believed me dead. But I am recovering now. All danger is past, and I hope within a few weeks to be strong and well again. During my illness I have had much time to think. Your pardons and restoration to citizenship are a result of this. I do not ask that you do not rebel against my authority again. But I do ask you to accept positions in my cabinet and aid me in making our country a better place to live in. Will you do this?"

Don Diego, the oldest of the three men, stepped forward. The glow of light from the council chamber streamed across his face, showing a weary look upon his features, his black eyes clinging to those of the man on the couch.

"I do not understand what lies behind this. There is some trick," he said simply.

"There is no trick, Manuel," the old man said faintly. "The position that I wish you to hold in my cabinet is a new one—the Secretary of Public Welfare. Will you accept it and work with the other members of my cabinet and myself to better the conditions of our people?"

Diego looked at him a moment. Then he said slowly, "I will accept But I make no promises."

"I ask none," the old man said, his voice barely audible. "In addition to the pardons which Colonel Moreno holds, he has also the appointment of yourself and your two companions to the cabinet. Will you take them? I understand that the square in front of the palace is full of people who have gathered to learn if the news of my death is true. Will you be so good as to announce to them, from the balcony, that not only am I not dead, but that I have pardoned you three and made you members of my cabinet?"

He dropped slowly back onto the couch and his eyes closed. Lieutenant Sanchez bent over him hurriedly, then straightened up, a look of relief on his face.

"He is asleep," he said softly.

The three pardoned rebels filed slowly into the next room. They did not see the gesture by which the Lady from Hell detained the five conspirators. But no sooner had the door closed on the three men than Colonel Moreno turned on her with fury in his eyes.

"What does this mean—this imposture?" he demanded. "It is outrageous—it is treason—it is punishable by death."

"You mean," Vivian said quietly, "that it is punishable by death *if it is discovered.*" Then her voice became hard. "Listen, you five fools. I hold you in the hollow of my hand. I give you choice of a dead dictator, with revolution, anarchy and death to yourselves to follow in the wake of the discovery of his body—or a live Dictator who will continue to rule over the country for many years to come"

She paused, and there was silence in the room for a moment.

"You mean—" almost whispered General Miguerra, staring at the still figure on the couch.

"Exactly," Vivian told him sweetly.

"The Dictator is dead. Long live the Dictator! In other words, since you were so careless as to permit the man on whom your fortunes depend to die, I have brought him back to life for you."

"You couldn't get away with a thing like that," Rodriquez said. But in his tones a certain grim doubt belied his words. **"AND WHY NOT?"** Vivian wanted to know. "For the past five years the public appearances of the dictator have been becoming fewer and fewer. The people have become accustomed to seeing him infrequently. And for weeks the only people who will see him will be ourselves and the three men who have just been added to the cabinet. There will be no suspicion in their minds, and their acceptance of him will be sufficient to allay any suspicion that might arise. That, gentlemen, was a master stroke, bringing the dictator's three greatest enemies into his cabinet—the one thing that makes it possible for us to carry the imposture on for years."

"Who is this man, this impostor?" demanded General Miguerra, waving a hand at the silent figure on the couch.

"This," Vivian said softly, "is His Excellency, President Rajas."

"She is right," Colonel Moreno said suddenly.

The dictator sat up suddenly and spoke. It was Wylie's voice.

"Of course she is right, gentlemen. I fooled you—and you knew President Rajas intimately. I could not hope to fool you at close range, nor for any great length of time. They accepted me as President Rajas. They will pass that belief on to the people at large. It will not be necessary at first for me to see anyone who knew the President intimately. Gradually I can be seen more and more, and any change in me can be accounted for by the serious illness from which the President has just recovered."

"The appearance, that I can understand," Colonel

Moreno said thoughtfully. "A matter of make-up and wigs and uniforms. But the voice—that I cannot understand. It was the voice of His Excellency."

Wylie smiled. "You have forgotten that His Excellency has many times recorded patriotic addresses on phonograph records that are on sale in most of the shops. And I have a very quick ear."

Vivian cut in swiftly. "You have your choice. Exposure—and death at the hands of the mob, or, at most, flight without funds to a foreign country. Or, acceptance of my scheme, retain your positions as cabinet members of the country, and continue as you have been doing."

Secretary Pillar's eyes flickered over the little group. What he saw in the eyes of the others told him that they were in perfect agreement with him—that there was only one choice.

"We accept," he said slowly. "But," and he voiced the unspoken query of the other four men, "what is your position in this matter?"

"I," the Lady from Hell told them with calm certainty, "will be the one who pulls the strings of the republic from behind the scenes."

www.ingramcontent.com/pod-product-compliance
Lightning Source LLC
Chambersburg PA
CBHW051137030726
47504CB00004B/922